MISSING POWERS

MISSING POWERS

REG RAWLINS, PSYCHIC INVESTIGATOR
BOOK SIXTEEN

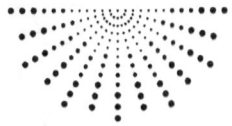

P.D. WORKMAN

PD WORKMAN

ISBN: 9781774682838 (KDP Hardcover)
ISBN: 9781774682784 (KDP Paperback)
ISBN: 9781774682814 (Large Print)
ISBN: 9781774682821 (Lulu Paperback)
ISBN: 9781774682791 (Kindle)
ISBN: 9781774682807 (ePub)

ALSO BY P.D. WORKMAN

FIND MORE BOOKS AT PDWORKMAN.COM

MYSTERY/SUSPENSE:

Reg Rawlins, Psychic Detective
Paranormal Mystery & Adventure
What the Cat Knew
A Psychic with Catitude
A Catastrophic Theft
Night of Nine Tails
Telepathy of Gardens
Delusions of the Past
Fairy Blade Unmade
Web of Nightmares
A Whisker's Breadth
Skunk Man Swamp
Magic Ain't A Game
Without Foresight
Careful of Thy Wishes
Time to Your Elf
Undiscovered Tomb
Missing Powers
Thrice Spared (Coming Soon)
Cloaked Campaign (Coming Soon)

*For friends who would walk
through flood or fire*

CHAPTER ONE

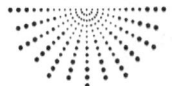

$\mathcal{R}$eg met with Davyn for her lesson on firecasting in a forested area outside of Black Sands. The woods in Florida were a beautiful, lush green. Davyn wore his usual black cloak, hood pulled up over his head so she couldn't see much of his face. He had been selecting different areas for her to practice in each time they met lately, which she supposed was to help her be prepared to use her craft in whatever circumstances she found herself in. He did seem to prefer remote outdoor locations. Easier to avoid detection. Less danger if her fire got out of control. Assuming that she didn't accidentally start a fire that was too big for Davyn to control. She worried about things like that sometimes. She'd had at least one experience where he had been unable to stop her and didn't want to experience that again.

"How are you feeling today?" Davyn asked. It was a routine question, but Reg felt something different from him. Not the usual concern of a mentor for the young, red-haired firebrand he was training, but something more. Deeper. His dark eyes were piercing under the hood of his cloak.

She looked at him, trying to mask her curiosity about his emotions. He would reveal himself sooner or later. If there were something wrong, she would find out. But she didn't want to pry into his personal life. There were things about Davyn Smithy she didn't want to know. Reg gathered her red box-braids in one hand and pushed them back, over her ears and shoulders.

She shrugged casually. "I'm fine."

"Got a good sleep? Hydrated?"

"Yeah. All ready to go."

Davyn started to form a fireball between his hands, cupping the glowing ball. Reg mimicked him, calling on her own fire. She tried to mimic every movement he made and every change he made to his fire. Bigger or smaller, warmer or cooler, changing in color. It was a routine warm-up exercise.

"I just wondered... how you were handling the news about Corvin."

Reg grimaced and kept her focus on her fire, which immediately flared at Corvin's name. She calmed it down again and watched Davyn's fire closely for any changes. He would be examining her to see whether she could maintain her focus when he distracted her with talk about her archenemy, the warlock who had once stolen her powers but then given them back to save her, something unheard of for his kind. The warlock who would like to take them back again, and this time keep them for himself. It would be one thing if she and Corvin were just enemies and she could keep a wall between them. But having shared her powers and part of her consciousness, Corvin was bound to her in a way that couldn't be dissolved. They had helped each other out of sticky or dangerous situations. They had dated and flirted, and Reg couldn't help but be tempted every time he tried to charm her.

But she was strong. She had learned to use some of the powers that she had never realized before she took up residence in Black Sands. She could hold Corvin off. Usually. If she wanted to, she believed she could overcome him. But she didn't want power over him. She didn't want to destroy him or take his powers or to drown him in the depths of the ocean.

Usually.

There were times...

But she tried to suppress those impulses.

"Corvin being allowed back into the coven doesn't affect me," she told Davyn, keeping her eyes on his ball of fire. "I knew that he was going to be allowed back in sooner or later. I don't like it, but I always knew that Corvin being shunned by his coven was only temporary."

"You think it is too soon."

"I don't think anything. It isn't anything to do with me. I'm not the one who brought charges against him in the first place. What you people choose to do with him is your own business."

Davyn was part of the tribunal that had judged Corvin and imposed the sentence on him for his attacks on Reg. For breaking a promise and trying to wrest her powers from her without her consent. They didn't care about the time that he *had* taken her powers because, in their eyes, she had consented to it—but of course Reg hadn't. She hadn't understood anything about what he was or what he was capable of. She had no idea what she had been agreeing with. She hadn't even understood anything about her powers. She had thought that the voices in her head were just that, voices in her head. Not that she was really hearing the voices of those around her, both living and dead.

Corvin's silencing of those voices when he took her powers had been terrifying. Reg didn't know how the people around her could walk around with empty heads, hearing only their own inner voice. To her, the silence had been like a cacophony. Overwhelming and terrifying.

"Focus," Davyn prompted quietly.

Reg looked at her own fire, growing smaller and darker. She instantly fed the flames and it burned brightly.

"I'm ready to play. Can we get on with it?" Reg asked impatiently.

"I just want to make sure that you're ready. That you're not too distracted."

"I don't care what Corvin does or what the coven does with him. He can do whatever he wants. It doesn't have anything to do with me. Let's just play."

Throughout Reg's childhood, her various foster parents, teachers, and leaders had always warned her not to play with fire. It was too dangerous. They said that she couldn't control what happened once a fire was started. A fire could get bigger, jump to a new location, hurt someone. Even hurt Reg herself. Fires were dangerous tools; not for children, not something to play around with or experiment with.

But now, with a firecaster for a mentor, Reg *was* allowed to play with fire, and it was one of the best parts of her week. If Davyn would just stick with the lesson and stop trying to distract her with talk about Corvin.

Davyn gave Reg a tolerant smile. His concern was still there, under the surface. Maybe he was doing more than trying to distract her this time. Maybe he really was worried about her mental state and how the news of Corvin's reinstatement in the coven had affected her. But it wasn't time to think about Corvin or about Davyn's concerns. It was time to play.

"What is your fire drawn to here?" Davyn asked. He closed his eyes for a moment, then opened them and looked around.

Reg mimicked him, closing her eyes and reaching out with all of her senses, trying to identify what things attracted her fire. Her fire was like a separate entity, a different Reg that dwelt inside her, with its own agenda. She knew it was part of her, but was sometimes surprised at its strength of will and how it could be so different from her conscious desires. She opened her eyes.

"There is a crow's nest in that tree," Reg nodded to an ancient tree that towered over them. "Very big. Lots of sticks that are as dry as a bone."

Davyn nodded.

"And... deadfall, over here..." Reg indicated an area where she could see the trunk of a tree that had fallen years ago. There were other remnants of the tree scattered around it. Wood that had been there a long time and had time to dry out.

"Yes," Davyn agreed.

"Dried mosses," Reg closed her eyes, trying to envision everything clearly in her mind's eye and to feel the stirrings of her fire. "Other birds' nests, little ones."

"What would you choose to burn?"

Her mind went again to the crow's nest. It was huge. So much tinder. But she was hesitant to choose a nest. She could see that it wasn't abandoned, but was still in active use. She couldn't tell if there were any eggs in it, but it was home to at least one bird. She turned her mind back to the deadfall.

"The fallen branches over there, I guess. I could gather them together. Make a nice bonfire."

A warm feeling in her chest, her fire responding to the idea. *Bonfire. Bonfire was good.*

"Why did you discount the nest?"

"There's something still using it. The bird. I don't want to burn up its home."

"There is other wildlife here. Smaller. Less visible. Did you consider the creatures that might live in the deadfall?"

Reg shook her head. "Bugs? Termites in the wood or maggots underneath? Gross. No. I don't care about those."

"Is that the only life that would be affected?"

"Yes." Reg focused on the dry wood again, checking her premise. Was there only insect life? What about mice or squirrels making a home in a hole in the trunk? Woodpeckers drilling for the bugs? She couldn't feel anything else and shook her head. "I don't feel anything else."

"You always need to be aware. Sometimes, there is more there than you can see."

CHAPTER TWO

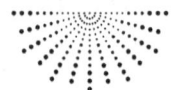

*I*s there something else?" Reg asked, a little impatient. "Did I miss something?"

"There might be other kinds of creatures that you are not aware of."

"Like what?" Reg thought about Sarah's garden. There had been a number of visitors there. "Like elves, you mean? Are there elves or some other magical race out here?"

"I don't feel anything either," Davyn admitted. "But you do need to be aware when you enter a new environment. If you burn a tree attached to a tree sprite, or that elves have made a home in, or some other being, you could end up in a lot of trouble."

Reg glowered at him. "So, this is just a safety lesson?"

"Safety is important. Not just your own, but of other creatures too. You don't want to end up cursed or the target of a malevolent force, do you? I've been trying all along to teach you how to use your fire responsibly. Firecasters… can be very dangerous and tend *not* to have good control. There's a reason for the expression 'a fiery temper.' Not only can that lead to the firecaster's early death, but also to a certain amount of prejudice from other practitioners."

"You're not like that."

"Prejudiced?"

"No, I mean, you don't have a temper. You're never out of control."

He shrugged. "You can master it. But mastering your fire is a lot easier than mastering yourself. There are a lot of things that can trigger your temper or distract your focus. It's much easier to let your fire burn than to keep it confined or put it out."

Reg nodded slightly. She'd had more than one experience where it had gotten away from her. But it was hard to see Davyn ever losing control. He always seemed very disciplined and calm.

"So... can I burn some of the deadfall, then?" She motioned to the trunk and branches. She ached to get a really good fire going. The warm-up exercises were fine for a start, but she wanted to ignite a nice big fire. She wasn't allowed to practice by herself, only when she was under Davyn's supervision. And that made it way too long between opportunities.

"Go ahead," Davyn agreed, nodding. "But keep it to the log and the larger branches. Don't let it spread to the undergrowth."

That was a little tricky. But Davyn knew that she was good at small, targeted fires. Reg focused on the log to start with. It was very big and dry, and she was excited about setting it blazing. Davyn stood nearby but didn't give her any instructions. She didn't have to make it burn with a blue flame or rise to a certain height. Davyn was allowing her free rein. Almost. She couldn't allow anything else to catch fire, but other than that...

The wood started smoldering. A thin column of black smoke rose from the surface. In a moment, it was blazing merrily away like a log in a campfire. The flames warmed Reg's face and hands and, even though it was already quite warm outside, Reg enjoyed the almost-scorching feeling she got from standing close to it. An ordinary person would not be able to get that close to it, but Reg didn't have to worry about being burned. She could tolerate any fire as long as she was concentrating.

Reg let her mind drift as she watched the fire. She wasn't taking her focus off of the fire. She was just allowing the back of her mind to work through some other things. Watching her subconscious thoughts as well as the flames.

It was Davyn who had brought up the subject as Corvin, as he often did, knowing that it was a good test of how well Reg was able to focus on her work. That and Davyn's… *friend* Julian Sabat, someone Reg had known when she was still a child. A tormentor that she was not interested in having back in her life. Bringing up Corvin or Julian was a great way to raise Reg's blood pressure and pull her attention away from her fire.

But Julian was not in town. He had work to do with Magical Investigations. And Corvin being reinstated back into his coven— maybe that was a good thing. Being shunned by his coven, he had no one to keep him company or focus his attention on, other than Reg or non-practitioners in the neighborhood. The other covens supported Davyn's and Corvin's coven by not having anything to do with him. Now that he was going back to his own kind, he would have other things to do, other people to talk to, and he would leave Reg alone.

Hopefully.

She told herself that it would be okay. She did not need to worry about late-night calls or dinner invitations from Corvin.

"Reg." There was a hand on her arm. "Regina."

Reg turned her head toward Davyn and looked blindly in his direction for a moment before she could see his face or the rest of the forest around her. He had lowered his hood so she could see more of his handsome, clean-shaven face and dark hair. And over in the dead-fall, a pillar of fire rose straight out of the log toward the sky. Not a campfire, but a solid pillar of fire that looked like something off of some sci-fi TV show. Reg pulled back, but her fire was happy where it was. Happy to be allowed to play, to pull in deep breaths of oxygen and grow and strengthen. Davyn tried to use his fire to contain Reg's. Like stopping a forest fire with a back burn so that there was no fuel left for it. Reg fought the anger that flared up in her at Davyn's interference.

"Wait. Just let me."

Davyn withdrew his hand from her arm, but she could tell that he was still cautious, eager to step in and contain Reg's fire before it could get beyond his control.

Reg thought about the little fire in her hands when she started an exercise, encouraging her fire to shrink down and not to consume the wood so quickly. She breathed slowly, trying to cut down the amount of oxygen it was sucking in.

"Come on," she murmured to herself. "Just a campfire. Not too big."

The wood crackled. Reg reached out, letting the fire warm her cold fingers.

"Just take it easy."

She didn't know whether she had said the words to the fire or whether Davyn had said them to her. Maybe both. Maybe they were that synchronized after the warm-up exercises.

"A nice calm fire."

The pillar of fire that had seemed to be reaching directly for heaven gradually shrank down until it was closer to the size of a campfire. A large campfire, to be sure. But there was nothing wrong with a campfire.

"Good," Davyn approved, relaxing his stance. "That was quite the display. You'll attract unwanted attention with a fire like that."

"We're out in the middle of nowhere," Reg dismissed. "No one would see it."

"We're not that isolated. And it can still be seen from the air." Davyn raised his eyes over the treetops. Reg had to concede that it had certainly been high enough and large enough to attract the attention of someone in the air. What would they do? Call in those firefighters that jumped out of airplanes to fight forest fires? What were they called? Fire jumpers? Smoke eaters?

"No one saw it."

"Were you aware of its size?"

Reg hesitated. It would be easy to tell him that she had known it was that big. That she realized what she was doing and had it all under control. Davyn was not a human lie-detector like Damon Knight, but he would probably know she wasn't telling the truth.

"I... lost track for a minute."

"You need to work on that. When you're kindling or tending a fire, it's not a good time to daydream, however hypnotic it might be."

"I wasn't *daydreaming*." Daydreaming would imply that she was thinking about something she liked, not that she was thinking of her enemy, worrying about how things would change when he went back to the coven. It would be good, wouldn't it? It would be good not to be Corvin's sole focus in life.

"Bring it down," Davyn told her, jerking his chin toward the fire. "There is more to tell you."

CHAPTER THREE

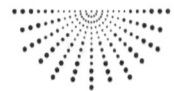

*R*eg didn't like the sound of that. She took her time bringing her fire back down to size and then putting it out. The longer she took to put out her fire, the longer it would be before she had to hear Davyn's bad news.

Eventually, she brought the fire back to her hands, molding it and playing with it between her hands, pulsing between the size of a softball and a soccer ball.

She looked past the fire to Davyn's face. He was cautious. Worried about her response to his news. What could be worse than hearing that Corvin was rejoining his coven?

"There's more," Davyn told her again.

"Okay. What?"

He still weighed his words, trying to decide if it was the right time and what was the best way to tell her. His anxiety was so clear that she could almost taste his words. There would be no need to tell her if he held back much longer, because she was going to read it before he got that far. She wasn't breaking the rules and invading his mind; he was just projecting so strongly that she couldn't help it.

"It's more about Corvin, isn't it?" Reg discerned, before he spoke. "What's going on? He's... doing something. A new project... something he's been wanting to do. Waiting to do..."

Davyn nodded. He licked his lips. "He's… running for leadership of the coven."

Reg blinked, trying to process this. She shook her head. "I thought you are the leader of the coven."

"I am. At the moment. But we rotate the leadership regularly, to allow others to lead if they are interested."

The dread grew in Reg's belly, weighing her down like a lead ball. "So… what happens?"

"He will need to get enough support in the coven to take over the position. A simple majority will do it."

"But he won't get it, will he? Everybody knows what he is. Everyone knows that he's broken the rules and been shunned. They wouldn't turn around and put him into a position of authority."

"Leadership of the coven isn't exactly a position of authority. It is… spiritual leadership. Guidance. The leader doesn't really tell the members of the coven what to do or not do."

"He doesn't make or enforce rules? Everyone can just do what they like?"

"Well… no. Our rules are traditional, and the coven votes on them if there is any difference of opinion. The leader is there to help others, to guide them in their spiritual journeys. If there is a breach of the rules, like with Corvin, then the person can be judged by a tribunal, as you saw. If it is serious enough."

"Corvin wouldn't have any power if he was the leader of the coven."

Davyn shook his head, but Reg could feel something different from him. "What?"

"Corvin does have… influence."

"Because he's older? More experienced?"

"Yes…" Davyn trailed off. That wasn't what he had meant, obviously.

Reg shrugged in frustration. "What, then?"

"You know. His glamour. His charm."

Reg knew far more of Corvin's ability to charm people than she would have liked to. She knew how he could exude pheromones and whatever other inborn magic he had, work his way into her brain, and persuade her to do what he wanted.

"But he can't charm other men, can he? And the rest of the coven are male…?"

"He doesn't have the same level of ability to charm men as he does women, but it is certainly still there. I don't know of anyone in the coven who is immune to it."

"Great. If he becomes the coven leader, he could still influence them to do whatever he wanted to."

"We all have the ability to choose our own paths, and he doesn't have any *right* to authority over the coven."

Reg rolled her eyes. There was no point in arguing with Davyn about it. He was doing his best to deny that Corvin could do anything wrong if elected to the leadership of the coven, but it was obvious that he would. It might not be written into the bylaws, but it was part of his gift, and no one could change that just by telling him not to use it. He would continue to use his gift, even if he were going against the coven rules.

"Has he been the leader of the coven before? If you guys rotate leadership, and he's so old, he must have been a leader before."

"Not necessarily. Sometimes people aren't ready to take leadership, haven't reached that point in their spiritual journey. Or they might not be able to get the votes to be elected."

Reg couldn't see how he could have failed to be elected before, when he could use his glamour to charm members of the coven into voting for him. It might be difficult to charm them all at once but, if he was strong from a recent feeding, she couldn't see how he could fail.

Davyn shifted his stance, clearly uncomfortable. Reg stared at him, trying to figure out the rest of the story. If Corvin was one of the senior members of the group, having been around for hundreds of years, what other reason was there for his failure to be elected a leader of the coven?

"Up until recently," Davyn said reluctantly, grimacing as if the words had a bad taste or hurt him to say aloud, "there was a rule against any warlock of his kind running for leadership of the coven."

Reg rolled the ball of fire between her hands, looking at it instead of Davyn. He hadn't started with that? He thought she could be convinced that Corvin was just not powerful enough to get the votes that he needed? She knew better than he did just how powerful Corvin had become.

"And… why did they change the rule?"

Davyn cleared his throat. "It was previously believed that a warlock of Corvin's ilk could not be allowed to take leadership of a coven because of his ability to gain in power and to use glamour to change the minds of the members and therefore the course of the coven."

"Exactly. So why would they change that rule?"

"It was determined to be… prejudiced. In the coven, we are all supposed to be equal, with the same opportunities for advancement and progress. A rule like that, which prevents a warlock with his gift from having the same privileges and opportunities as everyone like that… is prejudiced against his kind."

"For good reason!" Reg snapped.

"It has been debated for many years, in many different venues. But there have been a few covens in recent years which have reversed similar policies, and warlocks like Corvin have been shown to be beneficial in leadership positions. They have been even-handed and fair and have not shown themselves to be the destructive force people once feared. The prevailing wisdom is that his kind have been unfairly vilified in the past and that the prejudice and fear we have for them is unwarranted."

Reg sucked in her breath slowly, trying to keep herself from blowing up at the stupidity of their politics and negotiations. Denying warlocks like Corvin, who could steal the powers of others and influence their actions with magic, wasn't the same as keeping racial minorities or women out of positions of power. There was very good reason for it.

"I'm sorry," Davyn murmured. "Maybe I shouldn't have said anything."

"That wouldn't stop it from happening."

"No. But now you're going to be worried about it. I feel like it is cruel to bring it up when there isn't anything you can do."

Reg tried to come up with something that she could do. But she wasn't even a member of the coven, so what *could* she do? The change in policy had already been made. She wouldn't be able to change Corvin's mind about running for leadership. The only possible course of action was to convince the coven members not to elect him. And that was going to be pretty difficult to do considering Corvin's ability to influence people.

"Isn't there anything *you* can do to stop it?" Reg demanded.

Davyn took a deep breath. He lifted his hands in a gesture of surrender. "I will run against him. But if the other members of the coven want him to lead them, then I will accept that as the will of the coven." He sighed. "Perhaps it will be beneficial, as it has been in other covens."

Reg shook her head angrily. "They had better not elect him."

CHAPTER FOUR

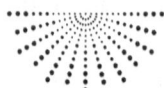

*R*eg was angry when she got home and didn't want to do anything that would help to calm her down. She didn't want to meditate or sit in the beautiful garden or pet Starlight. She *wanted* to be angry. She wanted to stay angry for as long as possible and to convince everyone she could not to vote Corvin into leadership or support him in his campaign in any way. She wanted to be a one-woman tide of destruction that would sweep away any support that anyone had for him.

It was unbelievable that they would reverse the rule against warlocks like Corvin running for leadership. That they would think it was safe or a good idea. It wasn't the same as having rules against other minorities. It was there for a reason!

Reg slammed the door behind her when she entered her home, the guest cottage in Sarah's backyard. Sarah, a grandmotherly-looking witch with a soft spot for Reg, gave her the cottage for much lower rent than she should have, claiming that she needed to have someone nearby to help her out and that she needed the cottage to be occupied to deter thieves. In reality, Reg depended on Sarah's help and protection far more than Sarah depended on Reg's. Starlight, Reg's tuxedo cat, was snoozing on the wicker couch, and looked up at the door slam. He didn't look spooked by it, but critical. He stared at her with his one blue eye and one green eye, clearly wanting to know what the problem was. Reg shook her head and slammed her purse down on the kitchen table for further emphasis.

"You wouldn't believe me if I told you," she advised.

That didn't stop him from looking at her, waiting for an explanation. He got up and stretched, his whole body quivering.

"Stupid Corvin," Reg blasted.

He put his ears back, flattened against his skull. Starlight was no fan of Corvin either. And Corvin was anti-cat, so it was mutual.

"Stupid Davyn. Stupid coven of *stupid* warlocks!"

She went to the fridge to get some tuna out for Starlight and slammed the container down on the counter.

He jumped down from the couch and approached warily. It wasn't like she would take her anger out on him. But she supposed it wasn't exactly fair of her to be shouting and slamming things around, either. She wouldn't like it if someone were behaving like that around her. Raised voices and slammed doors always increased her anxiety level exponentially.

"Sorry. You hungry? Come on; I'm not going to throw anything."

He skulked closer, still keeping a wary eye on her as he approached the side of the kitchen island his food dish was on. Reg took a deep breath in and let it out slowly, looking over the appointment book on the island. Sarah, her landlady, sometimes added new appointments. She was very helpful in finding Reg new clients and ensuring that she kept busy with paying work. Reg knew she needed just to settle down and not indulge herself in a temper tantrum. It wasn't going to do her or anyone else any good to be angry at Corvin, Davyn, and the other warlocks and take it out on everyone else.

The container of tuna rattled on the counter. Reg looked down at it, startled.

"What...?"

She looked at Starlight, sitting on the floor beside her, as tall as possible, staring at her. Was the white star on his forehead glowing even more brightly than usual? Reg couldn't usually see the magical aura around him unless she was trying to draw on her own powers.

"Sorry, I was just thinking..."

She stooped and picked up his food dish, set it on the island, and put a large spoonful of tuna into it.

"Did you move the dish? Or did I just bump it?"

He waited for her to put it back down in front of him. Reg obliged and he immediately stooped down to eat, making loud slurping noises. Reg rolled her eyes and turned back to the fridge to see what there was to eat. As it often had been lately, the fridge seemed packed almost to bursting with food, much of it the foods that Harrison loved.

But Reg found that she didn't feel like chocolate cake or ribs. She'd had too much of them recently. Starlight's food actually smelled better and appealed to her more than any of the other dishes she could see in the fridge. There was a loaf of bread that was reasonably fresh. Reg rummaged around in the fridge until she found a jar of mayonnaise, which she mixed in with the tuna still left in the container to make herself a nice sandwich. The smell of the fish had her stomach rumbling and mouth drooling, hardly able to finish making the sandwich. She wanted to snarf the food down as fast as Starlight was. It was probably his behavior that had made Reg so hungry in the first place. That and the hard work managing her fire during her firecasting lesson with Davyn. The concentration required to control her fire always made her tired and thirsty.

Reg took a big bite out of the sandwich as soon as she was finished making it. As she chewed it, trying to force herself to go slowly and enjoy it, she also got herself a glass of water. She didn't feel dehydrated, but that didn't mean she wasn't. She always needed to remember to drink after using fire.

Water and fish. A chant started up in her brain. Words that she couldn't understand, but she knew it was something to do with water and fish. Reg took another bite, closed her eyes, and tried to will the voices to be silent.

She'd never been particularly successful at silencing the voices. Plenty of foster parents had tried to discipline her for talking or playing with what they thought were imaginary friends. And plenty of doctors had tried to medicate the voices into silence. That didn't work either. Reg had done her best to suppress them so that she could function in the real world. But since moving to Black Sands, they had come back in full force. Now that she was practicing as a psychic, actually seeking communication from the spirits, there always seemed to be a chorus of voices surrounding her, trying to tell her their stories, to get in contact with their loved ones, or just talking inanely or commenting on her life.

The chant, though, was different. Not ghostly. The women's voices would eventually rise to a shriek, a siren song. The sirens seemed to be more and more insistent in reaching her. They were so annoying, Reg could understand why the sirens needed to have such large territories or they tended to kill each other. They were driving her crazy.

It's time to take your place, one particularly familiar voice drawled. Her mother, Norma Jean. *You must anoint the waters and claim your territory.*

"I'm a little busy with other things right now," Reg said aloud. "How about you just stay out of my business?"

You must take your place and defend your territory.

"I'll get right on that," Reg muttered.

She winced as the chorus of voices shrilled loudly in her head. Would she eventually acquire the ability to understand everything they said? Or would she have to take siren as a second language? Reg pressed her fingers to her temples, trying to banish the voices or at least to turn down the volume.

"It would almost be worth it to take Corvin down to the ocean just to make them all shut up," she told Starlight, who was gazing up at her attentively. "That would solve two problems at once."

She took another bite of the sandwich, but the bread was balling up in her mouth and getting stuck in her teeth, annoying her almost as much as the voices. She pulled the two halves of the sandwich apart and went straight for the tuna and mayonnaise filling, scooping it into her mouth and licking it off of the slices of bread. It occurred to her as she messily chowed down that Sarah could walk into the cottage at any moment and would probably be alarmed if she saw the state Reg was in. She licked the last few bits of fish off of the bread and threw them into the garbage.

"That's disgusting," she criticized herself. She wiped her mouth with the back of her wrist. "What are you, an animal?"

Starlight, wiping his face with his paw as he groomed himself, paused to glare at her.

"Okay. Sorry, sorry. I know a cat would never behave like that. You're very clean and civilized. I'm the one who is disgusting."

Starlight went back to washing. He radiated waves of concern over her. She hadn't realized that her behavior was unusual enough for him to notice it. Cats tended not to take too much notice of human problems.

Or maybe it wasn't her behavior that had him worried, but her agitation. She had been emotional from the time she had walked in the door.

"I'm just tired. Hard session with Davyn."

Starlight murmured a sound and wrapped himself around her legs, rubbing against her.

"It's Corvin. He's running for leadership of his coven. Against Davyn. And I think that's a really bad idea. I can't understand why they would let him do it. He'll have too much influence over the other warlocks. I don't think we want a dozen—or however many of them there are—warlocks running around Black Sands under Corvin's power."

Starlight continued to rub against her. Reg bent over and picked him up. She scratched his ears and he started to purr.

"Forget Corvin," Reg told herself. "It's got nothing to do with me."

The phone started to ring.

CHAPTER FIVE

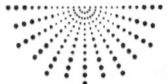

*R*eg knew even without looking at the phone who it would be.

She should have known better than to be ranting about him. Of course with their psychic bond, he would know that something was going on and would be drawn to talk to her. She looked at the phone for a minute, deciding whether to answer it. If she didn't answer, would he just leave her alone? Or would he be persistent, calling her back and even trying to come to the house or bothering Sarah to check on Reg?

She tapped the screen and reluctantly brought it up to her ear. "Corvin."

"Reg."

Not the usual purr of "Regina" that he used when he was trying to charm her. But he didn't sound angry, either. He'd been quite irritable lately, which Reg thought was probably related to his effort to be reinstated to the coven. Maybe now that he had been reinstated, he would be happier.

He had certainly been jubilant when he'd received the news. Reg had felt it, even though they had been apart and not communicating with each other. His joy at being reinstated had seemed over-the-top.

As a powerful warlock, he shouldn't really care so much about the companionship and approval of the coven. Should he?

Reg waited for a few long seconds, waiting for him to speak, but he didn't.

"You called me," she reminded him. "What did you want?"

"Maybe I just wanted to hear your voice again."

"Okay, and now you have. I've got appointments to prepare for tonight, so if that is all…"

"Wait."

Reg didn't actually need to prepare anything for her appointments. She would give them each a reading when they came, but she didn't research clients ahead of time or do anything to predispose herself to a specific outcome. If she really was a medium—and she no longer seemed to be able to deny it—then she was only the conduit through which messages passed. There was no need to spend time preparing a message that would impress her client.

"What?"

Again, there was a pause. Corvin didn't usually have any problem starting a conversation or stating what he wanted. Reg wasn't sure why he was being so slow to express himself.

"Where were you today?"

"I was out. Had some errands to do."

"Errands where? In town? Did you go into the city?"

"No. Why do you care? It's got nothing to do with you."

"I think you know something."

Reg's arms broke out into goosebumps. "Sure, I know lots of things," she agreed casually.

"What do you know about… *me?*"

"I know lots of things about you." More than she liked to, actually. Was he going to tell her something else? Something she didn't even want to know?

"Did you hear about my reinstatement to the coven?"

"Oh, yeah. Might have heard something about that."

He made a growling noise that raised the hairs on the back of her neck. "Don't play games with me, Reg!"

"Fine! Yes, I heard about you being reinstated. Good for you. You must be pleased."

"I am," Corvin agreed and, for a moment sounded like his old self, "very pleased." Reg recognized that little self-satisfied purr in his words. Yes, Corvin was always doing whatever he could to boost himself a little higher in everyone else's view. Maybe being part of the coven meant more to him than she had thought.

"Well, congratulations."

"I am also running for leadership of the coven. Davyn is stepping down."

Reg caught herself before correcting him. She swallowed and considered her words before speaking. She didn't want to give away that she had already known about his bid to lead the group.

"Wow, that will be something new, won't it? Or have you been the coven leader before?"

"You already knew." His voice was disappointed. "How did you know?"

"Heard some gossip while I was out running errands. That's great. I'm sure you'll be great about *serving* them."

Maybe that was her own little dig. Reminding him that he was supposed to be a spiritual leader and help and serve others, rather than becoming the leader for his own advancement.

"It is a great opportunity. This coven has been around for hundreds of years. It was one of the first covens to form in North America. We have a very long history of preeminent leaders."

"I didn't know that." Was it true, or was he just puffing himself up? There must be hundreds of covens across North America now. How would anyone ever prove that they had been one of the first? Maybe they had some history books. Maybe photographs of some of those early warlocks. Maybe Corvin had been a young man then, excited to join the coven because it was something new. Something that few people had the opportunity to do.

And now he had another opportunity—the opportunity to become the leader of one of the first covens in North America.

"For years, they have been able to keep me out of the leadership of the coven, but times are changing. Other covens have changed their rules to allow my kind to lead. We are natural-born leaders. That's why they have kept us out to begin with. They are afraid we will take over and not give anyone else the opportunity."

Or maybe they were afraid of what he could do and letting someone like that continue to grow in his powers over years, maybe even decades or centuries. Reg was pretty sure that the rules hadn't simply been the result of prejudice, but an effort to prevent people like Corvin from taking advantage of those who didn't have the strength to fight him.

Reg didn't say anything. She didn't know what to say. She had already congratulated him. What more did he want?

"Times are changing," Corvin repeated.

"Is that why you called me? To tell me that you were going to be running for leadership of the coven?"

He didn't answer immediately. Reg felt unsettled. He wasn't close to her, they were just talking on the phone, but she could feel his anger and dissatisfaction building. He had been happy when he called. She didn't know what had changed.

"Who have you been talking to?" Corvin demanded.

"I talk to a lot of people."

Too late, she realized the mistake she had made. He had told her that Davyn was stepping down so that Corvin could take over as the coven leader. But she had referred to his *running* for leadership, as Davyn had told her. She knew that it wasn't a "given." Corvin wasn't just going to walk into the position.

"You've been talking about me. Or reading me. You know that isn't allowed."

As if he were careful to follow all of the rules himself. Reg had seen him slip too many times to believe that was true. Even now, he was probing at the edges of her consciousness, looking for the answers to his questions, not satisfied with her responses.

"I'm glad that you're going to be able to join your coven again," Reg said. "You'll be happier. Not so lonely."

"I'm not lonely," he growled, as if she had insulted him. "It will give me the chance to expand in areas I haven't been allowed to before. I have a talent for leadership, but it has always been denied me before."

How could he know that he would be a good leader if he had never led? A lot of people thought that they could do things better than the political or corporate leaders around them. But it wasn't actually true. They were just good armchair quarterbacks.

She supposed it was different for Corvin. He could look to history. Some of his earlier ancestors must have had the opportunity to lead at some time. That was how kingdoms were built. Warlocks like he was had attained great wealth and power. There were examples throughout history of fabulously powerful men.

"Why don't you have your own coven?" Reg asked. "For warlocks like you."

"I have a coven."

"No, I mean... other warlocks who have your... abilities? If other covens wouldn't let you have any positions of authority, why didn't you form your own coven?"

"My kind have been dying out for many years. They have been targeted by both practitioners and non-practitioners and executed. Burned at the stake. Stakes driven through their hearts. All manner of cruel deaths."

It was true of many of the practitioners of magic, not just those like Corvin. But to be hunted by their own kind was particularly troubling. It was one thing for non-magicals who didn't understand what they were dealing with to lash out and try to destroy it. But for one warlock to kill another because he had a certain power or gift... that seemed unfair. Reg feared Corvin's ability to take her powers away, but she knew it wasn't his fault that he had been born that way. No more than it was Reg's fault for being able to hear the voices of the dead or that her mother was a siren. Those were things beyond her control. How could anyone kill another for his inborn nature?

"Imagine that," Corvin said, his voice husky in her ear. "Imagine what it would take to do that to another witch."

"I'm not—"

"Call yourself 'just a psychic' if you want. You know that your powers go well beyond what most of the witches in Black Sands can do. Well beyond most of the witches I have ever met." The phone picked up the sound of his breathing. "Why do you think you are such a temptation to me?"

"Corvin." Reg shuddered. It was like he was right in the room with her, even though she knew he was not. "Too much. Back off."

He continued to breathe but didn't say anything.

"I need to go," Reg said uncomfortably. "Um... I'm sure we'll talk again. Good luck with the coven."

"Thank you."

Reg hesitated for a moment, then touched the red hang-up button on her screen. She let out her breath, her heart beating quickly. She didn't know what had gotten into Corvin lately. He didn't seem like his old charming self, but even this irritable, short-tempered Corvin left her breathless and struggling to remember why she had to turn him down.

She closed her eyes, breathing slowly and waiting for her heart-beat to return to normal. The siren song started again and, below the wailing, she could hear them whispering and giggling about Corvin. When they said teasingly that he looked tasty, Reg didn't think they were talking about the attributes that would land Corvin on a racy calendar raising funds for orphaned witch and warlock children. They meant it quite literally. Reg had—perhaps unwisely—claimed Corvin as her own to keep Norma Jean from seducing him and dragging him off into the ocean. The sirens were still waiting for Reg to seal the deal.

Reg wiped the drool from the corner of her mouth and turned to the fridge to find some more fish.

CHAPTER SIX

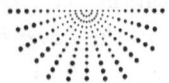

*R*eg had a restless night. First, she had her psychic consultations in the evening, then a seance at midnight, and then, sometime after three, she tried to get to sleep, but found herself still too wide awake and anxious. It was probably all the talk about Corvin and his reintroduction to his coven. And that really didn't affect Reg, so she wasn't sure why she let it bother her. Corvin would be busy with the coven; that was a good thing.

She awoke to Starlight sitting on the bed next to her, staring intensely into her face. Reg startled and gave a little yelp of surprise.

"Gee, that's not creepy at all! What do you think you're doing?"

Starlight didn't move, staring at her unblinkingly.

"I'm getting up. But you could let me sleep a little longer. You know how late I was up last night."

She rolled over, turning her back to him. But she could tell that he wasn't moving. He was still just sitting there staring at her.

"Go away. Go look out the window. See if there are any birds."

No response. Reg took a tentative look behind her, wondering if he had just crept quietly away without her realizing it and she was foolishly talking to herself.

But no, he was still there, sitting and staring at her.

"Come on. Just a little longer."

Reg closed her eyes. She hoped that she would be able to get back to sleep, but she knew better. She might just doze a little, but then she would be more irritable and short-tempered because of it. Something like Corvin had been lately. Was it possible that he wasn't sleeping? Maybe the tribunal taking their time to consider his application for reinstatement to the coven had kept him from being able to get a good sleep. And now, he had to plan his campaign to take over leadership of the coven from Davyn. Was Davyn the only opposition, or was someone else in the coven also running against them? Reg wasn't sure who else was in the coven, but she probably knew a few of them. She'd just never asked before who else was part of their circle. She didn't know if it was considered impolite to ask that kind of thing.

Reg opened her eyes and gave a louder shout than when Starlight had startled her. Right in front of her was a man's face, with a thin, drooping mustache and a little red beret. His eyes popped at her response and he fell over backward into the wall. Reg was instantly up on her hands and knees and looked over the side of the bed at him.

"Uncle Harrison! What are you doing here?"

Harrison struggled to unfold himself from the space between the bed and the wall and to get to his feet. He was wearing what Reg thought was a silk pajama top, embroidered with dragons, and form-fitting black yoga pants that ended just below his knees, leaving his long shins and feet bare except for a pair of Birkenstocks.

"I am... watching."

"I told you before not to watch me sleep! You're not supposed to come into my bedroom. You're supposed to knock on my door and wait until I let you in. You can't keep materializing in my house."

He gave her a doubtful look. "Yes, I can."

Reg rolled her eyes. "Well, you're not supposed to. You're supposed to be polite and ask to come in."

He shrugged, a gesture that indicated he had no idea why she would ask him to do such a bizarre thing.

Reg tugged at the t-shirt that she wore as a pajama top to ensure it was not skewed to show off anything it shouldn't. She rubbed the center of her forehead. The third eye position, like where Starlight's star marking was. She was still tired and was already developing a headache.

"I need coffee," she told him, and slipped off of the edge of the bed.

"As do I," Harrison agreed, and followed her out to the kitchen. Starlight purred loudly, rubbing around Harrison's legs and giving excited little trills.

Reg made sure there was a carafe under the coffee machine drip spout and pressed the button to start it brewing.

"You stole my coffee pot before," she accused Harrison. "I have no idea why. I had to go buy a new one."

"I do not steal." Harrison put his fingertips on his chest as if shocked that she would make such an accusation.

"You do too. It was right in the middle of brewing, and when you disappeared, the coffee pot did too. And got coffee all over the counter and floor."

Harrison chuckled in amusement over this suggestion. "Coffee on the floor. Ha!"

"It wasn't funny!"

Though, thinking about it now, it was sort of funny. Reg kept a stern expression. "Don't take anything of mine without asking."

He stroked his mustache. "Reg, may I have—"

"Before. You ask before you take something."

"I am!" Harrison insisted.

"Okay, may you have what?"

"The mealtime, is it... tea?"

"Not unless you want to actually drink tea. Breakfast?"

He nodded sagely. "I must break the fast."

She was getting used to the fact that he liked to eat with her when he took on a mortal form. It was, apparently, one of the few benefits of taking on a physical body.

"Sure. What do you want?" Reg opened the fridge door and looked at the overflowing contents. "You have to stop making all of this food materialize in here. One person cannot eat that much before it goes bad."

"You could," Harrison argued.

"I would be sick."

"Yes," he conceded.

"So just stop messing with my fridge. I don't need that much food. Thank you, but no."

He raised an eyebrow. "I did not fill the fridge."

"Oh, really?" Reg gestured to the contents. "I believe you didn't put the Tupperware dishes in there. That would be Sarah, trying to pawn off her leftovers on me, saying that I need to eat less junk food. But the chocolate cake and the ribs? Any of the other junk food or takeout in here? That's you."

Harrison shook his head.

"It is. Just admit it and stop filling it up. Maybe you can bring food when you come for a visit. One thing. But don't put anything straight into the fridge."

Harrison smiled and twirled the ends of his mustache. "It is not me."

"Who, then?" Reg had sudden doubts. Maybe it was Weston, another immortal, who *might* be Reg's father. Or was there someone else? Another immortal she had not met or some other person or creature who had taken it upon himself to provide for Reg?

Harrison pointed at her. "You."

"Me?" Reg shook her head and laughed. "I can't make food materialize out of thin air."

"Thin air," Harrison mused. "No."

"It came from somewhere. From you." Reg remembered Julian being amazed when he saw Harrison materialize a huge breakfast without any apparent effort. He had said that it was impossible for Harrison to produce something from nothing. That it must have come from somewhere. Matter couldn't be created or destroyed... something like the arguments that Reg had heard against time travel, which had all turned out not to be true at all.

"It came from somewhere," Harrison agreed. He pointed at her again. "You put it there."

"You think I went out and bought all of this food and put it in my fridge. And then can't remember doing it. Am I sleepwalking? I know my memory has been bad since—well, you know—but it isn't that bad. If I had bought all of this, I would remember it."

"You did not buy it," Harrison said, watching the coffee drip into the carafe with fascination. "You… called it." He picked up Starlight and cuddled him against his face, murmuring and making kissing noises.

Reg opened her mouth to say that she couldn't call it, but she had learned over the past little while that she did, in fact, have the ability to call a person or object to her using magic. But that was through effort of will. It wasn't something that could just happen without her knowing or remembering it.

Could it?

Harrison was nodding at her, emphasizing the point. "You called it."

Reg opened the fridge door and looked at the contents in dismay. Some of the food was in branded bags or containers, so that she knew which restaurant or store it had come from. Was it possible that she had magically transported the food directly from the stores to her fridge and wasn't even aware that she had done so?

"But I don't… need all of this food."

"Humans need food to live."

"Yes. I know. But not this much. There is too much. And I can afford to buy food, I don't need to…" she dropped her voice to a whisper, embarrassed, "magic it off the shelves."

"You said it is fun."

Reg blinked at him, shaking her head slightly. "When did I say that? I never told you that."

Harrison held his hand out low beside him, indicating a height below his hip. "You were small."

"When I was little? Living with Norma Jean?"

Harrison nodded and smiled. "Yes. Little Reg."

"When I was little, I probably *did* need to magic it to me," Reg admitted slowly.

Norma Jean had been an addict, walking the streets to support her habit, partying with anyone who would have her, giving little thought to the child back in her filthy flophouse apartment. Without

Uncle Harrison to help Reg or the long series of foster families she had been placed with once she entered the system, she would have died. But she had thought that Harrison had provided all of the food. She didn't remember being able to call it herself.

"So you taught me?" she asked slowly. "You showed me how to call the food so I would have something to eat?"

Harrison nodded. "You learned very quickly."

Hunger would do that to a person. Reg felt suddenly weak-kneed. She looked around for somewhere to sit and eventually staggered into the living room to sit down on one of the wicker chairs.

All at once, the pieces were falling into place. Being accused by foster parents of hoarding food when she hadn't been the one to stash it. She had assumed that one of her foster siblings had done it and thrown the blame in her direction. Foster parents found other things in her room too. Watches, handheld games, money, items that other children had shown her school class for show-and-tell. Things that Reg had never touched. She hadn't stolen them; someone else had put them there. But no foster parent had ever believed her.

And as Reg aged out of foster care and took jobs here and there to support herself between one brilliant con and the next, there were other things. Not food or games, but jewelry that had been given to her by her employers. If Reg found a necklace or heirloom brooch in her luggage that she had not put there, the only possible explanation was that her employer had put it there, making a gift of it as a show of gratitude. Such gifts had frequently gotten Reg in hot water.

"The coffee is ready?" Harrison suggested.

Reg rubbed her eyes and tried to focus on the present.

CHAPTER SEVEN

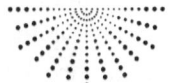

he coffee. Yes." Reg massaged her legs and then got slowly to her feet. She seemed to be steadier now. She went back to the kitchen and poured herself a mug of coffee. Harrison, she remembered, didn't actually drink coffee. He just liked to watch it being made and Reg drinking it. She added sugar and opened the fridge once more to select something for Harrison to eat for breakfast. There was most of a Black Forest cake piled high with frosting and cherries on the top shelf, so she pulled it out and set it in front of Harrison. She handed him a fork rather than allowing him to eat it with a spatula or serving spoon that he would have grabbed himself. He could be a very messy eater.

Reg took a long swallow of the scalding coffee. "If I'm the one making the food appear in here, then… why? Why would I do that?"

Harrison wrinkled his brow in a dramatic "thinking" face. "Because you are hungry?"

"But I'm not. I've been putting on weight. Sarah is always bringing food over. I eat out at The Crystal Bowl. I order in. Sometimes I even buy groceries. I'm not starving. There is plenty of food here without me overfilling the fridge with food."

"You like to eat," Harrison pointed out.

"Yes. And these are all things that I like… but I'm actually getting tired of chocolate cake, if you want to know the truth. Having it all the time, it can get to be a bit much."

Harrison put a huge bite of cake and frosting in his mouth. Reg was afraid it would all come squirting out when he tried to chew, but he was able to keep it in his mouth, though his cheeks puffed out like a hamster's.

"*I* like chocolate cake."

"Hmm. Does that mean I make it appear for *you?*" That made some sense. Reg had been worried about Harrison being angry with her when he had tried to keep her locked in the cottage and she had found a way past his magic. They had disagreed before that, too, about Harrison bringing Horace back from Egypt to Reg. As it had turned out, it had been the right thing to do, but Reg had not known that at the time.

Maybe all of Harrison's favorite foods in the fridge was her way of making up with him. Even if she had done it without conscious thought.

"Are we okay now?" she asked him.

Harrison didn't appear to harbor any resentments against her, but who knew what an immortal was thinking? They could hold on to a grudge for the smallest thing for a very long time, if the mythologies she had studied in school were any indication.

"We are okay."

Reg was not reassured. She didn't think he understood what she was asking. "I mean… you were mad at me before. Remember? Are you still mad at me?"

Harrison took another massive bite of chocolate cake and tried to say something around it. She shook her head and waited until he had swallowed the bite. "I couldn't understand you. What did you say?"

"I want Reg to be safe."

"I know. You've protected me for a long time. You've been very good about it."

He nodded his agreement.

"You're not still mad about me getting out of the cottage when you told me to stay here? Or when I got upset about you bringing Horace back from Egypt?"

"Horace is back in Egypt again in this time," Harrison said, his expression serious. "Why did you take him back?"

"He's not with the warlock again. You were right to take him away from there. But... I took him back so that he could be happy. So that he could join with Merneith and not be so sad about that piece he was missing." Reg took a sip of her coffee, shifting uncomfortably. What if he didn't accept her explanation? She couldn't exactly go and bring Horace back. He couldn't live with her, as Harrison had suggested. She couldn't have another cat living in the cottage, or Sarah would kick her out. And Horace was a *big* cat. "Merneith wanted a physical form and Horace needed something to fill the empty space. So... it seemed like a good solution. He's happy there. That's what you wanted, isn't it?"

"Merneith wanted a cat?"

"Yes."

Harrison started plucking the cherries from the top of the cake and putting them into his mouth. "The warlock stole his flame."

"From Horace... yes. Kareem stole the piece of the Witch Doctor that Francesca had bound to him. But you know he doesn't have it anymore."

"No. It is stolen again. And missing."

Reg didn't want to think about what might have happened to that missing piece of the Witch Doctor, her mortal enemy. He was supposed to be bound for a thousand years so that he would not be a problem again until hundreds of years after Reg was dead and buried. But she worried that with one piece being loosed already, the other eight were more vulnerable than Francesca had thought.

"I don't know where it is," Reg says. "But I think that Horace is safe and happy where he is now. Don't you?"

Harrison shrugged and didn't answer. He always seemed to either avoid her questions or to leave her with some kind of ambiguous or impossible answer. She should know by now not to ask him to explain anything.

"I think—"

There was a quick knock at the door, and Reg turned her head to see Sarah letting herself in.

"Oh, hi. I was just—" Reg looked back at the Black Forest cake sitting on the island, but Harrison was gone. Apparently, he wasn't in the mood to talk to anyone else. Reg rubbed her forehead and took another sip of coffee. "Never mind."

Sarah looked at the half-eaten cake, huge, ragged chunks ripped out of it, and raised her brows. "Morning snack?" she asked. "I'm surprised to see you up so early. Or have you not gone to bed yet?" She stood with her hands on her well-padded hips, a grandmotherly look of concern on her face.

Reg sighed. She wished she was still in bed. "*Someone* got me out of bed a lot earlier than I intended. And no, I wasn't the one eating the chocolate cake."

Sarah looked at it again and shook her head. "Do you want this back in the fridge, then?"

"No. You can toss it out. I'm not in the mood. I need to get the fridge cleaned out like you said, so I can see what's in there. It's packed so full there could be a whole rotisserie chicken in there and I wouldn't even know it."

She thought belatedly that she should probably not have pictured a rotisserie chicken jammed in among the fast-food containers and plastic containers. If she were unconsciously calling all of the food into her fridge, that was probably all it would take for a chicken to have disappeared from "Mary Jane's Chicken Delite" and appeared in Reg's fridge. She sighed.

Sarah shook her head at the waste of food and put the remains of the chocolate cake in the garbage. "You do need to keep on top of these things," she said, nodding toward the fridge. "I don't know why you keep buying so much food."

Instead of denying yet again that she had been the one to put all of that food in the fridge, Reg tried a different tack. "Maybe I was stressed."

"Ahh." Sarah nodded wisely. "Comfort eating is not good for you." She patted her own thickened waistline. "Goes straight to the belly."

Reg ran her thumb behind the waistband of her shorts. The shorts were significantly tighter than when she'd bought them. "I know."

"Well. Speaking of stress, I don't suppose you've heard the news yet."

"About Corvin being reinstated? Yes, I have."

"And that he's—"

"Hoping to become the new leader of the coven. Yes. That too. Davyn told me. And Corvin called yesterday to gloat about it too."

"Well, that's not what I meant, but yes. What I was going to say is that he is missing."

CHAPTER EIGHT

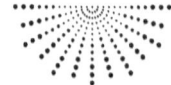

*W*ho is missing? Corvin?"

Sarah rolled her eyes and shook her head. "No, no such luck! It's Davyn who is missing."

"Davyn." Reg shook her head, not comprehending. "He isn't missing. I just saw him yesterday. For training."

"You should probably let the police know that. You might have been one of the last people to see him."

"He's not *missing*."

"He is," Sarah insisted. "He didn't show up at his office today and, when the police went to his house to check on him, he wasn't there. His car is. His wallet and phone. But he is not."

"But..." Reg tried to wrap her mind around this fact. "I just saw him. He can't be missing. Are they sure?"

"Where would he be without his car, phone, or wallet?" Sarah demanded.

"Well... I don't know. Out for a walk?"

"Without his wallet or phone."

"He could be. Maybe he didn't want to be disturbed."

"You know Davyn. He doesn't do things like that. And he didn't show up for work. He wouldn't go out for a walk instead of to work."

"No. I guess not. But it just seems so bizarre. He didn't say that he was going anywhere."

"I'm sure he's just fine," Sarah said brightly. "He'll show up again. The problem with Davyn is that he is *too* predictable and responsible. He takes on too much and was bound to burn out sooner or later. I have seen it happen to too many warlocks. They seem to have everything under control, and then boom, it all comes crashing down and they're running around town with their undershorts on their heads."

Reg blinked, trying to erase the mental image of Davyn sprinting along with a pair of tighty-whities stretched over his head. "You think he's had some kind of nervous breakdown?"

"It was bound to happen sooner or later. This strait-laced type doesn't know how to take a break or balance the load. Eventually, they just break."

Reg shook her head. Davyn did seem to be organized and responsible and have it all together, but she had never seen that as a disadvantage. She supposed it was true; she had release valves. If a situation got to be too much, she could back out. No one expected her to be that responsible. If she ducked out of something she had promised to do, people would just roll their eyes and go with the next person available. She didn't have a whole coven of witches expecting her to tell them what to do. If she were the leader of a coven, the members would pretty much just have to fend for themselves. She didn't know a higher way. She would probably be expecting them to tell her what to do.

"What will the coven do?" she asked.

Sarah raised her brows. "I'm sure the coven will be fine. A coven leader isn't always available. People have to realize that. You can't live your whole life for everyone else. If Davyn hasn't ever taken a vacation... well, he should have. They should know how to get along if he has to deal with something else or take a break. It isn't like they *need* him to tell them what to do every step of the way."

"So they'll be okay."

"Of course. Witches are pretty independent, you know. Many choose a solo practice. Those who join a coven... well, most of them are just loose affiliations. It is good for moral support, especially if you don't live in a place like Black Sands where you know any other practitioners. It's nice to get together for celebrations and holy days. But no one needs permission to practice."

"What if he doesn't come back before the election?"

"Oh, he'll be back before then."

"But what if he isn't?"

"I don't know. It will depend on if there is anyone else campaigning for leadership. If there isn't, and Corvin is the only one who makes a run for it…" She shrugged. "Then I guess he'll get what he wants."

Reg's heart pounded. "They can't make him their leader."

"If he is the only one who wants to… I suppose they can say that they won't recognize him, but that would be quite a scandal. I don't think most of the warlocks would be willing to do such a thing. Especially when there has been all of this publicity about allowing someone *like that* to run."

"Has there been a lot of publicity?" Reg shook her head. "I only just heard about it. I never even knew that he wasn't allowed to run before. Actually… I never knew that they did have elections and campaigns and that kind of thing. I thought that Davyn was just the most powerful warlock in that group, so he got to be the leader."

"He has achieved a higher level of understanding than most of them, but that doesn't automatically give him the authority or the responsibility. He has to accept it. Be willing to serve."

"If this is a service thing, where the leader is supposed to be doing things for the other members, then how is Corvin going to do that?"

Sarah raised her brows, shaking her head slightly. "What do you mean?"

"I mean… he isn't going to serve anyone else. He isn't going to do anything for anyone else. All he wants is his own glory."

"Well, that's not the way it works. And Corvin *has* been of service to others. As much as it pains me to say it, he has been helpful at times. To me, when I lost my emerald. Fighting the Witch Doctor. Helping you with your… various things. I would not recommend relying on someone like him and trusting that he will do the right thing, but he is capable of serving others."

"And do you think he would? He's been so grumpy lately."

Sarah made a motion as if to sweep this away. "You cannot go by a few days or weeks. A person's character is established over time. Years, decades, centuries. I know what kind of a person he has been. A few grumpy days does not make him incapable of leading a coven."

Reg opened the fridge and looked for something to eat with her coffee, but she didn't know what she wanted and there was too much to go through.

"What happens when a coven gets a leader who is… evil? What if he tells them to do things they shouldn't? Or hurts people? Takes their powers?"

"Other covens have worried about this, but the groups that have experimented with allowing his kind to lead them have had favorable results so far. They are clearly able to control themselves. To differentiate between hunting and leading. So far, the experiments have been positive."

Reg wasn't at all sure that Corvin leading the coven would prove to be a positive thing.

"Maybe those other covens have just been lucky. Are all of the warlocks who are *like Corvin* the same? Maybe some of them are… more enlightened?"

Sarah chuckled. "I can't imagine that they are all that different from Corvin. Their needs are still the same. They can't control their… hunger. All they can do is… choose where and when to satisfy it."

"By not consuming the powers of their coven members."

Sarah nodded. "Well, yes."

"So maybe it's actually safer to be in their coven than anywhere else."

"I hadn't thought about it that way. Perhaps you are right. But as you are not a warlock, you will not be able to join his coven."

"No gender equality in covens?" Reg asked. "Aren't you supposed to be open to all seekers?"

"No. Certainly not. We are quite selective about who we allow in our coven. Not just gender, but personalities. We don't accept just anyone."

"Then Corvin's coven didn't have to accept him? They could have denied him membership?" Reg was surprised by this. She had assumed that they weren't allowed to turn him away. Otherwise, who would agree to accept a power drinker into the coven? Maybe they hadn't known.

"No. It took him a long time to be accepted. There were a lot of the old guard who did not want him in the coven. It wasn't until recently that they agreed to allow him membership. There was talk about whether they would allow him to be reinstated. They could agree that his sentence was complete and he would no longer be shunned, but still not allow him to rejoin them."

"Why didn't they do that?"

Sarah patted at her hair like she was getting ready to go out somewhere and had to make sure she was presentable. "I imagine that it has to do with the powers he holds. They would prefer that power to be held by the coven. For them to have the ability to access it."

"He has to share?"

"He is expected to serve, even if he is not the leader of the coven. If someone has need of his gifts, he is expected to be selfless and to use them for the good of the coven and its members."

"He *has* to? Can they make him?"

"No, they can't make him. But I would imagine that he has already demonstrated the aptitude to be selfless. They would perhaps not be so quick to allow him back in if he had refused to help before."

Reg's mind was whirling with all of the new information. She wasn't sure how to take any of it. She needed to talk to Davyn, to ask him how—Reg stopped herself and shook her head. Davyn wasn't there to answer any more questions about Corvin and how the coven worked. Davyn was missing. And he wouldn't even answer her call if she tried to reach him on the phone, because his phone was at home and he was not.

CHAPTER NINE

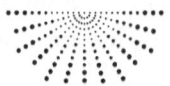

*A*fter Sarah was on her way to a lunch date with a friend, Reg wandered out to the garden. She was feeling out of sorts and hoped that the peace and tranquility of the garden would boost her spirits and help to clear her mind. She didn't know if the elves' presence made the garden so peaceful or whether it was just because of the green plants, sweet-smelling flowers, and the breeze blowing through the wind chimes. Forst, Sarah's garden gnome, had made the garden a paradise in the time he had been working on it. Maybe the calming feeling she got from the garden was just the natural result of all the work he had done.

She sat with her coffee on one of the benches, dappled leaves shifting overhead and the wind chimes tinkling gently.

There was no reason for her to be so worried about what had happened to Davyn or what was going to happen with Corvin and his bid to become the leader of the coven. It had nothing to do with her. Sarah was undoubtedly right, and Davyn would return after a few wild days and resume his position until Corvin beat him out. Corvin would serve as he was expected to and would be so wrapped up in the management of the coven that he wouldn't bother Reg. It would all work out to her good.

Unless, of course, something had happened to Davyn and he

wouldn't return, and Reg would not have a mentor in firecasting. Corvin would gain control of the coven unopposed and then would proceed to do all of the things he had been planning to, sucking power from the other members of the coven until he was strong enough not just to attack Reg, but to overwhelm her defenses and take her powers.

Does Reg Rawlins bring the thunderclouds?

Reg looked around for Forst, hearing his "inside words" in her head. He stood nearby, resting his arms across the handle of a shovel. The cheeks that showed above his beard were rosy red. He was dressed in drab browns and greens, with a red cap.

What? Reg looked up at the sky, expecting to see gathering clouds, but it was clear, bright and sunny.

Not those thunderclouds, Forst told her with amusement. *The ones on thy face.*

Oh. Reg rubbed her face with both hands, trying to relax her muscles and lose the scowl. *I'm sorry. I'm sitting here thinking negative thoughts.* Reg looked around at the garden. *That's probably not very good for the plants, is it?*

Forst gave a grave nod. He patted the trunk of the big tree like he might a close human—or gnomen—friend. *They are strong now. You will not hurt them.*

Good. Yeah, I don't want to make them sick with all my negativity.

Why so thunderous? Forst inquired.

Reg sighed. *Davyn, my mentor, is missing, and I want to ask him questions. About Corvin—the one who is a power drinker.*

Reg Rawlins should not associate with that one.

I know. I'm just worried about what he might do.

Forst stroked his beard, thinking about that. *What is coming is coming,* he told her finally. *Reg Rawlins cannot change that.*

You're right.

Reg tried to keep the scowl and worry lines from tightening across her face again. *I came here to feel better.*

The living always help, Forst agreed sagely, looking around with satisfaction at the garden bursting with life. *They are real friends.* He reached out to touch and stroke the leaves of one of the nearby shrubs.

A year or two ago, Reg might have scoffed at anyone taking such a personal interest in plants and claiming that they were his friends. But things had changed a lot in that time. Reg herself could feel emotions and sensations from gemstones. Was it really any different from being able to communicate with the dead, who were also inanimate? She knew how dearly the dwarfs treasured gemstones and gnomes their living plants. The plants were just as alive as Starlight, and Reg had no trouble communicating with him. Why not plants?

Reg leaned forward to bury her nose in a large yellow flower nearby. She closed her eyes and breathed in the scent, then sat back again.

Do you communicate with other creatures in the yard? she asked Forst.

He rubbed his brown, lined forehead. *At times.*

Orri, the elf, he said that I need to protect the creatures in the garden. Reg looked around. *I suppose he meant the birds and the bees. Maybe the elves, even though I can't usually see them. Are there other things? Other creatures he was talking about?*

He gave her a big smile, his eyes twinkling. *There is much Reg Rawlins does not see.*

I guess human eyes are not very quick.

No, he agreed. *Not very good. Many times, you do not even see Forst.*

And look how big you are. I assume you're the biggest creature in the garden. Tell me there aren't any panthers or crocs in there. Reg peered at the thickly growing foliage around her.

Nothing that eats humans, Forst assured her. Then he frowned and cocked his head, thinking about it. *No,* he confirmed. *not that eats humans.*

Reg got goosebumps on her arms. She put down her coffee mug and tried to rub them away. Forst was just teasing her, she was sure. There were no large predators in the little garden. She would know if there were. And Sarah had even performed a spell to help keep venomous snakes away so Reg wouldn't have to worry about running into any of *them* again. The garden was perfectly safe, guarded by magical wards and by the garden gnome. There wasn't anything there that could hurt her.

Why can't I see any of these other creatures? Reg asked. *Do they hide from me?*

There are many things unseen. Especially for humans.

Reg really didn't like the sound of that. It was fine if they were things like butterflies or elves, but she didn't like the idea of any *dark* creatures lurking in the garden.

Reg's phone rang, making Reg jump. She grabbed it from her pocket and turned it to look at the screen. It had better not be Corvin again. She didn't have anything to say to him.

Instead, she saw Marta Jessup's name on the screen. Detective Marta Jessup. *I-have-to-follow-the-law* Marta Jessup. Reg considered not answering the call but, after a couple more vibrations, decided that she'd better. Jessup would keep calling or would show up on her doorstep. And, unlike Corvin, Jessup was not specifically barred from the cottage. No one could enter who intended harm but, as a peace-keeper and law-abiding citizen, she was sure that the wards would not keep Jessup away.

She swiped the call and put her phone up to her ear.

"This is Reg."

CHAPTER TEN

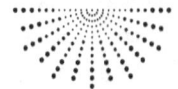

*R*eg, it's good to hear your voice," Jessup said pleasantly. "It's been too long since we talked last."

"What do you want?" Reg asked. Not in an angry or demanding voice. Just straightforward and to-the-point. She was not going to be friendly toward Jessup. She had answered the call as a courtesy and to ensure that Jessup didn't show up at her house, not because they were friends.

"Well... I was wondering if we could get together and have a visit. I could bring takeout if you like and we could sit down and chat."

"No."

There was silence as Jessup considered this. "Is there a better time?" she asked. "It doesn't have to be right now. Later in the day, maybe..."

"I'm not interested in a chat. It seems like too many of our chats end up with me at the police station."

"Oh, this is nothing like that." Jessup tried to laugh, but it sounded nervous. "You are not a suspect in any case, not even a person of interest. I was just hoping..." she trailed off and didn't finish.

"Hoping what?"

"To tell the truth, I am looking for a consultant on a case. It's right up your alley." When Reg didn't reply, Jessup tried again. "I could pay you as a consultant."

"I have enough jobs right now. I'm not looking to pick up any new clients. Especially the police department."

"Well," Jessup cleared her throat. "I thought you might be interested in this one. I don't know if you have heard yet, but…"

Reg hoped she wouldn't say that it was something to do with Corvin. Corvin acted as some kind of consultant or informant for the police department now and then. Reg assumed that it was off the books, since most of the police didn't have a magical bone in their bodies, and it would be difficult to explain hiring someone for magical purposes.

"Did you know… that Davyn Smithy is missing?"

"Sarah mentioned that, yes."

"Oh. Okay. So you know. Well, there isn't very much evidence, and I would like to get some outside help. Sometimes… well, I know usually it is just a TV thing, but sometimes psychics do contact the police department with insight on a case."

"I didn't call you, so you don't have anything to worry about. Nothing to explain away."

Jessup cleared her throat again. "Reg, you're making this really difficult. I know you have some powerful gifts and I was hoping that you would be able to give me some help on Davyn's disappearance. I'm quite concerned about him."

"Sarah said that he probably just got overworked and burned out. Took some time off for a few days to recover."

"If that was the case, then I would expect him to be at home. Wouldn't you?"

"Not if he didn't want to have to talk to anyone."

"Well, no, I suppose not. Is that what you *feel* about this case? That he doesn't want to talk to anyone?"

"I don't feel anything about it. How about I give you a call if I have any thoughts about it?"

"That would be really good! Maybe I could come over this afternoon and we could talk things over? Just to make sure that you have all of the pertinent details. Then if you see or feel anything, I can take immediate action…"

"No. I said I'll call you. If I think of anything."

"Well, yes. But you don't know anything about the case, and you would be more likely to have an insight on it if you knew all of the details, wouldn't you? Maybe if you had something of his to touch."

"I don't want anything of Davyn's. If he wanted me to have something of his, he would have given it to me."

"Maybe later this evening or tomorrow morning?" Jessup pressed desperately.

"No," Reg told her firmly. "Don't call me back. And don't come over here. If you do, you'll be trespassing and I'll call your boss."

There was a hurt silence from Jessup. Maybe she was trying to think of a comeback. Or any other way that she could make Reg help her with the case. Reg tapped the end call button on her screen and lowered the phone to her lap.

Forst was still there, watching her and taking it all in. Apparently, gnomes did not have any prohibition against eavesdropping on other people's calls. Forst smiled at her. *Reg Rawlins has very strong outside words,* he told her admiringly.

Gnomes had a difficult time speaking aloud with humans. Which was why they were often silent around humans or were perceived as terse or uneducated when they did manage a few short "outside words."

Reg chuckled. Yes, she could be very strong with her outside words. She hoped that she had been clear enough that Jessup would not dare bother her any further with requests to help with Davyn's missing person case.

* * *

Reg thanked Forst for spending the time with her and for taking such good care of the garden and returned to the cottage. She was still in her pajamas, though the shirt and shorts that she wore for sleep were not obviously sleepwear, and probably no one else could have told whether she was still dressed for sleep or ready for the day. But *she* knew, and she needed a hot shower before she did anything else.

After a nice long shower, Reg changed Starlight's kitty litter box and decided it was time to tackle the problem with the fridge. It was still earlier in the day than she usually got up, and she wouldn't have any appointments with clients until the evening. Maybe if she worked hard for an hour or two, she could completely straighten out the kitchen, and would be so tired that she would be ready for an afternoon nap and catch up on the rest of her sleep before any clients showed up.

The part about making herself tired cleaning up the kitchen certainly worked. Reg went through the fridge, emptying half of what was in there into the garbage and taking it out to the bins behind the fence. She went through the cupboards, which were not quite as full as the fridge, and at least most of what was there was in cans and would not go bad if she didn't get to it right away. There was quite a bit of tuna, which was becoming a staple for both Reg and Starlight. It was nice not to have to go to the grocery store to buy supplies, but she felt guilty knowing that she had probably called those items to her home from the store without the store being compensated for them. But it hadn't been intentional, so it wasn't exactly stealing. Was it?

She washed and put away all the dishes and scrubbed down the counters and sink until everything gleamed.

Then she felt ready to drop.

But she was also famished.

Reg had cupboards and a fridge full of food, but she didn't have the energy to warm anything up. And she didn't want more dirty dishes in the sink she had just cleaned, or to have to wash and dry them and put them away. Reg sighed tiredly and shook her head at her own silliness. All the food she could want, and she couldn't bring herself to eat it.

She could try to force herself or talk herself into it, but why bother with that? She would just end up cranky and out of sorts when she had her readings and seance. It wouldn't do to be grumpy with paying customers. And she didn't want to channel angry spirits. Clients paid for comforting messages from their loved ones, not negativity.

It was really in her best interest to go out to eat, rather than stay home and make something. It was better for everyone involved.

CHAPTER ELEVEN

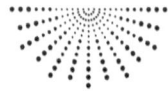

*T*he first restaurant that Reg had gone to upon her arrival at Black Sands was The Crystal Bowl. It was a hangout for all kinds of practitioners, and they served tasty food in a comfortable, though somewhat dramatic, atmosphere. It was close to home and remained her favorite eatery in Black Sands. So, tired though she was, it didn't really take any effort to hop in her car and drive the few blocks to The Crystal Bowl for a meal.

There *had* been some trouble getting service at The Crystal Bowl when her siren parentage had been revealed. She was told that they didn't serve her kind there and she would have to leave. But Sarah had promised that people would forget about it quickly enough, and she had been right. Corvin had eaten with Reg there a couple of times, and his charms ensured that no one would kick her out. So things had gone back to normal again. Maybe Reg should have held a grudge against management for treating her that way, but Reg preferred eating there to the meager satisfaction of withholding her patronage because they had done her wrong.

Everyone made mistakes. It was best to leave the past in the past and move forward. From what Reg had learned about time travel, she wouldn't want to remain in the past or change anything for a better future anyway. Things never seemed to work out for the better when tampering with the timeline.

Reg greeted Bill, one of the bartenders, at the bar and had a refreshing first drink to slake her thirst and calm her nerves. She could just relax and enjoy the ambiance of The Crystal Bowl on a lazy afternoon before the dinner rush. With a warm, comfortable feeling, Reg slid off of the barstool to find herself a table.

She should have recognized that the flush of warmth wasn't caused by a malfunction in The Crystal Bowl's air conditioning or her drink. She should have known that familiar feeling for what it was.

Corvin was standing behind her, dark hair and eyes, carefully sculpted beard, a shark-like smile fixed on his face.

"Oh!" Reg froze, startled to see him there. "I didn't know you were there."

"Ready for dinner?" Corvin asked, looking like he was more interested in consuming her than eating *with* her.

"No—" Reg could just go home and eat there. She didn't need to stay around Corvin. But was she going to let herself be run off by him? From her favorite restaurant? She couldn't stop going to The Crystal Bowl just because he knew it was her favorite place to eat and he would be able to find her there for dinner at least half the time. "Uh… yes. But I was planning to eat alone."

"Then isn't it fortuitous that I am here and can keep you company?" Corvin touched her arm to escort her to a table. There was a buzzing electrical charge between them when he touched her and she couldn't resist his encouraging smile.

She shouldn't be with him. Not when she was exhausted from her housework and already had one drink on an empty stomach. It made her too vulnerable. Too susceptible to his charms.

Reg walked with him over to the booth that he picked out, smiling like she really wanted to be there. And she did. She enjoyed the feeling of his touch on her arm, the heat of him standing beside her, the heady smell of roses that he exuded when charming her.

"No, I shouldn't…" Reg murmured. But she knew it wasn't a real protest, and so did he.

"We could go somewhere else," Corvin suggested. "Somewhere more private."

"No." Reg's protest was more emphatic this time. She knew that she shouldn't leave with him. As long as she was at The Crystal Bowl, Bill and the other staff would keep an eye on what was going on. She was safe where there were people. If she were to leave with him and go to his private club or to either of their homes, things would not go well. Reg knew only too well that he would not be able to control himself, even to get the pro forma consent that the magical laws required. "No, I want to stay here."

"You would be more comfortable, and we would be more free to discuss things openly…"

"No." Reg pulled her arm away from him. "I said no."

The resistance required an effort. Reg tried to shield herself from his charms to allow her head to clear a little. She was feeling warm and contented and a little muddled. She needed a clear head if she were going to stay in control of the situation.

Corvin didn't try to touch her again. He motioned to the booth with a grand sweep of his arm, and Reg sat down. Corvin seated himself across from her. There was a slight scuffle as several waitresses tried to approach the table at the same time to talk to Corvin, but one of them came out the clear winner and placed herself at Corvin's side, looking down at him, eyes shining.

Corvin ordered a bottle of wine. Reg shook her head. "I'll have a glass of water—no, a Coke. Thanks."

The waitress looked disapproving, but wrote it down on her order pad, bestowed another adoring smile on Corvin, and walked over to the bar. Corvin raised his brows at Reg. "Teetotalling today?" he asked, shaking his head. "Coke won't exactly pair with your meal. You expect me to drink the whole bottle myself?"

"You can have however much you want. I need… a clear head."

He rested his arm on the table and extended his fingers to touch Reg's arm. Reg pulled back at the electrical charge between them.

"I won't even make it to dinner if you keep doing that."

He shrugged. "It's a bit early for dinner anyway. We could do other things. Worry about dinner later."

"No." Reg was as firm as she could be, keeping the shield between them and avoiding his touch.

Corvin pushed back against the shield, making Reg's body temperature go up. She broke into a sweat. She concentrated on using the shield to reflect his heat back at him and, in a few seconds, Corvin withdrew, wincing uncomfortably. Reg breathed more easily. If he would stop trying to ensorcel her, they could enjoy a meal together. But if he kept pushing it, Reg would have to leave.

"Just leave me alone," she told him in a low voice. "I'm hungry."

He gazed at her. "So am I."

"I could leave."

"I could follow you," he countered, his mouth curling up in a smug smile.

"If I can transport myself to and from Egypt, I think I can transport myself home from here. Or maybe send you *back* to Egypt. How about that?"

Corvin sat back and stopped trying to influence her. He shook his head. "Fine. If that's the way you want to play it."

Reg breathed a sigh of relief. "Yeah. It is."

The waitress returned with the bottle of wine and Reg's Coke. "And what can I get you to eat today?" she asked Corvin, without even a glance at Reg.

Corvin flicked through the pages of the menu, which he must know off by heart. Reg knew everything the restaurant offered, and she hadn't been in Black Sands as long as Corvin had. He placed his order, then looked at Reg for hers.

"What's your freshest fish?" Reg couldn't help thinking about going to the ocean with Corvin. Taking him to the water's edge. Her mouth was watering. But fish would have to suffice.

"The trout." This was obviously a question that the waitress was asked regularly, because she didn't have to think about it. Living so close to the ocean, people in Black Sands expected their seafood to be very fresh.

"I'll have that, then."

The waitress nodded. She smiled at Corvin, fluttering her eyelashes, then withdrew to place the order with the kitchen.

Reg tried to assess Corvin dispassionately. His eyes flitted around the restaurant instead of staying on her as they usually did. He normally gave her his full attention, or at least pretended that he was. Without his charms affecting her, Reg noticed something different about Corvin. His aura was dark. Something appeared to be worrying him or making him anxious. He didn't stop moving, but shifted his position every few seconds, eyes monitoring everything in the restaurant.

"What's going on?" Reg asked him.

"What do you mean?" Corvin's eyes touched on her briefly, and then his gaze was elsewhere again.

"You seem like you're worried about something. Is it… campaigning for the leadership of the coven?"

"What do you know about that?" his eyes narrowed suspiciously.

"You told me."

He eyed her for a moment, scowling, then he wiped his hand over his face in a tired gesture and smoothed the angry lines. "Yes. Of course I did."

Reg nodded. "I just wondered if that was what was on your mind. You seem… distracted."

"Maybe I am," he admitted. "You wouldn't think that it would be stressful to do something you wanted to—being reinstated to the coven and maybe taking over its leadership—but even positive changes can be taxing."

Reg nodded her understanding. Any new situation or big change was difficult. Living in her own little cottage in Black Sands, finding out that she had powers, coming into money, they had all been difficult for her.

"Is it going to be a lot of work, running for leadership of the coven?"

"Yes, of course it takes work."

She stretched out all of her senses, trying to feel more from him. The stress of running for Davyn's position in the coven didn't seem to fully explain the darkness around him. He was doing his best to keep his mind closed from her but, due to the way that they had been connected in the past, the conduit between the two of them could not be completely closed off. Reg shut her eyes, trying to visualize what was going on with Corvin. Trying to get some sense of what was going on with him.

"Mind your own business," Corvin told her.

Reg pulled back her mind and opened her eyes. "It isn't the coven?" she asked tentatively.

"What else would it be? That's the most important thing in my life right now. Getting back my life. Showing that I am as qualified for leadership as—even more qualified than—anyone else."

Reg nodded slowly. She took a sip of her soft drink and looked around the room, taking her focus from Corvin to sense the moods of the others around her. The Crystal Bowl was not very busy, so there weren't many other people to worry about. Even the voices in her head were relatively quiet and relaxed for once.

"You've never said very much about your coven," she said. "Is the membership secret?"

"No. We don't generally talk about what goes on in the coven. We afford people their privacy. But the membership itself is not a secret. Happily, we live in a society where mere membership in a coven is not enough for a person to be burned at the stake."

"Who else is in your coven? What are they like? The only one that I know of is Davyn. Damon isn't a member, right?"

Corvin shook his head, sneering. "He's not a member of any coven."

"That's right," Reg remembered. "He called himself a lone wolf or something like that. He said that with his security business, he can't afford to take sides or be associated with any particular group."

Corvin rolled his eyes. "Good excuse for not being able to get along with anyone else."

"Do you think so? He's friendly enough; I thought he got along with people. He was in charge of the security for the Spring Games. That was a big deal."

"That's his business, not his personal life."

"Well… yeah. I guess so."

"*You* don't get along with him," Corvin pointed out. He gave a slightly superior smile.

Reg struggled to answer his point. She had several reasons for not getting along very well with Damon Knight. "He's a nice enough guy, and good at his job… he can be fun. But…"

"You don't need a diviner analyzing whether every statement you make is true?" Corvin suggested.

"Well…" Reg's face warmed. Not finding out that Damon was a diviner until she'd probably told him several things that were not *quite* true had made her pretty uncomfortable. Reg wasn't quite as married to the truth as some people. Sometimes it served her well, and sometimes it did not. She didn't like being caught in a lie, even just a small one. "He was never mean about it. He said that everyone lies."

Corvin considered this. "Still probably didn't make you feel very comfortable around him."

Reg nodded.

"But that's not all," Corvin guessed.

"No…" Reg didn't want to get into why she was not comfortable around Damon and had decided that their relationship would not go anywhere. It was pretty personal, even if Corvin had been in her head before and would not be shocked by anything she had to say. She had asked him about his coven, and that was what she wanted to talk about, not Reg's suitors. "I guess… I had to keep telling him not to put visions in my head, but he acted like he couldn't help it. And then he used them to deceive me when we were looking for Wilson." Reg rubbed her forehead hard, trying to release the tension in the space between her eyes. "I've got enough stuff going on in my head without someone else adding visions of things that aren't true." She shrugged. "I can't deal with that."

Corvin nodded, looking very smug. It wasn't like he was a prize catch. She knew that things could never work out between her and Corvin either, no matter how attracted she was to him when she touched him or he was charming her. The only thing he wanted out of a relationship was her gifts, and she knew that her feelings were being manipulated. They weren't real. Two handsome bachelors in her life, and neither one was someone she could live with for a day, let alone long-term. Reg let out a long breath.

Before coming to Black Sands, she'd always been on the move, never in one place for more than a few months, so none of her relationships had been serious. She could have a fling, do what she liked, and then be gone by the time the relationship started to sour. Encounters could be as short as she wanted and not mean anything to her long-term. Now that she was settled down in one place, with a home of her own and stable employment, she had to consider where a relationship might take her and what would happen when she ended it. Would she end up awkwardly avoiding an ex at the grocery store? Trying to divide up their friends between his and hers? She had no idea how to navigate that kind of complex relationship. She would have to leave town, and she didn't want to be put in that position when she had finally found a place she belonged.

CHAPTER TWELVE

*C*orvin had been looking away from her, scoping out the room carefully as if looking for hidden dangers. He turned his gaze back to her, brows drawing together slightly.

"Belonging?" He echoed the word in her thoughts. "It must be nice to find a place you feel like you belong."

Reg shifted uncomfortably. "*You* belong here," she pointed out. "You're a warlock. You have a coven. You have a business where you provide magical services to people. You have your studies. You fit in here like a piece in a puzzle."

He shook his head. "It only looks that way from the outside. I have been different ever since I was born. Hated because I am what my father was. Excluded from polite society. I was allowed into the coven, but barred from progressing any further. You think that's a life of belonging? To be shunned everywhere I go, even, eventually, by my own coven? The people who were supposed to be my spiritual brothers?"

Reg shook her head. She wasn't sure what to say to him. He was twisting it around. She didn't know what his whole life had been like, all of the secret resentments he had against the people who had excluded him. But she did know that his coven hadn't shunned him for being a power drinker. He had been shunned for breaking the laws of their community that said he could not take someone's powers without their permission. Because he had tried to do exactly that and take Reg's powers from her.

"Neither of us belongs here," Corvin told Reg, his eyes reflecting a weird light as he stared at her. "I because of my curse. You because you are part siren, part immortal, and have more magic in your little finger than anyone else in this room."

He took another look around the room as if something might have changed since he'd checked last. He looked back at Reg.

"Except you," she said.

"Except me," Corvin said, smiling to show off his even white teeth. "You and I are more matched in our abilities. We belong together."

"You don't want me. You just want to hold my powers."

"There is more to you than just your powers."

Reg raised her brows. There certainly was, yet Corvin seemed to have little idea what her other desirable attributes might be. He had said that she was beautiful and given her other compliments, but all he'd ever had eyes for were her powers. She'd been too naive, had known nothing about his kind or his powers, and had let herself be taken advantage of. But that would never happen again.

The waitress appeared beside them at the table, startling Reg. She nearly knocked over her drink and grabbed it to keep it from falling over.

"Sorry, sorry! I didn't see you!"

The waitress smirked at Reg, then simpered at Corvin as she put his plate in front of him. "Is there anything else I can get *you*?"

"This looks fine. Thank you."

The waitress said nothing to Reg about the plate she had put in front of her. But the fish looked good, and Reg didn't think that the waitress had spit in it. Reg hadn't done anything to be rude to her. Though she might be a target just because she was there with Corvin and every warm-blooded woman in his orbit wanted to be with him instead.

They made noises indicating their enjoyment and talked about the food for a little while, but they hadn't really gotten together for the food. An undercurrent ran through every look and sentence.

"I'm starting to worry about Davyn," Reg said, pausing to take a drink and see if her comment elicited any reaction from Corvin.

"He's a grown man." Corvin dabbed at his mouth with a napkin. "I don't think there is anything to worry about."

"But men go missing too. They get mugged or murdered, or disappear, and no one ever hears from them again. It isn't just women and children who disappear."

"Of course not. But he can take care of himself. He is a powerful warlock. Even if you don't know that from your direct experience, you must know it by virtue of the fact that he is the current leader of the coven. I don't see what could have happened to him."

"Sarah thinks he had a nervous breakdown. That he's too serious and has too many responsibilities and was bound to break sooner or later."

"There is something to be said for that."

"Do *you* think that he just took an impromptu vacation?"

"Well…" Corvin eyed her, "Of course that is a possibility. And Sarah is right about him having a lot of responsibility, a lot of things to stay on top of, and that could easily become overwhelming. I would like to ease that burden a little, and he was very happy to hear that I would take over leadership of the coven from him. He deserved a break."

"He was happy about it?"

"You know what it is like to carry a heavy burden."

Reg had actually avoided taking responsibility for anything she didn't have to for most of her life. She didn't like to have people relying upon her. She didn't promise anyone anything, and then they couldn't say that she had disappointed them. If she did something nice for someone, it was just a bonus. Not something that she had promised.

But she had inadvertently taken upon her other burdens since she had moved to Black Sands. Trying to help people who were sick or injured. Trying to reunite jewelry and gemstones with their rightful owners. Protecting Corvin and Julian from siren attacks. It had been difficult, and she kept telling herself that she would soon be able to relax and just think about herself and her own needs. Soon. But other things kept coming up.

All the more reason not to take on the additional responsibility of helping Jessup and the police to track down Davyn. Davyn was just fine, wherever he was.

"Maybe he's gone to visit Julian," Corvin suggested. "The two seem very close, and it has been some time since they saw each other last. Long-distance relationships can be difficult."

"He would have told his office. He wouldn't just... not show up one day."

"You would think. But like Sarah said..."

Reg nodded. "I suppose. He might have just gotten burnt out. Decided that he'd had enough."

"I've seen it happen to other practitioners," Corvin assured her. "You might think that having gifts would make life easier for us, that these powers would pave the way. But they take a lot of energy and attention. This isn't a TV show where you can just flick a magic wand and have whatever you want without any energy expenditure. And for a guy like Davyn..."

"What do you mean 'a guy like Davyn'?"

Corvin raised his brows. "An inherently *nice* guy. Someone who truly wants to help other people with his gifts. Someone who has problems saying no, so he keeps taking on more and more."

"Oh. Yeah." Reg felt a slight twinge, realizing that he had also taken on her training as a firecaster without indicating that the time and energy it took were a drain on him. He was just there, every week, helping her to learn how to use her firecasting without putting anyone else in danger. He took it on because he knew that no one else in the area could mentor her. But he took time away from work to do it and, as Corvin had said, handling fire and helping Reg keep hers under control took energy and attention. Maybe he had been spread too thin.

"Someone should call Julian," Corvin said, his eyes moving away from Reg again. "He probably knows where Davyn is."

"Wouldn't the police have called him?"

Corvin raised his brows. "The police? Have they gotten involved in this?"

Reg nodded. She poked at her fish and ate a couple more bites. "Jessup called me about it."

"Indeed. I didn't know it had been reported to the authorities."

"You don't think it should have been?" Reg guessed from his tone.

"Matters concerning practitioners should be left to the magical community. No good comes from involving non-magical investigators."

He was probably right. Reg couldn't see what good it would do to involve people who had no idea what Davyn could do, what he spent his time on, and the people he associated with. They would think that he was just a regular office worker bee and would only look in the obvious places. It didn't make sense to involve them in something where they only had a fraction of the facts. Jessup might know more, having come from a practicing family. Still, she didn't have any powers to speak of herself, so she was a member of the magical community by tradition only, not a full participant in all that it had to offer.

"Do you think Jessup knows about Julian?" she asked Corvin.

"I don't know. Did she ever meet him?"

"I don't think so. But he is with Magical Investigations, so maybe he interfaced with the local police through her?" Reg tried to remember. Her brain was like Swiss cheese. Or like someone had rifled all of the drawers of the cabinets her memories were filed in and thoroughly tossed the place. Anything that had happened before Wilson's intrusion could be affected. "I think... Jessup knew that I was talking to someone from MI. But I don't think she ever met him. Not while I was there, anyway."

"Maybe someone ought to fill her in, then."

"Not me. I already told her I didn't want to talk to her about the case."

"Why not? I thought psychics were always trying to get in on this sort of thing. Big case. Get on the news making predictions and then become famous when they prove to be true..."

"I'm not looking to get on the news," Reg told him, horrified at the idea. "I like to keep a low profile."

"So you won't help her with her case."

"No."

"Then… I guess you're not concerned about Davyn after all."

"I… of course I am! I'm more concerned than you are!"

"But you won't go to the police with what you know."

"No. They can find that out from his other friends. I'm not the only one who knows about Julian."

Corvin nodded slowly. "Maybe they'll get around to it tomorrow or the next day."

CHAPTER THIRTEEN

*T*he trickiest part of a date with Corvin was always escaping at the end with her powers intact. She knew that Corvin would really turn on the charm as they were having their final sips of coffee and getting ready to go. That's when the rubber met the road, and Corvin knew that if he was going to get anywhere with Reg, he only had minutes to act.

"You enjoyed your fish?" Corvin asked, looking down at Reg's plate, which was nearly clean.

"Yes, it was very good." Looking at Corvin, Reg couldn't help but think about taking him for a walk on the beach, as she had once before. Actually, he had taken her, but the results had not been what he had expected. And Reg knew that she couldn't get close to the water, much less get her feet wet, with him at her side. Despite his powers, he might not be able to escape a second time. Reg was growing in her abilities, and the siren instincts were getting stronger.

Reg licked her lips, then turned away from him. She couldn't let herself think about what would happen if she gave in. What would the police do if another man she was associated with disappeared? They wouldn't just stand by, Reg was sure. She'd seen too many times how they would insist on being involved, turning over every stone and looking for anything at all suspicious, even when she was completely innocent.

"I need to go," Reg told him. She adjusted her grip on her purse on her lap as if she were going to have to race him to the door. "Sorry, I have a few appointments tonight."

He was looking away from her, across the room. But his eyes were so distant that she wasn't sure he was looking at anything actually in the room. He was somewhere else, lost in thought. After a moment, he seemed to realize that she had said something to him. His eyes returned to her.

"Sorry, what?"

"I have to go. I have to prepare for my sessions tonight."

"Yes. Of course." He stood up.

Reg stared at him. He had never before missed the opportunity to try to persuade her to go home with him. Or to another, more intimate location. Corvin stood there, waiting for her. He held his hand out to her to help her to her feet. Reg didn't take his hand, wary of the effect of his touch on her, and slid out of the bench seat of the booth.

"That was nice," she told him awkwardly. "And I hope that whatever is on your mind is resolved soon. If it's the coven... I hope everything goes well."

She didn't, of course. She didn't want him to take over as the leader of the coven. And he would sense that in her.

"Yes," he agreed. His lips pressed together for a moment, thinking.

Reg had fleeting images in her mind of gatherings of the coven, many of which seemed to be far in the past, of arguments and of Corvin stymied in his goals, prevented from advancing as he had wished. Arguments with other warlocks who must have been his coven members. Long, dark, lonely hours. And other impressions that went by too quickly for her to see or analyze them. A lot of dark memories.

She felt a little sorry for him, as she hadn't before. She had felt for the little boy that he had been and how he had been abused by his father and by the deep, painful hunger he suffered if he did not fill the void within him with the powers of others. But she had never understood how isolating life was for him, separated by his gifts from the rest of the magical community.

But she steeled herself against the pity she felt for him. He would use those feelings against her. The images that had flashed through her mind could be a ploy, another way to draw her to him and get her to let down the barriers she had to keep between them. It could all be another way to seduce her. So she didn't smile, touch his arm, or say that she was sorry. She gave a curt nod and walked briskly away from him, clutching her purse tightly.

He didn't call her back or follow her out.

Though distracted by thoughts of Corvin's strange behavior, Reg managed to get through her readings and seance without any issues. Her clients were happy with the results, and the woman who had set up the seance with her family members had even given Reg a generous tip at the end of the session. Reg enjoyed the satisfaction of her clients almost as much as the money. With the gemstones that she had been able to liquidate, she didn't need to worry about her bank account, and other measures of how her business was going came into play.

She went to bed satisfied with the day, despite all of the ups and downs and her concern over Davyn's disappearance. It wasn't her job to find Davyn. Jessup was on the case and others in the magical community were talking about it. Reg had no doubt that they would sort it all out soon enough.

Reg awoke a few hours later to whispering. She lay in bed, trying to figure out if it was the rustling of leaves outside the window, or maybe the fridge was making noises again. She was sure, to begin with, that her brain was just misinterpreting something else in her environment. No one could come into the cottage. Unless maybe they were outside in the garden. But even the garden was protected by charms and wards. Forst wouldn't be whispering; if he were talking to Fir or one of the other gnomes, he would use his inside words, not a whisper. And if he were talking to Sarah out loud, he wouldn't be whispering long sentences, but conversing in his usual brusque, one- or two-word answers.

She rubbed her eyes and grabbed her phone off the nightstand to check the time. It was way too early for her to be awake yet. She'd barely been in bed for three hours. Reg groaned and rolled over, pulling the blanket over her head to block the sun and the irritating whisper.

CHAPTER FOURTEEN

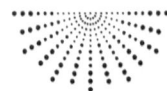

*E*ventually, Reg couldn't stand it anymore and rolled out of bed to see where the noise was coming from. She found Harrison in the kitchen with Starlight. Two mornings in a row. Harrison often went long periods without putting in an appearance, or only showed up when he was called. It was unusual for him to be there two days in a row.

Starlight was sitting in the middle of the kitchen island, his furry butt firmly planted in the middle of Reg's appointment book. He knew he wasn't allowed up on the counters. Harrison was standing facing him. He turned and looked as Reg walked out of the bedroom. He put his finger to his lips, telling Starlight, "Shh. Don't wake her up."

"It's a little late for that," Reg told him. "What are you doing here?"

"Whispering."

"Clearly," Reg laughed. "What are you two talking about?"

She didn't think Starlight had been whispering, but she couldn't be sure. And certainly, Starlight could have been communicating with a method other than whispering. Reg had found that there were many more methods of communication than just speaking aloud. Gestures and body language, telepathy, visions, feelings and auras, and probably several others she wasn't thinking of. Even non-magical humans had other methods of communication when someone did not want or was not able to use the spoken word.

"We are friends," Harrison stated.

"Yes. You and Starlight, or you and me? Or all of us?"

He raised his eyebrows, considering. "It is complex."

"Yes, it is."

"Humans have friends."

"Immortals don't?" Reg was sure that she remembered Harrison calling Destine, the Witch Doctor "my old friend." But had they really been friends, or had Harrison just been using a human figure of speech because he thought it was appropriate? They had probably known each other for a long time, but Reg wasn't sure they had ever been buddies. They had very different natures. Harrison was more concerned with human life, or at least the lives of a few of the humans that he knew. He tried to follow the rules the immortals had agreed to. The Witch Doctor preferred to find his way around the rules and was concerned with accumulating power and ruling over the human race. Or maybe the whole universe.

"Not the same," Harrison confirmed. "Tell me about your friends."

Reg was put on the spot. She looked at Starlight, then back at Harrison. "I just woke up. I'm going to need a cup of coffee."

He moved out of the way so that she could see the coffee machine. "Coffee!" he said, sounding delighted. "Look!"

"You made coffee?" Reg was impressed. Harrison's grasp of human machines was not great. She had shown him how to make coffee before, but the idea of using buttons to make the coffee brew seemed to be a bizarre concept to Harrison. "Good job."

Harrison grinned widely at her. Reg walked over to get out a mug and filled it from the carafe. She held the cup up to her nose to smell the coffee, but didn't inhale any steam. She tentatively brought the mug to her lips for a sip and found the coffee stone cold. She touched the side of the carafe and looked at the settings on the coffee machine. The warming element was not turned on. But for the coffee to be that cold already, Harrison had either brewed it several hours before or had magically produced the coffee and forgotten that it should be hot.

She cleared her throat and tried to smile. "It's better hot," she told him, hoping he would not be offended.

Harrison nodded. "Yes."

"Well… that was very nice of you."

"So." Harrison bent over so that he could put his elbow on the island and rest his chin in his palm. "Tell me about your friends."

He must have seen the gesture and expression on TV or from someone else. It was such an out-of-character performance from Harrison. Was he really trying to learn about human friendships? Or was he just mimicking something he had seen, thinking it would feel natural to Reg?

"I don't know…" Reg shifted awkwardly. "I have a lot of friends." It was true that she made friends easily. But she didn't retain them very well. She was used to moving from place to place, leaving friendships behind. It was harder to keep a friend than it was to make one in the first place. After a while, people started to irritate her. Or she decided they weren't the kind of people she wanted to be with after all. A twinge of guilt pricked at her heart when she thought of Jessup. But having a cop in her life really didn't work. It wasn't Reg's fault that that relationship hadn't worked out. She had tried to make it work—girls' night out or girls' night in to watch movies and eat ice cream. Going to events Jessup had invited her to. But then… being questioned as a suspect in a murder. Being accused of stealing jewelry she hadn't even touched. Repeatedly being put on the hot seat by someone who was supposed to be a friend.

"There's Sarah," Reg offered. "She has been a very good friend. Renting me this house, bringing me food, helping me learn things about wards and charms and other magical stuff. She even brings me in new clients for my business."

Harrison nodded sagely.

Was it weird that the first person Reg could identify as a friend was possibly centuries older and more of a mother figure than a girlfriend? She pushed any doubts aside and thought of who else. Corvin? She wouldn't call him a friend, but they had worked together, protected each other, and shared each other's thoughts and powers. It was a very intimate relationship, but she didn't know what to call it. They weren't really friends or lovers, but were bound together.

"Uh… there's Damon and Jessup and Davyn." Reg hoped to distract Harrison from the fact that they weren't close friends by giving him several names at once. Each of them had been a friend at one time, and Davyn had grown to be more of a friend, not simply a mentor. There were some non-humans that she considered friends, but Harrison had been asking about human friendships.

"They are all friends?"

Reg made a face and shifted uncomfortably. "It depends on what you call a friend."

Harrison cocked his head. "What *you* call a friend."

"Well, yes."

"How do you make them friends?"

Was Harrison asking because he wanted to be classed as one of Reg's friends? If so, she would be happy to call him one and avoid having to explain complex human relationships to him. She didn't think he was worried about his relationship with Starlight, since neither of them was human. Harrison scratched Starlight's ears and the ruff of his neck.

"Well, I can't make them friends unless they want to be friends. It is a two-way thing."

"Do they not want to be?"

"Yes, they do. I think. Jessup does for sure. Damon… I don't know. Maybe friends. Maybe something else. Davyn is my mentor, but he is a friend too."

"How?"

"Uh… he cares about me and my opinion. We talk about things other than just firecasting. I'm interested in his life and he's interested in mine." Reg wasn't quite sure that the last bit was true. She cared about Davyn, his opinion of her, and what happened to him. But her interest in his life had not extended beyond their mentorship role. She knew where he worked and she knew about his relationship with Julian, but she didn't want to know any details of either one. She and Davyn didn't have much in common other than firecasting. "And…

since we're the only two around here who are firecasters, that kind of bonds us together as friends. Other people can't understand how to handle fire like we do. How to *play* with it."

Harrison nodded slowly. "You like to play the same games."

"Yes, I guess so. And there isn't anyone else I can play them with."

She could just see Sarah letting her play with fire in the cottage or the big house. If she were lucky, Sarah might let her light candles with her fire. But that was probably as daring as she would get.

"You want him to live so that you can play with him."

Reg laughed awkwardly. "Uh, yeah. That's right."

"And the woman. You don't have a lot of woman friends."

"Sarah?"

He shook his head.

"Jessup? Uh... well, it's kind of hard to be friends with her, even though we'd both like it."

"But you are friends."

"Well... mostly. But there are reasons I can't be close friends with her. Reasons I don't want her in this house."

"Why?"

"She is a police officer... do you understand what they do?"

"Bind people," Harrison said promptly. "Enforce the human rules."

"Yes. Exactly. And... I don't want to be bound. So when she thinks I have done something to break the human rules, I don't want to be around her because I don't want to be arrested. Bound."

"But other times, you are friends."

"Mmm. Yes. We have been."

Harrison nodded. "It is time," he said obliquely.

"Time for what?"

"Human friends are time-based," Harrison said, with more clarity than usual. "Friends at this temporal point, but not at that. Changes over time. Not *always* friends."

"Yeah, I guess. Yes, it is time-based."

"Not *always*."

"No." As a non-time-traveling mortal, Reg wasn't even sure she could comprehend "always." Forever, always, and other words denoting eternity or some undefinable period of time were too difficult to wrap her mind around. Humans were time-based; she didn't think it was possible for them to clearly understand what it would be like to live without a linear timeline, being able to move in both directions through time or time that never ended. It was just too fast for her to conceptualize. "We can't *always* be friends. We don't begin to be friends until we meet and find similar interests. And we can't be friends forever because... we don't live forever. And sometimes we don't live in the same area for very long or find that we can't stay friends with someone for some other reason."

"This is so." Harrison nodded as if he understood it all, though Reg felt like she was more confused now than when they had started the conversation. "Human friendships are linear."

He petted Starlight again, kissed him on the top of his head, and disappeared.

Reg stood there staring at the place where Harrison had been standing, still holding her mug of cold coffee.

CHAPTER FIFTEEN

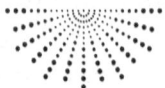

*R*eg dumped the cold coffee from her cup and the carafe and brewed a new batch.

She had thoughts of just going back to bed, since it was much too early for her to get up for the second day in the row. She could just go back to bed and finish her sleep.

But the thought of going back to bed wasn't as attractive as it usually was. Harrison's questions had her brain whirling away, trying to sort out everything she had told him and what was the truth. Had she been telling the truth or lying when she had listed off friends to him? Were those people unconsciously the most important people in her life, even though she had ended the friendships or hadn't officially become friends?

Had she pushed her friends away when things became difficult because she couldn't run away like she normally did? Were they still willing to continue to be friends and had been confused or hurt by her rejections?

Could she really say that she was friends with Davyn when she wouldn't take any action to find him and make sure he was okay?

"Human relationships are complex," she told Starlight as she waited for the coffee to finish brewing and he stared at her from his perch on the island.

He continued to stare, unblinking.

What did cats know about relationships? The only thing he cared about at the moment was when she was going to get around to putting fish in his bowl.

Starlight blinked and began to wash. *If she knew what he wanted, why wasn't she doing it?*

Reg shook her head and found some tuna in the fridge for Starlight. He jumped off the island and began chowing down, his purr filling the room.

Cats were easy. Humans, not as much. Of course, Starlight wasn't a regular cat, but he still had cat instincts and behaviors, so that was how she thought of him.

Someone should be looking for Davyn.

Someone *was* looking for Davyn. It just wasn't her. Reg sighed. She picked up her phone and hit the number on her recent calls list for Jessup. She touched the speakerphone icon and looked through the fridge for something that appealed to her for her breakfast. She didn't usually eat early in the morning and she wasn't sure she would. Maybe she would just have the coffee and wait until the rest of her body woke up.

"Reg?" Jessup's voice blared from the phone.

Reg reached over and turned the volume down. "Umm... yeah. Hi. Sorry, I probably called you too early. Were you already up?"

"Yes, I'm up. How are you doing? You aren't usually up at this time. Unless you're still up from last night. Is everything all right?"

"Sure. Everything is fine."

"Just... making sure you aren't calling me because you happened across a body. Or some creature."

Like Reg would call Jessup if she happened across a body. She would sneak away and do everything she could to avoid detection. Being at the center of a murder investigation was not an experience she wanted repeated.

"I was just thinking about your call yesterday. About Davyn."

"Ah. Do you think you could do anything to help? I know it's presumptuous to ask. It's up to you when and how you use your gifts.

But like I said, I would pay you as a consultant. It wouldn't just be a freebie."

"I don't know. I haven't had any impressions about where he might be. But I was talking to Corvin, and—"

Jessup snorted. "Are you still talking to Hunter? I don't think I would if I were you, especially knowing he's been allowed back into the coven. I really don't think they waited long enough. His punishment should have been more severe, considering how serious his breach was."

"We're not talking a lot, but… I just happened to run into him at The Crystal Bowl."

"Happened to? I doubt it. If he was at The Crystal Bowl, he was looking for you. It isn't one of his usual hangouts."

Reg considered this. She frequently ran into Corvin at the restaurant, so she had just assumed that it was one of his favorite places to eat too. Even though it wasn't like the places he took her to when he was taking her out. People didn't eat *every* meal at fancy restaurants. He must have some places he went just because it was quick and easy. Like The Crystal Bowl. Reg was sure that he went there for reasons other than just seeing her.

"So, we were talking," she said, deciding to ignore the tangent. Jessup was interrupting too much, not letting Reg get to the point. Reg hadn't called to gossip or talk about Corvin's behavior. She had just wanted to give Jessup a quick tip. One quick call, and then she could stay out of the case, confident she had done everything she should. "Talking about where Davyn could have gotten to. And Corvin said that he wasn't sure you even knew about Julian. And… I don't think I told you anything about him."

"Who is Julian?"

"Julian Sabat. He is with Magical Investigations. An investigator." Reg tried to remember the other details on Julian's card. "On… animals, I think. Creatures."

"Magical Investigations." Reg could practically hear the gears turning in Jessup's brain. "I wouldn't think you would want anything to do with Magical Investigations after the Everglades thing."

Reg cleared her throat. "He *was* the investigator on the Everglades

78

thing. And you're right; I don't want anything to do with him. That's why I'm telling you. I don't want to call him."

"So... explain to me why I should call this investigator about Davyn's disappearance? What does that have to do with magical creatures?"

"Nothing. No. I don't think Davyn was kidnapped by a goblin or anything," Reg hurried to assure Jessup. "No, Davyn and Julian are... *friends*. You know. Corvin wondered if maybe Davyn decided to take an impromptu holiday and to go see him. Because long-distance relationships are hard," Reg finished lamely. It didn't sound like as good of a lead as Reg had hoped. Maybe Jessup would just laugh it off.

"Oh, I didn't know Davyn had anyone. No one that we talked to so far said anything about that."

"Maybe he was trying to keep it quiet. But they've been out in public together. Julian stayed to watch the Spring Games."

"Everybody stayed to watch the Spring Games," Jessup laughed. "I wouldn't have thought anything about seeing Davyn there with a stranger, unless they were..." She cleared her throat. "Obviously *together*. I would have just thought that the stranger was an old friend from out of town."

"Maybe. So, that's all I called about. I just didn't know if you had that piece of information and thought that it might be important."

"That's helpful. I appreciate you calling about it. And do you think... we could work that consultation in? We're doing everything we can, but we haven't turned up anything concrete that indicates a direction he might have gone. It seems like he has disappeared off of the face of the earth."

"You don't think that he just went to visit Julian?"

"Without his wallet or keys or vehicle? How did he do that?"

"Oh. Well, I don't know. Maybe Julian picked him up. Maybe it was a surprise for an anniversary or something like that and Davyn just dropped everything and went with him."

"We'll certainly look into it, but I don't think that is very likely. Davyn isn't really the 'drop everything' kind of person."

"No," Reg admitted. "Sarah thought he might have had some kind of nervous breakdown. So I was just hoping..."

"I'll check it out. But assuming it doesn't pan out... can I come to see you? Maybe you won't be able to tell me anything, but at least I would know that I was checking every possible angle."

Reg sighed. "I suppose," she finally agreed.

Human relationships were complex.

CHAPTER SIXTEEN

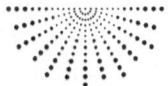

$\mathcal{R}$eg opened the door to admit Jessup, a slim woman with a golden-brown complexion and features faintly Asian. She invited her in. As Reg did so, she couldn't help thinking about how Jessup had treated her as a suspect in the past. Not just once, but multiple times and, in each case, Reg had been completely innocent. She hadn't had anything to do with the crime that had taken place. And Jessup's partner had been one of the people who had tortured Reg for information so, even if Reg had not already had a distrust of police, then she would have after that day. She ran her finger over the scar in the middle of her palm as she thought about it.

And here she was, letting a cop into the house—one who had betrayed her in the past.

What was she thinking?

Starlight came out of the bedroom and approached Jessup, sniffing the air.

"Hi, Starlight," Jessup greeted, putting her hand down to the floor to call Starlight and allow him to smell her hand. Starlight immediately sat back on haunches and began to wash, ignoring the outstretched hand.

Reg grinned. Cats really were contrary.

Jessup waited for a moment, making clicking and kissing sounds and wiggling her fingers, then finally gave up. She stood back up to her full height. She motioned to the living room area, and Reg nodded. "Have a seat."

Jessup selected a chair. Reg grabbed the kettle as it started to whistle, and poured boiling water into two mugs, which she took on the tea tray over to the table in the living room. She and Jessup went through the familiar routine of making themselves tea. Reg watched Jessup in her peripheral vision, not looking directly at her.

It would only take a few minutes, and then Jessup could leave to continue the investigation, either with new information or, as she had said, knowing that she had at least explored all of the avenues open to her. Reg didn't have to keep her entertained or to immediately resume the friendship they'd had prior to stumbling across a body in the graveyard.

Jessup tried to open with some small talk, but Reg ignored it. She got to her feet and went over to the shelf to pick up her crystal ball. She didn't need it, but found it a little easier to focus her brain if she used it. And Starlight helped too, if he were inclined. Reg sat down with the crystal and called Starlight to her.

"Do you want to help me, Star? We're looking for Davyn. You like Davyn, don't you?"

She knew that, unlike Corvin, Davyn had never been rude or aggressive about Starlight or the subject of cats in general. Reg didn't think that he had a familiar, but maybe if he did, it would have been a cat.

Starlight paused in his bath and looked at Reg. She patted her lap. "Do you want to help me?"

Starlight gave his fur a couple more firm licks and then padded across the room to Reg and jumped into her lap. Reg scratched his ears and rubbed his fur, though she tried to keep from ruffling his fur up so that he would have to lick it down again. "Davyn has disappeared and we're going to see if we can see him."

Starlight settled himself comfortably into Reg's lap and sat looking at the crystal ball.

"He looks like he knows exactly what he's doing," Jessup chuckled.

"He does."

Jessup rolled her eyes, but didn't argue about it. Reg reached out and touched the crystal with her fingertips, staring first at the reflection on the outside of the ball, and then into its depths. Nothing appeared to her. Reg closed her eyes and tried to reset. She was looking for Davyn. He had to be out there somewhere. All Reg needed was to see a flash of something. Some clue as to where Davyn was or what kind of shape he was in.

The crystal remained stubbornly dark.

"Come on," Reg murmured. "Show me Davyn Smithy. He must be close by."

But the universe and the spirits that surrounded Reg were not obliging.

"Can you do a *seek*?" Jessup asked after a few minutes, in a respectfully lowered voice.

Reg closed her eyes. Seeking had been hit and miss for her. It was a powerful bit of magic that really, she shouldn't be able to perform, but sometimes it worked perfectly. She had always been good at finding lost items when she was a little girl, so she must have an affinity for it. But since she had come to Black Sands, she hadn't always been able to find people or magical objects when she had tried. Sometimes there were counter-spells in place to prevent it.

She didn't want to do a seek, just to have it fail.

But she needed to get over the fear of failure. If she didn't try, she couldn't fail, but that meant she was stopping herself, rather than an outside influence stopping her. Which was more embarrassing? Failing at a seek or being afraid even to try?

She could just tell Jessup that the seek had failed. But didn't she want to find Davyn?

"Okay," Reg said, more to herself than to Jessup. "I'll give it a try."

She pictured Davyn in her mind as clearly as possible. *Where is Davyn Smithy?*

Starlight's claws pricked Reg's leg. Not hard, just enough that she knew that he was exerting all of the power he could to help her with her demand. With both of them working together, seeking Davyn should be a cinch. But she still couldn't see Davyn in the crystal or her mind. She reached out with all of her senses, trying to sense a pull in one direction or another. He *had* to be somewhere. She knew him well enough and was exerting all of the effort she could, including using Starlight's magnifying power. How could she use so much and still have no idea? Even when trying to find Wilson, someone she had never met before and had been missing for decades, she had felt a pull. She had been able to track him even though Damon had shown her the wrong image.

Reg sat back, letting out a puff of breath. "I can't. I'm not getting anywhere."

Jessup's brows drew down. "Nothing? Not even an inkling?"

"No. Nothing at all. It's like... he's not anywhere."

"Could someone or something be cloaking his location?"

"I guess. I don't know enough about that kind of magic. I can usually find what I'm looking for, eventually. But you know, a lot has happened that has disrupted things and messed with my brain and with what I can do. It seems like just when I get a handle on things, start to understand what I can do, something else happens that messes it up. It's always changing."

Jessup nodded. "That must be frustrating."

Reg had the definite feeling that Jessup didn't understand it at all. She was just saying something to placate Reg, to calm her irritation at not being able to find Davyn.

What if something had happened to him? She kept trying to convince herself that Sarah was right and Davyn had just taken some time off because things had become too overwhelming for him, but it didn't fit the facts. Why would Davyn leave his wallet and his phone behind? Even if he were going fishing or doing something else where he could be off on his own, he wouldn't have left his wallet and phone. And where would he have gone without his car? How would he have gone anywhere without it?

She had seen stories on TV about people who walked away from their lives. It did happen. Their friends and loved ones went on, thinking that they were dead, maybe kidnapped or murdered, only to find out thirty years later that they had just abandoned their lives and started over somewhere else.

Then there were those people who had amnesia. The victim got mugged or hit on the head by a falling bit of debris on the way home from work, and then suddenly, everything was gone. He couldn't remember who he was or the life he'd been living. Everything was a blank and he didn't have any choice but to start over again, leaving everything else behind.

What if something like that had happened to Davyn? Would the police be able to figure it out? To find him and bring him back home, where he could rest and recover his memory?

"Do you think... something happened to him? Was there any blood or evidence of... violence? What if he was kidnapped or murdered? What if he has amnesia and doesn't know who he is?"

"We're trying to figure all of that out. I can't tell you very much about the investigation. You know I have to keep that confidential. But we are looking at all possibilities."

"If he had amnesia—or something—" Reg didn't want to suggest that he was dead, "—then that would explain why I can't find him. If he isn't *himself* anymore, or isn't... you know, on this *plane*, then there wouldn't be anything for me to latch onto."

Although, she had been able to find Wilson when she had looked for him, even though he had a forgetting spell put on him. But he still knew who he was. Mostly. He hadn't remembered the part about being a wizard, but he had remembered his name and things about himself. He had still been himself, even if he couldn't remember certain things. Reg rubbed her forehead, trying to sort it all out. She wanted it to all make sense but, until they had some evidence, she wasn't going to be able to put the puzzle together in a way that would all make sense.

"I suppose so," Jessup agreed. She pressed her lips together in a thin line, thinking about it. "We are concerned, of course. If we weren't, we wouldn't be looking for him. It isn't illegal to disappear. But I don't think he just decided to take some vacation time and didn't bother to tell his work or anyone else. I don't think that he left his phone and wallet behind of his own volition."

"You think he was kidnapped?"

Jessup shrugged.

"Who would do that? Why would someone take him? There wasn't a ransom demand, was there? Wouldn't that be all over the news?"

"There hasn't been a ransom demand. There isn't any evidence of a kidnapping or who was involved, if someone else was involved or took him against his will. Forensics is going through all of the physical evidence, of course, but I don't have any great hope that they will find DNA or other trace evidence showing who else might have been there."

"I was just with him. I just had a firecasting lesson with him on Monday."

Jessup's brows went up. "Right before he disappeared?"

CHAPTER SEVENTEEN

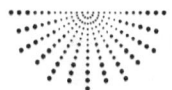

*R*eg grimaced. "I don't know if it was *right* before he disappeared. I saw him Monday afternoon…"

"And Tuesday morning, he did not show up at work. He disappeared sometime between when you saw him Monday afternoon and work the next day. Did he tell you what he was going to do? Was he going home right away? Or did he seem to have anything on his mind? Something bothering him?"

"I don't know where he was going. I think usually after we met, he would go home and have supper and relax… Firecasting takes energy, and if he was trying to control my fire, he would be tired."

"So if he went directly home after meeting with you and put down his phone and wallet while making himself dinner or sitting down to watch TV…"

"And then something happened? He didn't go to bed? Get up in the morning and something happened on the way to work…?"

"We don't know whether he disappeared before he went to bed or after getting up. He obviously wasn't driving to work, or he would have had his possessions with him."

"Right. Of course."

"Did you guys talk about anything? Did he seem upset or distracted?"

"You can't be distracted when you're firecasting. That's how forest fires start."

It was something that Davyn had joked about with her.

Only *you* can prevent forest fires.

Thinking about it made Reg feel hollow and empty.

"He talked about the coven. About how Corvin was being reinstated. He tries to talk to me about things that I will find distracting to break my focus."

"Didn't you just say that you have to stay focused?"

"Yes. That's how he tries to build up my ability to stay focused no matter what he is saying or what might be bothering me. Practicing under adverse conditions."

"Oh, okay. I guess trying to simulate real-world experience makes sense. You get stronger by adding more resistance. But you don't think he was worried or upset about Corvin's reinstatement?"

"He didn't seem to be *upset* about it. I guess... Corvin brings certain benefits to the coven. Something about them being able to access his powers. That it makes the coven stronger. And he's really powerful, so I guess that would make the coven a lot stronger. Even if Davyn thought that his punishment should have lasted longer—"

"Did he? I thought that they would listen to him on the issue of whether Hunter was ready to be reinstated."

"No... he never said that he thought it should have lasted longer, I don't think. But I guess... I felt like it should have been longer. But it isn't anything to do with me. It doesn't matter whether it is longer or shorter than I would have wanted. It's good for me if he is back with the coven and not just obsessed with me all the time. He can do his work with members of the coven instead of only being able to do non-magical work in the community. He has friends and everything there, I guess..."

Jessup pursed her lips and didn't comment on this, but Reg got the clear impression that Jessup didn't think Corvin really had any friends in the community, whether he was allowed to associate with them. Reg had just assumed that the reason he didn't hang out with any of the practitioners in the community other than Reg was because he was being shunned, not just by his own coven, but by the others as well, who had decided to honor the punishment his own coven had imposed in a show of solidarity.

He *did* have other friends in the community, didn't he?

"Anyway." Reg shrugged. "I don't think Davyn was upset about Corvin being readmitted to the coven. I think he was relieved that it was all over. Other than Corvin wanting to take over as the leader of the coven."

Jessup's brows went up at this comment. "He wants to lead the coven?"

"Yeah. You didn't know that?"

"No. We hadn't heard that from anyone we have contacted."

Reg shrugged. "I guess they have some kind of election process. It wasn't like Corvin had to take Davyn out in order to take his place."

"No… but it's worth looking at."

"Maybe. I don't think he's got Davyn tied up in his basement, though."

Jessup shook her head. "No, I agree with you on that one."

"He'll just charm the other members of the coven and they'll elect him."

"I imagine that is probably against the rules for an election."

"So? Since when did that stop Corvin? He'll make them think it was their own idea."

Jessup frowned in concentration. "I thought that he was not allowed to lead a coven."

"Apparently, there have been a bunch of rule changes." Reg fluttered her fingers in the air to indicate a flurry of activity. "So now in some places, there have been warlocks like him who have been allowed to lead covens, and it has all been just fine, so other covens are looking at them and hoping to copy their success."

Jessup rolled her eyes and grunted, clearly not liking this development. "I suppose that's a point in Corvin's favor, then. He didn't have to do anything to Davyn to get in. Davyn had already changed the rules of the coven to allow him to campaign for the position."

"*Davyn* changed the rules?"

Reg was pretty sure that he said that the coven had to vote on any rule changes.

"Well, it would have been with the consent of the warlocks in the coven, of course. He wouldn't just do it unilaterally. But yes, the administration of the coven was Davyn's responsibility. He would bring forward any changes that should be made for consideration. And he was the one who would keep the book of rules of the coven and note any changes."

Reg thought about that, wondering why Davyn would have allowed Corvin the opportunity to take over the coven. It didn't seem like a good idea to Reg, and there had long been rules in place to prevent it from happening. Why wouldn't Davyn just stick with tradition and not allow a power drinker the leadership opportunity?

She had thought that Davyn had told her about Corvin running for leadership because he didn't approve of it. But maybe he had just been checking to see Reg's position on the matter. Or had wanted to give her a heads-up so that she wouldn't be surprised by it. Had Davyn been the one to suggest the rule change, or had someone else in the coven? Maybe even Corvin himself. She could remember his mentioning the biases against warlocks like he was at his tribunal. He had not believed that the community's laws about what he could and couldn't do were fair. Maybe he'd been lobbying for those changes for years.

"I will have to have a word with Hunter." Jessup grimaced. "Find out what he knows about Davyn's disappearance, if anything."

"It isn't like he would tell you."

Jessup didn't argue or explain. Reg had wondered more than once just what power Jessup held over Corvin. Reg knew that the police had worked with him as a consultant in several cases, but she didn't know what kind of service he provided. Or why he would care about continuing to work with the police in the future. But Reg had never seen Corvin try to charm Jessup and he listened to her when she told him to back off and leave Reg alone. Jessup seemed to pay Corvin in the form of powerful magical artifacts, so maybe that was why he didn't want to get on her bad side. He preferred to drink the powers from live prey, but he could still use a magical artifact that had been imbued with power.

"Was that all you talked about with Davyn? The only thing you can think of that he might have been concerned about?"

"Did he mention any stalkers or death threats?" Reg rolled her eyes. "No, I'm pretty sure that would have stood out in my memory."

Jessup sighed and nodded. She gazed at Reg's crystal ball. "I was really hoping that you would be able to see something. Give us some clues, even if you couldn't see exactly where he was."

"Yeah. Sorry. I'll keep trying. Sometimes the spirits have the answers, but they don't always respond when you ask them. It can take a while."

"I appreciate anything you can do. Davyn is your friend. I'm sure you want him to be found safe and sound."

CHAPTER EIGHTEEN

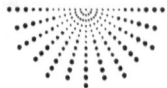

*R*eg did make a few other attempts to ask the spirits for any information about Davyn, gazing into the crystal until her eyes were gritty and she just wanted to close them and have a nap. She didn't try a *seek* again; it took too much energy, and she would need energy for her evening clients. She didn't like just to pretend to channel the spirits while cold reading her clients. Even though that was what she had done before arriving in Black Sands, she liked to provide a legitimate service when she was able to. And real encounters with spirits always made for happier clients and better reviews than the ones Reg just fudged.

There was a loud rap on the door. Reg glanced at it and continued to carry her dirty dishes to the sink. She wasn't expecting anyone, and it wasn't Sarah's knock. Sarah always just gave a quick tap in case Reg was meeting with a client, then let herself in. In Reg's experience, a knock like that could only mean trouble.

Starlight jumped down from the couch and walked toward the door, making an inquiring *mrrow*. Reg went to the window and looked out to see if she could see anything. Her visitor was too close to the door for her to see him. She approached the door and checked out the peephole. A slim, cloaked man.

Reg considered. It wasn't Corvin. It couldn't be anyone who

intended her harm because of the wards and charms in the yard and the cottage. No one with evil intentions toward her should be able to make it past the gate to the backyard.

The sharp rap came again, making Reg jump because she was right there on the other side of the door. She squinted through the peephole, still trying to make out the person on the other side through the distorted and scratched lens.

"Regina Rawlins. Open up."

Reg knew *that* voice. She continued to study the form through the peephole, then finally opened the door and looked at him.

"Reg." The blond-haired man with intense blue eyes nodded to her. "Thank you for letting me in."

Reg shook her head, staying in the doorway. "I'm not letting you in."

He stood awkwardly, waiting, apparently not believing she would keep him barred from her house. "This isn't really a conversation for the doorstep. I'm not here asking for charitable donations," he told her irritably.

Reg knew it would have to be a longer, more involved conversation, but that didn't mean she wanted him in her house. She considered the matter seriously, but she wasn't about to invite him into her house. The wards and charms were there for a reason. He might be able to use his wand to break them if she were the subject of investigation but, as she wasn't, he was prevented from doing so by his regulations, if not the power of the wards.

"We could talk in the garden," she suggested eventually.

Julian looked around and nodded. "Is there somewhere to sit down?"

Reg stepped out of the house, pulling the door firmly shut behind her. "Yeah, around the back of the cottage." She led him around the house to the bench by the pond.

Julian eyed the pond and looked at Reg speculatively. Reg gave him her best predatory smile.

"If you cause me trouble, I'll drown you in the pond."

He had the gall to look pleased at her threat. But then, he was the one who had been so delighted to find out that she was part siren, even when she had marked him as prey. It was quite a notch in his belt as a Magical Investigator in the Endangered Creatures department. Sirens were very rare and he was pleased to know one personally, even if she did consider him an enemy. Reg still remembered how he had tormented her when they had both been foster children in the same family. Or at least, she remembered parts of it. Her brain was too much like Swiss cheese lately. She couldn't always recall what she wanted to, much less the childhood memories she had tried to bury. Julian had shared his memories with her. He had been older than Reg, his memories of that time clearer.

They sat down side by side on the bench. Not too close together. Reg needed room to breathe.

It actually *was* distracting to look at the pond with him at her side. She had marked him for death, and even though she had made the conscious decision not to follow through, the siren hunger still niggled at the back of her mind. She tried to focus on Davyn, because it was surely Davyn Julian had come to talk to her about.

"So… how have you been?" Julian asked.

"You can skip the small talk. You don't care how I've been and I don't care if you ask."

"Of course I care," he reared back slightly as if offended. "The health of all of our endangered creatures concerns us."

"I'm not *your* creature. I'm just a person. Don't treat me any differently than anyone else."

Though, of course, she probably wouldn't like how he treated most people. He was arrogant and a bully. He hadn't grown out of either trait since she had known him as a child. The deference he treated her with now was solely due to the fact that she was a rare species. And possibly that she could kill him if she wished, though that seemed to come in a distant second.

He looked at her, considering his approach.

"I'm fine, okay?" Reg figured if she didn't actually answer his question, he was going to stay stuck there. "I am in good health, so your department doesn't have anything to worry about."

"Good, good." He nodded in satisfaction.

"But you're not here because of that. You're here about Davyn, right?"

Julian nodded. Worry and concern crept into his features. It was weird to see them there, as if Julian were actually a human being with regular feelings instead of just an uncaring jerk.

"That policewoman called me, but she wouldn't tell me any details. She said he was missing." He shook his head, brows drawn down. "I don't understand how he can be missing."

"No one knows what happened. Or I don't, anyway. I don't think Jessup does, but she wouldn't lay all her cards on the table for me either."

"What *do* you know?"

"I saw him Monday afternoon. Then he didn't show up for work Tuesday morning, and they called the police. They checked his house and he wasn't there. He hadn't left any kind of note as to what his plans were. His car is still there. And his wallet and phone."

"That doesn't make sense. Where could he have gone?"

"I was hoping he'd gone somewhere with you. To your place or on a cruise or something." The image of Julian on a boat made Reg salivate. She licked her lips and swallowed, trying to ignore her appetites. "Since he obviously didn't, I don't know. I keep telling myself that it was just like Sarah says; he had too much on his plate and had some kind of breakdown. But there should be some kind of trail to follow. And I know that sometimes people leave without their phones or ID and start over again somewhere else, but it's just that… I never saw Davyn as that kind of guy. He seemed normal on Monday. Not stressed out. If he was going to do something like that, wouldn't he have shown some signs? He should have acted stressed and overwhelmed. At least mentioned that things were bad at work, or that he was worried about the coven, or something about Corvin. But he didn't. He just acted normal."

"What did you two talk about?" Julian knew that Davyn was her mentor, so he wasn't surprised that they had seen each other.

"Nothing earth-shattering. Nothing like him being afraid of someone or thinking he just couldn't handle life anymore. I don't know where to go, what to think."

"You perform as a medium. I suppose you have some clairvoyance due to your siren blood. Have you tried to use it to find out where Davyn is?"

"Yeah, I tried to see him. But... nothing. Like he didn't even exist."

Julian paled rapidly. "You don't think that... he's dead, do you?"

Reg shook her head. Her heart beat faster thinking about it. She didn't want anything bad to have happened to Davyn either, and had been avoiding thinking about anything violent or permanent. Davyn was just fine. She didn't know where he was or what he was doing, but he couldn't be dead. That was impossible.

"No... I would... I just can't believe that. I don't know where he is, but I'm sure nothing like that has happened to him."

Images flashed through her mind, and she didn't know whether they were coming from her imagination or if she was reading Julian's fears. Fears that Davyn was hurt or killed. His body lying in a ditch, buried in a shallow grave, or worse. Reg tried to block the images, but they were very vivid. They had to be coming to her from Julian. She hadn't pictured anything like that when she had been alone. Since she and Julian had been so closely connected at one time, it was easy for her to read him.

She looked at Julian. His bright eyes seemed to have darkened. He stared away from Reg into the garden, his hands clenched into fists.

"Hey... it's okay... we don't know what's happened yet. We don't know anything has happened to him. Don't imagine the worst."

He shook his head. "How can I not?"

"You don't know. Everything could be fine. In the Everglades—" She cut herself off, unsure what to say to him. She had been about to say that she had found a wizard who had been lost there for 50 years, and he had been just fine. But Julian didn't know all of the details about Wilson and, if he did, he would probably not be comforted by the story.

Julian glanced at her and gave a hoarse laugh. "We all know what happened in the Everglades."

He wasn't talking about her finding Wilson, but being attacked by a swamp goblin.

Anything could happen. Julian's voice was in her head. *Anything could happen anywhere.*

"No, no. I didn't mean that. You don't know all of what happened. There were good creatures there too. Good, helpful creatures. And wherever Davyn is, people could be helping him too. People do that. They reach out and help even when they don't know the person." She stared into Julian's face. His look was black and despairing. As if he had never seen that side of mankind and didn't believe it existed.

Reg had never known the details of why Julian went into foster care. She didn't know anything about his history before he was put into the system, other than that he had once lived in a magical household. He had known of his powers before he went into care. Unlike Reg, who had no idea what she was, what gifts she had, or how to control them. When her emotions got out of control, things happened. She hadn't been able to control any of it. But Julian had been there and he could control his magic and see the magic in her.

"There are good people," Reg insisted. "Someone will help him."

"You don't know that. You have no idea where he is. You said it is like he doesn't exist anymore. Like he's been wiped from the face of the earth."

Reg tried to object. She shook her head. "It doesn't mean anything. There have been other things that I couldn't find. It just means that my gift isn't working. Or that his location is cloaked. Maybe I'm too stressed out or worried about him. That makes it harder to control things. Doesn't that make it harder for you?"

Julian nodded. "Yes."

"You see? It just means that I'm not doing it right. I'll keep trying, and maybe in a couple of hours, I'll be able to settle down enough to get a real answer."

"Unless he's not there. He's already gone." Julian's mouth twisted in grief. "This is what happens to me. I let down my guard, let someone inside, and something happens to them. I lose everyone."

"You haven't lost everyone," Reg wanted to reassure him. *People* that he cared about that were still alive. *He was just looking at his life with a filter, ignoring everything that didn't fit.* But she didn't know enough to say that. She put her hand on his arm in comfort, but then had to pull it back as her skin warmed and she started thinking about just how close to the water they were. She could *help* Julian. She could make him forget the bad news. Forever.

Anoint the waters, the siren chorus started in her head. *Make your claim. This one is yours.*

They had focused on Corvin up until then. But now that Julian was sitting beside her, another man she had claimed, they cheerfully changed their tune.

Any blood would satisfy them. But Reg wasn't a predator and she wasn't going to do anything to "prove herself" to them. She wasn't a creature who couldn't control herself. It was difficult when her blood was up or she was in the water. But so far, she had been able to prove herself a rational human being rather than a creature of instinct.

Reg pulled her hand back and folded both of them in her lap.

CHAPTER NINETEEN

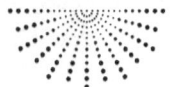

*H*e's gone for good," Julian said. "He's never coming back."

"You don't know that. We might still be able to find him. Or he might turn up again on his own. Maybe it is all just a misunderstanding."

"How could it be?" he demanded. "He isn't at home, but everything else is. Something happened to him."

Reg pressed her fingers to her temples, trying to concentrate. "Maybe... he's closer to home than we realize. Maybe it is amnesia or he had an accident and is waiting to be rescued..."

Julian shook his head. "The police searched for him. If he was close by, they would have found him."

Reg tapped her fingernail on the bench, thinking about it. "Or... maybe they wouldn't have." She turned her eyes back to Julian's. "What about his invisibility?"

Julian blinked, staring at her. Reg raised her eyebrows.

"Well? Maybe they couldn't find him because he was invisible."

"Why would he be invisible?"

"Because he was afraid. Or confused. Or if he has amnesia, maybe he doesn't even know he's invisible, and can't understand why no one is talking to him."

Julian didn't look any more enlightened by this explanation. He licked his lips, then scratched the back of his neck. "Davyn has invisibility?"

"Yes." Reg nodded emphatically. "Didn't you know that?"

"No. He never mentioned it."

Reg tried to imagine how or why Davyn had kept that little tidbit a secret. Julian knew Davyn was a firecaster, knew about his family background and upbringing. He knew that Davyn was the leader of the coven. Why didn't he know that Davyn could cloak himself in invisibility?

"If Davyn cloaked himself... would I be able to see him with my powers?" Reg asked, warming to the idea. "Maybe that's why I couldn't picture him and couldn't see him in my crystal ball!"

Julian lifted his head, grasping this new thought. "I don't know. Can you usually see things that are not visible to others?"

"Well... yes." Reg's enthusiasm dimmed a bit. She could see the pixies when they retreated to the world of shades. Not clearly, but as a shadow. She could see auras. If she concentrated, she could see the light around objects that had power or had been enchanted. And, when Davyn had been following her while cloaked, she had still been able to see a shadowy figure. He wasn't completely invisible to her as he was to others. "I guess... I could see him a little bit when he was cloaked before. But I wasn't thinking about that when I was looking for him in the crystal before. I wasn't looking for his shadow. I might have missed it."

Julian sighed.

"But I haven't looked for him in person," Reg pointed out. "If he was cloaked when the police searched the house and the area around it, they wouldn't have been able to see him. But I could."

"We should go there." Julian's voice was subdued. It was the logical thing to do, but he wasn't optimistic that she would be able to find Julian any better than the police. "Have a look around."

"Yeah. I think we should. And maybe if I'm there, where he lives, I'll be able to sense something else. He'll have left an imprint there, and I'll be able to sense him better."

Julian nodded and rose to his feet. He looked a little unsteady.

Reg thought that she should step forward and help him. But that would be a bad idea. With her hand on her prey, unsteady on his feet, just inches away from the little pond... she might not be able to resist.

She stood back and waited for him to lead the way out of the garden and to the front of the house where he must have parked his car. Julian stumbled on ahead of her, getting farther away from the pond, which was a relief. Reg stopped at her door.

"I just need to get my things. My purse. Car keys."

He gave a little nod and stopped where he was. He stared off into space like a zombie. Reg went into the cottage to quickly gather her things together and was back out the door a minute later. Julian's eyes turned to her.

"What things are in this garden?"

Reg frowned. "What? I don't know. I'm not a gardener. I can recognize a few flowers, but that's about it. You'd have to ask Forst."

"A garden gnome?"

"Yes."

"Ah." Julian looked around. "That would explain it, then."

Reg started to walk toward the gate. "Explain what?"

"There is a lot of magic here. And it seems to be... filled with life."

Reg nodded. Forst and Fir often referred to plants as "their living." The garden was overflowing with green and blossoming things. They all thrived under Forst's care.

"Not just plants," Julian said. He blinked, looking around. "There are many other living things here, too."

Reg nodded. "There are elves. Birds, bees, other insects."

"More than that." Julian nodded to himself. "Have you seen the elves?"

Reg chuckled. "Oh, yes. I've seen them."

"You are very lucky. It is a rare thing."

"Are elves endangered too?"

"No. Just shy. It's hard to catch a glimpse of them."

Even Forst had been delighted to catch a glimpse of the elves.

And Reg would have thought that as a gardener, he would have seen a lot of them.

They left the garden and walked up the sidewalk to the curb where their vehicles were parked. "Do you want to go together or separately?" Reg asked.

"We may as well go together. I can drop you back here when we are done."

Or if he decided for one reason or another to stay at Davyn's house, Reg could find her own way back across Black Sands.

CHAPTER TWENTY

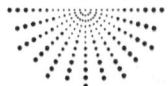

*B*lack Sands wasn't a very big place, so it only took a few minutes to get to Davyn's house. Reg wasn't surprised to find that it was on a large lot just past the town corporate limits. Somewhere he would be able to light fires without breaking bylaws. The house, though not huge, had large chimneys, and Reg sensed a fire pit around the back of the house. Definitely the home of a firebug.

Julian parked in the driveway and they both got out and went to the door. Reg extended her senses as much as possible as soon as she was out of the vehicle. Was Davyn there? Inside? Outside? Was he hurt? Being on his property made it real and that much more urgent to find him. There was no way she could just ignore the fact that Davyn was missing and wait for him to return home in his own time.

Julian knocked on the door, pounding loudly a few times before trying the doorknob. The door was locked. He knocked again. "Davyn? Are you there? It's Julian. Call out if you're there and need help. Davyn?"

Then he was quiet, and they both stood there straining their ears. But there was nothing to hear but birdsong and the wind in the trees. No sounds came from within the house. Julian tried the door handle again, as if he might have been wrong about it being locked the first time.

"Let me." Reg put her hand on the doorknob once Julian had withdrawn his hand. She focused on the tumblers within the lock. She used to have to use a credit card or lock picking tools to get past a locked door. But she had been refining her ability to manipulate objects with her mind, and locks were the perfect objects to practice on. Manipulating a few small tumblers could open up new possibilities for her. Literally.

She felt the tumblers falling into place and turned the handle. Julian looked at her, brows raised. "How did you do that?"

"What, can't you do that?" Reg asked with a grin. She knew that he was capable of telekinesis. He should be able to do the same thing if he practiced a bit.

"I never tried," Julian admitted. "I'm not sure why not. It seems like a very practical skill. Might even help me in my work."

Reg wouldn't want Julian, the Magical Investigator, on the other side of her door. A lock should do what it was supposed to and keep uninvited guests out. She should probably put extra wards on her locks, now that she'd given him the idea. She wasn't likely to be the target of another investigation, since they had confirmed that, as a siren, she was an endangered creature. But things could change. Like the policy banning warlocks like Corvin from leading his coven.

Reg pushed the door open slowly, wary of any charms or wards Davyn might have in place to keep unwanted guests out. The doorknob didn't burn in her hand. She was not prevented by an invisible barrier from stepping through the doorway. There wasn't a guard dog or some magical Harry Potteresque creature barring entry. It was all a little anticlimactic. Reg looked at Julian as she stepped through the doorway. "Wouldn't you have expected wards to keep us out?"

He shook his head. "There are rules against barring Magical Investigations from entering a scene. Of course, the real criminals aren't afraid to break that rule." He shrugged. "Besides, I've been here before. He has allowed me entry. I'm a friend."

Reg was glad that they hadn't been confronted by a three-headed dog. If Davyn were having some kind of psychotic break, he could definitely have barricaded himself in, setting up all sorts of booby traps.

The lack of barriers, wards, or booby traps made the house feel empty and hollow. She knew right away that Davyn wasn't there. That he hadn't been there for several days. Probably not since he had returned home from firecasting session with Reg.

What had happened? Reg walked around the house, looking for any clues the police might have missed. The police were generally non-practitioners or, like Jessup, had minimal powers. If Davyn had left a magical message or trace behind, maybe Reg had some hope of finding him. She reached out with all of her senses, opening her mind, hoping to find something there. She could see a glow around various items in the house. Wards and charms, just like at her house and Sarah's. Blessings of health and happiness. Guards against strangers and enemies.

Jessup had said that Davyn's wallet and phone were at the house, but Reg didn't see them. She supposed the police had taken them into evidence. Would Jessup let her see them? Touch them? They were something that Davyn carried around with him everywhere he went, held against his body. Reg might be able to get a better impression off of them than anything else in the house.

She wandered around, looking for anything that might indicate where Davyn had gone or what his state of mind had been before leaving. There was no broken glass, no empty whiskey bottle on the counter; there were no papers filled with demonic scribbles. No voodoo doll stuck with pins. Everything looked neat and tidy, like Davyn himself. Always properly squared away. He had a very different personality from Reg's, and she was sure that they would not have been friends if it were not for their shared firecasting ability. Especially not after he had led Corvin's tribunal, asking her questions that were accusatory and made it clear that his bias was in Corvin's favor, not Reg's.

But all of that had changed. Maybe he had only been playing his appointed role that day and had always been on her side. It was hard to say with someone like Davyn. He was good at keeping his emotions wrapped up tight, difficult for her to read. As it was, even though she thought she had completely botched her answers to the tribunal and that they were not going to do anything to punish Corvin, they had given him an indefinite sentence, something Jessup said was never done. The first couple of times that Corvin had applied to be reinstated, he had been turned down.

And Reg had gotten to know Davyn, his sense of justice and willingness to look at both sides of a story. She remembered how he had protected her from Corvin in the dwarf mountain. And the patience he had as the teacher of a late-blooming firecaster who could literally set the town on fire if she didn't learn self-discipline.

"Nothing seems out of place," Julian said, looking around and shaking his head. His voice was a whisper, as if he might wake someone up. "You said that if he was here, you would be able to sense him."

"I *should* be able to," Reg agreed. "But I'm not getting anything. I haven't seen, heard, or felt him here. Just… his absence."

Julian nodded his agreement. They continued to explore the house. Every room, even those that did not appear to be in regular use. There was a big central fireplace that, when lit, would heat the entire first floor, with glass doors facing into each room. Perfect for a firecaster. There was a narrow door and set of stairs leading down to what must once have been a root cellar or filled with shelves of preserves, but stood empty now, a dark, low-ceilinged place that Reg wanted to get back out of as quickly as possible. The last thing she needed was spiders in her hair. She had never fully recovered from the visions and spiders she had encountered while investigating a previous case.

Julian led the way up a large staircase from the first floor to the second, into nice, bright, airy rooms that looked down on the woods. He went first to the master bedroom and looked at the neatly made bed and other tidy furniture and decor. Reg looked from behind him. Davyn wasn't a messy, careless bachelor, leaving clothing, plates, and beer cans on the floor. It looked like he had just made the bed, tidied everything up, and stepped out of the room a moment before. The bed glowed slightly with a purple aura. On a bedside table was a picture of Julian laughing. A picture that made him look so relaxed and attractive that even Reg would have looked at him twice. Julian stared at the room, then turned around to look at Reg, a red flush rising from his throat to his ears. She shrugged and pretended not to notice his embarrassment.

"He's not in here. I guess we should check outside. The woods. Maybe he went for a walk and twisted his ankle. Or was kidnapped by a witch in a gingerbread house."

"That's not funny."

Reg looked at him, frowning. Why wasn't that funny? Just because he was worried that something had happened to Davyn? "Don't tell me that witches really do build houses out of gingerbread and kidnap people who walk by. None of the witches I know would do anything like that."

"No," he shook his head in irritation. "But all fairy tales begin with *some* truth."

They left the bedroom and quickly checked the other upstairs rooms. Even Davyn's home office was neat and tidy. No stacks of papers in his in basket. No open books and scrolls spread out over his desktop. All neat and contained, just like every other part of his life.

"You may not be familiar with them," Julian said, as they walked down the stairs to the main floor again, "but there are witches and warlocks who are a danger to those who encounter them unaware. They may not physically consume them, but…" He shook his head. "I wouldn't want Davyn to cross paths with one of them."

Reg might not be aware of them?

Had Julian been that clueless when he had been investigating her or had he forgotten what he had known at the time?

"But they have rules they are supposed to follow," she reminded Julian. "I know, I've met them. Or one, anyway."

He turned his head to look at her, then led the way out the door. Reg shut the door and focused on the tumblers to relock it. No point in leaving it unlocked so anyone could wander in. Did Davyn have his keys with him, wherever he was? Or had he left those at the house too, and the police now had them in evidence? If he did come back home, would he be able to get in? Maybe he had a key hidden somewhere nearby. She scanned the ground and the area around the door for one, but wasn't drawn to any particular rock or other object.

"There are not a lot of them left. Did Davyn know about this witch?"

"Warlock," Reg advised. "I'll say he did. He's in Davyn's coven."

Julian cocked his head at Reg in surprise. "Are you sure? Maybe we're not talking about the same thing. It is something of a taboo amongst the magical community..."

"A power drinker," Reg said baldly. She hated the fact that it was a taboo topic. How were people supposed to discuss real dangers when some silly tradition forbade it?

Julian's face was pale. He nodded. His lips were light pink, almost bloodless. "A power drinker," he agreed. "Davyn has one in his coven?"

Reg nodded. "Corvin Hunter. You've met him."

"Hunter... yes, during your investigation..." Julian shook his head. "I did not realize what he was." He smiled, and his voice went up in pitch. "All of the rare and endangered creatures around Black Sands! How did the two of you manage to find each other?"

"They're rare too?"

Reg guessed she had known that. More than one person had referred to them as a dying breed. As far as Reg knew, Corvin was the end of his line. He had inherited the power from his father.

"Maybe not as rare as sirens," Julian said with a shrug. "But, yes, they are not seen very much anymore. They have been rooted out of many magical communities. Hunter is lucky to have survived in Black Sands."

"Everyone seems to treat him just fine. I mean... no one is trying to kill him, as far as I know."

"Fascinating. I must talk to him. Get his history. Preserve what knowledge he has before it is lost."

"I'm sure he'd be happy to have an audience. It doesn't take much to put Professor Corvin into lecture mode."

Reg led the way into the trees, following a path worn in the grass. "I thought that it was mostly passed father to son, though. I didn't know that there were women with it."

"Rarer than their male counterparts. But they do exist. I know of a few that we have locations on. Three, maybe...?"

"But none here."

"No. I didn't even know of Hunter. Though maybe I should have guessed from his name. Chances that there would also be such a witch in these woods are..." Julian stared into the densely growing trees, "very slim. And if so, probably a relation of his."

"And Davyn would probably know about her."

"Possibly. They do not generally mix with the community. They have been shunned and excluded for many centuries."

"But now they can even lead a coven."

Julian glanced at Reg. "Perhaps."

"Corvin is trying to be elected leader to replace Davyn."

"He's the one? Davyn said that someone was running, but he never said he... was cursed that way. Sort of burying the lede." Julian tapped the side of his leg restlessly as he walked. Reg split her attention between looking back at him and ahead at the thick forest. Had the police had dogs out there to search for Davyn? With how dense the woods were, they would need dogs to do a thorough search.

"What did Davyn tell you about Corvin running for the leadership? Did he say what he thought about it?" Reg ventured.

"He was open to someone else taking over. He didn't seem too happy about Hunter being the one. I didn't understand why until now."

"Yeah. He didn't say what he thought about it to me, but I know Corvin, so... maybe he was afraid word would get back to Corvin if he said anything to me."

"You are close friends with this soul drinker?" Julian asked in surprise.

"Not... friends. He's always trying to charm me. To get my power from me. But I won't let him."

"How would Davyn's words to you get back to him, then?"

"Because... we've been connected. We are bound together. I can't keep him completely out of my thoughts. So I guess if Davyn told me he didn't want Corvin to take over, Corvin might hear that from me. Even if I didn't mean him to."

"You must practice keeping him out of your thoughts."

"It doesn't work. He has held my powers. He has given me strength and taken it from me. He's been in my head too much for me to lock him completely out. Believe me, I've tried. I don't *want* him reading me."

"He has held your powers?"

"It's a long story."

"You can't keep him out… Is the opposite true? Can he keep you out?"

"Umm… I don't know. Not completely, I don't think. But I try to stay away, not to test it. If I am in his mind, then he is in mine."

"That is fascinating. A siren and a soul stealer. Which is stronger?"

Reg didn't want to think about that. It wasn't a question that she wanted to answer. She was a few yards into the woods, and then she stopped. Julian came to an abrupt halt behind her, almost running into her. Reg looked around, seeking out any magic, any spells used in the woods, any trace of Davyn. She had just been in his house, steeping herself in the imprint Davyn left behind. She was at her strongest and should be able to tell which way Davyn had gone.

CHAPTER TWENTY-ONE

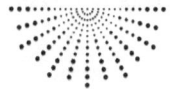

*R*eg blew her breath out slowly and looked around. She closed her eyes and tried to relax every muscle in her body. Other than those needed to stand upright and keep her body alive.

Where is Davyn?

She sent the question out into the ether. A breeze blew through the trees, playing with her hair and causing goosebumps to rise on her arms and neck.

Did Davyn come this way?

The spirits normally attached to her were quiet, also listening for an answer. Reg sent her thoughts out, searching for spirits that inhabited the woods. There must be some consciousness nearby who knew Davyn, his routines, where he would go, and maybe where he had gone. Some spirit must have observed him as he moved around his property, in the house and the woods. Must have watched him kindle fires and perform rites and rituals. He was the spiritual leader of the coven, so he must have had plenty to do. He wasn't just a half-hearted warlock who liked to play with fire occasionally. He was involved in the lives of the members of his coven.

The breeze swirled around her again. Reg raised her hands, fingers spread wide, and let the wind blow through them, trying to capture the words. The wind or something on the wind was speaking to her. But the whispers were too quiet to hear. Too insubstantial.

Reg began to walk again, taking the worn pathway deeper into the woods. Julian followed her but, for once, had the wisdom not to speak and question her. Maybe he could hear the questions she sent out to the universe or hear the wind following her and whispering to her as she strode deeper into the wood. Or maybe he was just interested in the crazy lady fluttering her fingers in the breeze and walking with her eyes mostly closed.

The path branched several times, but Reg had no difficulty staying on the right course. She knew without a doubt which way the path and the wind were pushing her.

They came to a clearing in the woods. It was, as far as Reg could tell, a perfect circle. There was no sign that the trees had been cut down or the undergrowth cleared by hand. How long had Davyn been coming to this place? Reg made her way to the middle of the circle, where there was a long, smooth slab of rock. It had scorch marks and bumpy drips of wax here and there. Candles on an altar. A firecaster's offering. Reg sat down in front of the rock. She knew she should probably kneel, but she wasn't praying there. She wasn't making an offering of her own, just trying to see what Davyn had done there. What his intentions had been and whether he had been worried or afraid. If someone had followed him there. If he was there in the woods somewhere or farther afield.

Julian stood back a respectful distance, watching Reg and looking around at the circle of trees.

Reg touched the rock. The cool, smooth surface felt good under her hand. She put both hands on it and heated the rock. She wasn't sure why, but she followed her instincts. She knew that Davyn would have told her that she could not play with fire alone and needed to follow the rules he had taught her. And she wasn't going to break them. The last thing she wanted to do was burn Davyn's grove to the ground. That would not make him happy.

The rock heated steadily under her hands, the heat spreading evenly throughout. She worried as it got hotter that it would crack, the heat finding the cracks and imperfections in the stone and expanding them. But it was quite warm, almost glowing under her touch, and did not split.

Where is Davyn?

The wind blew hard through the clearing. Reg listened to it. But no matter how hard she looked or listened, the answer was the same.

Not here.

But Davyn had to be somewhere. Maybe she *was* having trouble finding him because he had cloaked himself. But she needed to reach past that veil and find him.

* * *

Davyn saw a crack of light in the darkness. He stared at it, trying to will himself to be able to see it, to sense who was on the other side of the door.

A wind swirled around him, making his cape flap wildly and chilling him to the bone.

Davyn. Davyn.

It was Reg. He was sure that it was Reg's voice. Not loud enough for him to hear more than the whisper of his name, but he was sure she was there. He concentrated, trying to send her a message. Reg's psychic powers were very strong, and she had read him inadvertently before. He knew that she could hear him if he intended her to.

Where are you, Reg? I'm here.

The wind grew stronger. If he had been speaking aloud, the words would have been ripped out of his mouth. But the wind couldn't steal his thoughts.

She was there. She was somewhere close by.

He didn't know where he was. He had been trying to figure it out every time he awakened the first time and found himself in that cold, dark place. He hadn't gotten any closer to determining whether it was underground or in a building. Or maybe he was wearing a blindfold, though he didn't think that was the case. At first, he thought he had been drugged, and maybe he had been in the beginning. But he was clearer now and, if he tried hard enough, he believed he could reach Reg.

* * *

Reg found herself in nothingness. Cold, black nothingness. She could no longer feel her legs or bottom resting on the mossy ground. She wiggled her fingers, feeling for the breeze that had been guiding her earlier. The wind wound its way around her fingers and surrounded her body, moving faster than any wind had the right to. She wasn't prepared to take on a hurricane.

The darkness was disorienting. Reg tried to open her eyes to see the glade around her, but she wasn't able to see anything. It was as if she had been pulled from the clearing, sucked by a vacuum into the dark nothingness of outer space. Only there was no light from stars or planets around here either. Maybe it was like being sucked into a black hole.

But she still existed. If she were in outer space, the air would have been sucked out of her and she would have been floating frozen and lifeless.

* * *

"Reg. Reg Rawlins."

Fingers dug into her arm. Someone shook her body, trying to take her out of the dark place she had ended up in. Reg peeled her eyes open. It felt like it had been years since she had opened them last, and even the shadowy, dappled light of the clearing was so bright it sliced into her brain.

"Reg!"

She tried to nod and to speak. Julian crouched beside the altar stone, staring into her face, trying to get a coherent response.

"I'm here," Reg croaked. "It's okay. I'm fine."

Julian heaved a huge sigh of relief. "What happened? You just went into a trance. I didn't know if I should do anything. If I should try to bring you out of it or let you be."

"It was just for a minute," Reg assured him. "I would have woken up just fine."

He shook his head. "It wasn't just a minute." He looked at his watch. "It's been almost an hour."

Reg rubbed her arms, cold in the shadows of the clearing and the wind that kept racing around and around her. "An hour?"

"Yes. I left you alone to start with, but... I don't know how long you would have stayed that way if I hadn't tried to wake you up."

"An hour... I guess that was long enough."

"What happened? You had a vision. Did you see Davyn? Do you know where he is?"

Reg rubbed her forehead and thought about it, trying to translate the impressions and sensations she'd had into words. It wasn't easy.

"He was there... somewhere close by. I could feel him. Hear him in my head."

Julian's face brightened. He clutched Reg's arm. "You could? Where is he? Do you know where to find him?" He looked around the clearing.

"I don't know. I'm not sure where I was."

He shook his head. "What do you mean you don't know where you were? You saw something. You must have a clue, at least."

"I was... in nothingness. There wasn't anything to see."

"But he was there. So... he's still alive. Right? You were still earthbound."

Reg wasn't sure. She rubbed the back of her neck and shoulders, trying to relax her muscles. Julian wasn't making it any easier to process with his questions. "I'm... yes... he is still alive. I could sense him. He didn't feel like a ghost..."

It had been hard for her to tell the difference as a child. Ghosts and living humans were both equally clear to her, and it was confusing that foster parents and other children could only see some of the people around her. They had played along when she was still very young, like adults frequently played along with children and their imaginary friends. But as she got older, that had stopped. People told her to stop playing around or making things up. They told her that she was too old for imaginary friends. When she didn't stop, they started sending her to doctors and therapists. Some of them believed that she needed to express herself using these stand-ins to work through her trauma and let her talk about them in therapy. Others thought, especially as she got older, that she was experiencing psychosis and needed medication and intensive treatments to banish the hallucinations.

So she had learned to keep quiet about them. She had learned to pick up on the little things that differentiated the living from the dead to know when to keep her mouth shut. Over time, it became easier not to see them, though their voices were still in her head. As an adult, she rarely mistook a particularly vivid, recently deceased spirit for the living in the first few moments, but it did happen on occasion.

Davyn had still felt alive. Distant, separated from her by that dark, cold expanse, but still alive.

"If he is alive, we can get him back," Julian said, trying to reassure himself.

Reg nodded vaguely. She had made contact with Davyn. Therefore, she should be able to go to him and find a way to release him from that in-between place. But how? She didn't want to go back there and, if her first journey into the expanse was any indication, if she dove too deep into that place, she might not be able to get back on her own. Without Julian there to wake her up, how long would she have sat there on the ground in a trance? It had not felt like any time had passed, but it had been an hour. She could have stayed there for hours or days before she felt the passage of time. And would her body be preserved, or would it still be subject to the physical world and waste away if she didn't have food or drink?

CHAPTER TWENTY-TWO

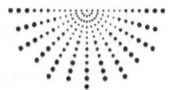

*R*eg's pocket was vibrating. She moved slowly, feeling like a stranger in her own body. Her fingertips touched the phone in her skirt pocket. She wrapped her fingers around it and pulled it out, looking at the screen.

Corvin.

Reg groaned. It really wasn't a good time for her to talk to him. She didn't like an audience when she spoke to him on the phone. Friends listening in and criticizing her for even taking his call, telling her that she needed to stay away from him, cut off all communication. They didn't understand that she couldn't do that. She couldn't keep him out of her mind. And it was easier to talk to him on the phone than to have him burrowing into her brain, which he would do if she refused to answer him.

Reg swiped to answer the call. She looked at Julian, directing the thought to him that he needed to walk away and give her some privacy while she was on the phone. Julian stood there looking at her, apparently impervious to the suggestion.

"Get out," Reg told him tersely. "Give me some space."

"What?" Corvin demanded.

"Not you." She looked at Julian. "You. Go back to the car. Or go look around some more."

Julian rolled his eyes, his lip sticking out in a pout like he was a five-year-old. But he did turn away from her and wandered a few feet away, looking up at the branches of the trees.

"What do you want?" Reg asked Corvin.

"Me?"

"Yes, you," she snapped. "You called me. What do you want?"

"Who is there with you?"

"No one now. What is it?"

"Where are you? I need to see you."

"I'm busy. Investigating—following up with a client. He needed me to go somewhere else to do a reading. You know, restless ghosts in his house or whatever. Why do you care?"

"I've been trying to get you. Where have you been for the last hour?"

She could feel him close to her. Not like he was across town in his own house, but like he was in the clearing with her.

Not in the clearing. In her brain.

Reg focused, trying to push him out. She had left herself too open after the disorienting journey into nothingness. She walled Corvin off, trying to shut up all of the cracks he could climb into until she felt like her thoughts were hers again.

"Reg…" Corvin's tone was a growl, not the seducing, wheedling tone she was used to when he was trying to worm something out of her or get her to do what he wanted her to.

"It's none of your business where I've been. I've been busy. I can't always take your calls. I have work to do."

"You're not working."

"I am too."

"Who is your client?"

"None of your business."

She could feel his anger rising. Whatever was going on with him lately made him irritable and easily angered. He could go from cold to hot in an instant. The Corvin she had grown to know was mellow, taking his time and using all of his wiles to persuade her to do what he wanted her to. Even when he got angry, it was controlled. But this new, short-tempered Corvin was the opposite. He was impatient and jumped immediately to threats and force rather than using his charms.

"Where are you now? When can I talk to you?"

"You're talking to me right now. I'm not sure when I'll be home, but I have appointments tonight. I don't have time for… whatever."

"I could not feel you here. You disappeared. Have you been off to Africa again?"

She had been a lot farther away than that. But Reg wasn't about to tell him anything about it. "Yeah. I had some business to attend to."

"Restless ghosts in his house," Corvin repeated her own words back to her, "in Africa. Why would someone all the way over there expect you to come to deal with his restless ghosts? There are plenty of practitioners there to take care of such things."

Reg couldn't come up with a logical explanation. It wasn't like she knew a lot of people across the ocean. The journeys that had taken her to the continent had been to little huts with no phones and no internet. Or to the tombs in Egypt. Those people would not be calling her about exorcising restless spirits.

"What does it matter to you?" she asked. "You're not in charge of me. I don't have to report anything back to you. I have my own life and my own business that has nothing to do with you."

"I'm worried about you, that's all."

Said a hundred husbands and boyfriends to the women they tried to control and manipulate.

"You don't need to worry about me. I'm fine, and it's not your place to track my movements. Just stay out of my head and out of my way."

"I will not—"

He was irritating her. Reg tapped the red button and cut him off mid-sentence. She wasn't even sure why she had answered his call in the first place. She knew that he was going to be intrusive and over-bearing. She didn't have to answer his calls or report to him.

Of course he tried to call her back. Reg ignored the phone as it buzzed and buzzed. If he kept it up, he would run her phone out of juice. She sent the next couple of calls directly to voicemail rather than letting the vibration motor run down her battery. Her thumb hovered over the "block caller" button. The calls stopped. Reg put the phone back into her pocket. She straightened her legs and rose unsteadily to her feet. Her joints felt rusty after sitting on the ground for so long. She stretched her arms and shoulders and rubbed her knees.

Julian walked back across the clearing to her. "The power drinker."

She shrugged. "Yes."

"You should not talk to him."

"My life, not yours."

How many warlocks did she have to tell that she was her own person and didn't need them to interfere with her business?

At least two, apparently.

Reg looked around at the ground, up at the trees, and scanned the ground again.

"What are you looking for?" Julian asked.

"Something for the altar. I think… If the altar helped me make contact with Davyn, I shouldn't leave it bare. But I don't know what to leave there."

"Oh." Julian joined her in looking at the plants growing in the clearing and deeper into the trees.

After a few minutes, he motioned to her and pointed to a cluster of small purple flowers. "Violets."

"You think they would be okay for an offering?" She didn't know much about what different plants and herbs meant or what they might mean. She could burn sage or another savory herb, but she didn't see any growing wild and hadn't thought to bring anything with her.

"They can signify wisdom."

"Okay. That sounds good." Reg bent down and pinched off a few small flowers, leaving the rest to grow there. She returned to the altar stone and laid them there. "Just like that? Or should I burn them?"

"Like that, I think."

Reg nodded. She paused for a moment, thinking about Davyn and how far away and untouchable he seemed. She needed to find out more about where he was and how to reach him. She badly needed more wisdom than she already had, so the violets seemed appropriate.

"You should not have anything to do with the soul eater," Julian said again, picking up on his earlier line of communication.

"Why? Because you think I can't stand up to him?"

"Because… his kind and ours should not mix. That may go against the new *enlightened* ideas that excluding them from our society is unfair, but creatures like him should have their own communities. Should gazelles let lions join their herds?"

"*Creatures* like him?"

Julian nodded. "He may look like us physically, but his nature is very different. We can't let predators like him infiltrate every part of our lives."

While Reg had previously had some of the same thoughts, she wasn't sure that Julian was right. Was Corvin really any different from her? Other than the fact that his hunger drove him to steal the powers of others, of course. Reg had called on Corvin's powers more than once. It was different, because she didn't intend to steal them all away from him. But she also didn't have that big hole inside her that needed to be filled as he did.

She had felt Corvin's hunger herself and she didn't know how she would have survived having to deal with that pain all the time. She would have hunted to fill it too.

"He's still human," she said tentatively. "I know he is different in some ways, but he is not *that* different."

"The soul eaters are *not* human. They are a very ancient race and have had years to learn how to imitate humans, but they are not human."

Reg tried to reconcile that with what she knew. Corvin had said that his curse was usually passed from father to son. His mother had not been like him. Julian had said that there were female witches with the same affliction, so it wasn't always passed from father to son. Corvin had admitted to having a wife a long time ago but had never said that she was one like him. How did that make any sense if humans and Corvin's kind were incompatible?

"But… they can… uh… *pair* with humans," she pointed out to Julian. "I mean… that's the whole point to their glamour, isn't it? To pair with witches—or warlocks—to steal their powers?"

"They are compatible," Julian said, making an impatient gesture with his hand to push this argument away. "But they are not the same kind."

"So if a human and a power drinker get together, what is the baby? I thought the curse was passed from father to son, usually."

"They can have either one."

"Then… they must be the same species. Right?"

Julian shook his head. "They are not the same. They are nonhuman. Predatory creatures that camouflage themselves to look human."

Reg rolled her eyes. It was the first time she had heard this argument and she couldn't reconcile it to what she had experienced. How could she get into Corvin's head or he into hers? How could they reproduce? How could Corvin's kind be allowed to mix in Black Sands society if he were not human? It couldn't be true.

But then, she had learned that in the magical world, reproduction was not all the same as what Reg had learned on the playground and in science class. The fairies stole babies from other species and magically transformed them into fairies so that their nature was entirely different from what it had been and they had different physical attributes. It wasn't just a change that could be attributed to clothing or diet or bearing. Calliopia was as different as she could be from Karol, her pixie sister. And then there was the whole thing about Norma Jean supposedly getting pregnant with Reg by an immortal, and all of the stories in mythology of the immortals bearing mortal children in bizarre circumstances and combinations.

"Corvin isn't a monster," she said tentatively. "He's just like anyone else I know. Except for his curse."

Julian closed his eyes and shook his head at her folly. "You are playing with fire," he warned. "He is just waiting until you let down your guard. And when you do…"

"I can protect myself."

"Until you can't."

"Well, I happen to like playing with fire," Reg pointed out to him. "It's kind of my thing."

CHAPTER TWENTY-THREE

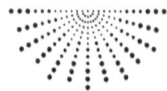

*I*t had been a long day. Reg let Julian drive her back home rather than transport herself directly there and let him find out about another of her powers. He knew far too much about her as it was. Julian opened his door to get out of the car at the same time as Reg.

"Stay put," Reg told him. "I'm fine. I'll let you know if I figure anything out. About Davyn. You'll be among the first to hear."

"I'll walk you in," Julian declared.

"I don't need an escort. I'll see myself in."

Julian looked around. "How do you know that soul drinker isn't close by, just waiting for you to come back home? He knows where you live. You cut him off; he will want to talk to you again."

"He can't come into the yard. He is barred from it. He can't get into the garden or the cottage. I'll be just fine there."

"It isn't safe," Julian warned. "Associating with him, you open yourself up to all kinds of dangers. He could be here. You don't know."

"I *do* know. I would be able to feel him here." Reg insisted. "Goodbye." She slammed the passenger-side door closed.

Through the window, she could see Julian shaking his head at her.

But he pulled his door shut and didn't attempt to follow her or walk with her into the yard.

Reg was tired and riled up at the same time. First Corvin demanding to know where she had been and trying to control her life, and then Julian, her self-appointed guardian, trying to keep her from doing anything he might consider dangerous. As if Reg didn't know what she was doing. She had a lot more experience than he did with Corvin's kind. At least she assumed so. With Corvin, anyway. Even if Julian knew other power drinkers, he did not know Corvin. Warlocks were individuals, just like any other class of people. There were bound to be both bad ones and good ones. She couldn't judge just by the reputation of the class. That was prejudice.

She paused at the gate to the backyard and took a quick look around. Corvin had startled her there before. It was as far as he could go before the wards would stop him. But looking around, she didn't see him anywhere. He was probably pretty angry after Reg had hung up on him, but he hadn't come to the house to confront her about it. She would already know about it.

Reg unlatched the gate, pushed it open, and entered the garden. She could feel the warm, welcoming glow of her home and the enchanted garden. It was a place she could be perfectly comfortable and at home. Safe from any outside influences. Julian had been able to enter the garden, but he wasn't Corvin. And he wasn't someone who had tried to enter with evil intentions. The fact that it was against the magical community's rules to bar a magical investigator from entering was not something that Reg had ever discussed with Sarah. It had never come up. Sarah had not been cowed by Julian and his threats to arrest Reg or anyone who interfered with the investigation. Sarah *knew people*.

Reg didn't sense that there was anyone in the yard who shouldn't be there. She followed the stone path to the door of her cottage. Sarah appeared to be home in the big house. There were several lights on. Taking a moment to feel for Sarah's presence, she knew that Sarah was there, along with a few guests. Maybe members of her coven.

Reg unlocked her door and let herself into the cottage. Starlight jumped down from the windowsill in her bedroom and came out to talk to Reg, meowing loudly about what he had seen outside and Reg being so late to feed him dinner.

"Oh, you're just fine," Reg told him sternly. She walked around the kitchen island to look down at the bowl on the floor. "You've even got kibble in your bowl, so it isn't like you're starving. You could have eaten that if you were hungry."

Starlight meowed crossly a few more times, ending in a low vocalization that sounded almost like a growl.

"All right, food is coming," Reg promised.

After feeding Starlight, Reg picked through the fridge, tasting a dish here and there, but not sure what she wanted to eat. Maybe she wasn't really hungry. She should eat since it was suppertime, but it wouldn't hurt her to skip a day. Her waistbands were getting tighter lately. It was nice not having to save and scrounge for food.

She sat down on the couch in front of the TV but didn't turn it on. She stared at the blank screen, trying to decide what to do. She wasn't sure she had made any headway on the case. She knew she had gotten close to Davyn, that he was there somewhere, but she didn't know how to get him back or exactly *where* somewhere was.

But she really did know what she should do. She just didn't feel like doing it.

Eventually, she picked up her phone and called Jessup.

"Reg!" Jessup's voice was way too enthusiastic when she answered the phone. "Hi! I was trying to decide whether to call you."

Reg cleared her throat and shifted uncomfortably. "Well, I was trying to decide whether to call you."

"You... found something?" Jessup suggested.

"I don't know. Not anything helpful. Nothing that the police can use."

"I'll be the judge of that. Tell me about it."

"Well, I saw Julian today."

"I talked to him on the phone. He didn't seem like he had much to contribute to the case. He hadn't heard from Davyn lately and didn't even know he was missing. They hadn't had any plans and hadn't talked in the past few days."

"Yeah. Doesn't seem like he knows anything about it."

"So you didn't get anything from him either."

"No. We went over to Davyn's house together to see if there was anything out of place, or something that might suggest where he had gone or if someone had it out for him."

"The police have already searched the house. We didn't find anything of note other than that he had left all of his possessions behind. Not like he had planned to go anywhere."

"Yeah. Boy, that guy keeps a neat house. Talk about repressed."

Jessup chuckled. "He is tidy; I'll give you that."

"We took a look around the grounds. It's pretty wild out there."

"Yes. We couldn't find anything of note. Had dogs out there but, of course, his scent is on everything. They couldn't lead us to him. No body, though, that's a positive. I am beginning to get worried. The longer we go without finding any indication of what happened to him… our chances of ever discovering him go down and down."

"There was a path into the woods that we followed to a clearing, with a stone for an altar in the middle of it."

She could see Jessup in her mind's eye, nodding at this information. "Yes. Saw that. No way to tell when the last time he used it was, though. Not very helpful."

"I tried to find him again from there, where his imprint was strong."

"Did you find out anything?" Jessup asked eagerly. "Any hint at all of what happened or where he is?"

"I don't think it is anything the police will be able to follow up on," Reg warned again.

"I can say that we got an anonymous tip. Or if it's really weird, that I consulted a psychic. I might be the laughingstock of the department, but they would at least have something to look for. They'd follow it up even if it sounded ridiculous."

"He's in a place… that's dark and cold."

"Uh-huh…?" Reg could hear papers rattling as, presumably, Jessup turned to a new page in her notepad and prepared to take down all of the details Reg could provide.

"That's all I know about it. Except… I don't think it's part of this world. Not this plane. This visible world."

Jessup made an exasperated noise. "What does that mean?"

"As I said, I don't think it is anything the police can investigate. They can't exactly find it; go there to get him. Wherever it is, this void, he can't get out, and I don't know how to get him out."

"Did you see this place? Can you tell me how to get there?"

"I saw it... I was there. Close to where he is. I could feel him close. But there wasn't anything else. No... doorway or exit that I could find. No ground to stand on. It's just... nothingness."

"But if he wandered in there, or someone put him there, there has to be a way to get in and get him back out again."

"You think that he got there by himself?" Reg asked, rubbing her forehead where the muscles were bunched up, pulsing with pain.

"I think it does happen. That people sometimes wander out of this world into another. Falling unintentionally between the cracks, the borders of the world. There have been enough strange disappearances over the years that I think something like that must be possible."

"I don't think he got there himself."

"Maybe not. Maybe someone sent him there." Jessup thought about it, humming a little. "If someone sent him there, do you think you could *call* him? Maybe you don't need to find an entrance or exit. Maybe just do a call."

Reg hadn't considered that. She was getting better at both calling others and transporting herself and others to other places. She hadn't traveled that way a lot, but it certainly made it a faster trip across the ocean. And maybe to the place where Davyn was.

"I guess I could try," she agreed reluctantly. She already feared that it wouldn't work. So far, nothing she had attempted on the case had succeeded.

"Should I come over?" Jessup suggested. "Then I can talk to him if you're able to call him. Or if he needs some kind of treatment, I can get some help..."

"No. It probably won't work. There's no point in coming over."

"Not with that kind of attitude," Jessup disapproved.

"I just don't think... the place where he is. I don't think I can reach it with a *call*. I couldn't do a *seek*. Not until I was actually at his altar."

"We could go over there so you could call from there. Maybe a midnight call? You could light some candles. Get prepared that way. It would be much stronger."

Reg still didn't see herself as a witch, despite the gifts that she was able to call upon. She was a medium, yes, a psychic, but the stuff that Jessup was talking about definitely had a more witchy feel to it, and Reg wasn't comfortable with it.

"No?" Jessup asked after a minute, her voice more subdued. "If you don't want to try that, then whatever you're comfortable with. If you want to try a *call* from your house, that's fine. It's more than I can do. Much more."

"Was your family magical? You grew up as part of this community?"

"Yes. I didn't really mind that I didn't have magical gifts... In all families, there are people who have gifts and those who don't. All different degrees and different talents. I was more interested in the physical world. Sports. Cops. Tangible things. I didn't have much of an affinity for the unseen. I guess if you can't ever see it, you don't miss it. I participated in rituals and celebrations with my family, but they were just... family traditions. I didn't feel like they were a big deal."

Reg shook her head. "I can't imagine what that must have been like."

"A lot like any other family. Some people are athletic; some are musical. Some are brainiacs. Everybody has different strong and weak points. Sometimes we were brats to each other, but mostly we supported each other in whatever studies or careers we wanted to go into."

"Sounds like a good family."

Not like the families Reg had grown up in. They were not at all like Jessup described.

"Do you want to just put me on speaker while you do the call? Or do you want to phone me back after and tell me how it went?"

"It might take me a little while. I'll talk to you later."

"Let me know, okay? Either way. If it works or if it doesn't."

It wouldn't. Reg was sure of that. "Okay. I'll let you know."

After Reg hung up, she wondered why she had bothered. *It might take a while?* She knew that it only took a moment or two of concentration. If it was going to work, it worked right away. Almost instantaneously. One minute, she would be thinking of Davyn and saying his name and the next minute he would be there.

The truth was, she wanted a little time to fortify herself. Have a drink. See if Starlight would help her. Work up her courage to try the spell she was sure would fail.

When she was little, she had always thought that being magic when she grew up would be great. She could be like Harrison, having whatever she wanted—coming and going as she liked, never going hungry or having to deal with abuse. Now that she had discovered her powers, it seemed unfair that she couldn't do whatever she wanted. Her attempts frequently failed. She was good at talking with the dead or doing some minor magic she had retained even though the adults had tried to break her. But the big things that she'd never had a chance to develop... like any skill, were hit-and-miss. She never knew if they were going to work or if she were even doing them the right way.

It was Calliopia's sister, Karol, who had first prompted her to do a call, and Reg had done just that, called Calliopia to her while she was visualizing her in the crystal. Calliopia had been transported to her, nearly on top of her, and Ruan with her, because they were holding hands.

But what if that had just been beginner's luck? It seemed sometimes like the skills that she needed the most failed her when it was most important.

CHAPTER TWENTY-FOUR

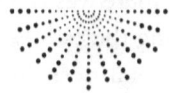

*E*ventually, there wasn't any way for Reg to stall any longer without admitting to herself that she was only looking for ways to delay the potential failure of a call. She sat with Starlight on her lap, staring at the crystal ball, as focused as she could be after a long day and one visit to the void already.

"Okay." She closed her eyes and prompted herself. Sometimes it was easier to concentrate over the other voices if she spoke aloud. "It will only take a minute, and then I'll know."

She pictured Davyn as clearly as she could. Not the black, cold place where she knew that he was, but Davyn as he was when he mentored her, working alongside her as she developed control over her fire, helping her find an outlet for the desire to burn without putting anyone in danger. Smiling, his eyes bright and alert, his black cloak flowing around him in the breeze.

"Davyn Smithy. Come."

She felt the tug immediately. She was prepared to see the void again; she knew that when she did a call, her perspective changed to that of the person she had called, a confusion of light and color and sound as they tumbled through space. She would see what Davyn saw as he traveled to her. She saw and felt the darkness again. She could feel the tug as she tried to pull him to her. But it felt like someone else was on the other end, holding Davyn back, keeping him in that black hole. The formless entity resisted, keeping a tight grip on Davyn. Reg focused, digging her fingers into Starlight's fur and using as much of his strength as she dared, hoping that their combined powers would be enough to shift the balance to her side.

Davyn cried out in pain. Reg relaxed her grip on the cord that bound them together. She didn't want to tear him in half.

The thing that held him there was too strong for her.

She breathed out, releasing the call. Leaving Davyn in his prison.

"I'm sorry." She took several deep breaths, reorienting herself to her cottage. Sitting on her couch, with Starlight on her lap. "I'll try to figure it out. I'll find a way. I just need time."

Starlight dug his claws into her leg for a second, then jumped to the floor and padded over to his bowls, where he noisily lapped water for several minutes. Reg supposed she should rehydrate too, but the kitchen seemed a long way away, and she needed to rest for a while before she could manage.

After a few minutes of just breathing and trying to ready herself for the rest of the night's activities, Reg pulled out her phone to call Jessup back. There was a long list of missed calls on her screen, and the time was eleven o'clock. Reg looked behind her at the dark window. Eleven o'clock? That couldn't be right. But it was dark outside and, when she looked at the time on the satellite receiver under the TV, it verified the lateness of the hour. How long had she been fighting to get Davyn out of the void? As in the glade, it seemed like only a few minutes had passed, but it had been hours. She had missed all of her evening readings. She must have been sitting there in a trance while they each knocked on her door and called her on the phone, trying to get ahold of her. Reg was surprised that Sarah hadn't shown up to find out where she was and why she was not there to take her appointments. She must be out with friends.

Luckily, Reg did not have a midnight seance to prepare for. That would be too much. She needed to rest and regenerate, not to have to reach out to the spirits, carrying messages back and forth.

Jessup had called a number of times, every twenty to thirty

minutes during the time that Reg had been in a trance. Reg tapped the last missed call.

Jessup answered before it had even rung on Reg's end. "Reg! I've been trying to get you! What's going on? Is everything okay? You said you would call me back."

"Yeah, sorry. It… took longer than I expected. I missed all kinds of calls."

"You've been trying to do it since we talked?" Jessup's voice held a note of disbelief. Did she think that Reg was lying? That she had gone out partying and just not bothered to call her back and ignored all of her calls? Reg might have a complicated relationship with the truth, but she wouldn't have made up something like that. Well, that probably wasn't true. But the fact was, she wasn't lying, and she expected Jessup to believe her when she told the truth. However, history had shown that Jessup had often been skeptical of Reg's answers.

"Yeah. It didn't feel that long, but I guess it was. The same thing happened when I tried to find him from the grove. Julian said I'd been a trance for an hour, but it seemed like it had only been a minute or two."

"Oh. Hmm. Well, I guess you'd better be careful if you try it again. I don't want you to get lost there too."

"Yeah."

"Do you want me to come over there? Are you okay? You sound tired."

"I am. I'll probably hit the sack soon. So, no, I don't need anyone here."

"Reg Rawlins going to bed before midnight? That's something I never thought I would hear."

Reg laughed weakly. Not that it was really funny.

"Before you go," Jessup said, her voice getting a little louder, "I did phone you for more than just to find out if you were able to make any progress with the call."

"Oh. What is it?"

"I found out that you were not the last to see Davyn. We were able to narrow the window for his disappearance down further."

"That's good! What did you find out? Who saw him?"

"He went to coven at midnight Monday night. A dozen people can vouch for the fact that he was fine after you saw him. That narrows his disappearance down to between one o'clock or whatever time he left the coven to eight o'clock when he should have shown up at work."

"What happened to him?" Reg cleared her throat. She felt a little sick to her stomach. She knew without a doubt that Davyn had not just wandered into that netherworld by accident. Something was keeping him there. Something did not want him to leave. And whatever it was, it was strong.

"I don't know. We'll do some more investigating. But it's good to be able to narrow the time down more. It helps to eliminate suspects."

"What about Corvin?"

She didn't like to think that Corvin might have done something to Davyn. But he was the one who had a motive to get Davyn out of the way, opening up Corvin's path to leadership of the coven. And the last place that Davyn had been was the coven.

"The latest information actually clears Corvin. He had a clear alibi. He was still with the coven when Davyn left. The others can vouch for him. Whatever happened to Davyn happened after that."

"He could have followed Davyn home…" Reg frowned, replaying what Jessup had said. "When Davyn left? Why did Davyn leave before the others?"

"He got a phone call."

Reg waited for more information, but Jessup was being stubborn about it. She needed to either give Reg all of the information about the investigation or leave her out of it. Reg couldn't work with only half the story. How was she supposed to figure anything out from what Jessup was giving her?

"And? A phone call from who? Why did he go home? He left early, before anyone else?"

"Yes. He said it was an emergency and he had to get back to his house."

Jessup again stopped, but Reg was determined to wait her out this time. She pressed her mouth closed and didn't ask for anything else. Jessup could give her the details, or she could hang up and go about her police business and not concern herself with psychics and the knowledge that Davyn was stuck in some magical prison beyond her reach.

"He said it was a call from the police and that his house had been broken into."

"What?" Reg's head spun as she tried to make sense of this. "His house was broken into? I didn't see any signs that the door had been forced or a window broken. How did anyone get into his house?"

Of course, *Reg* hadn't needed to break a window or the door to get in. They must have picked the lock, either magically like Reg or with standard lock picking tools.

"No one broke into the house. We didn't find any sign that anyone had been there other than Davyn. It's possible that he leaves his door unlocked. Some people do, but he had wards guarding against intruders. And... it wasn't the police who called him."

"I thought you said..."

"He told them it was the police. We have to assume that the caller told him they were the police. But it wasn't. There was no incident report of a burglary at Davyn's address or anywhere in the neighborhood. There is no record of a call being placed to him for any reason."

Someone had deliberately called him away from the coven— someone who had wanted to get him on his own. At night, when there were no witnesses.

"And Corvin was at the coven when Davyn got the call?" she checked.

"Yes. We have confirmation that he was definitely there when Davyn got the call. He isn't the one who placed it."

So someone other than Corvin had gotten Davyn out of the way. All along, Reg's suspicion of Corvin had been growing in the back of her mind. He was the one person who seemed to have a reason to make Davyn disappear, at least for a while. If it wasn't him, then who could it have been? Another warlock? Someone he had crossed without even realizing it? A random attack? Jealous lover? She knew so little of Davyn's personal life that it was hard to think of who else it could be. And the man seemed so tidy and squared away that she couldn't imagine a messy, emotional situation in his life.

Reg rubbed her forehead. "I'm really wiped out. I'm going to go to bed... sleep on this... maybe it will make more sense in the morning."

"You're more likely to be able to see things clearly if you're well-rested," Jessup decided. "Go ahead and get some sleep, and if you have any new ideas or impressions in the morning... give me a call, okay?"

Reg nodded. "Sure. Of course."

In the morning, maybe something would occur to her.

CHAPTER TWENTY-FIVE

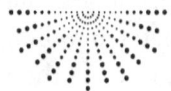

*U*nfortunately, the night didn't bring Reg much rest, and she hadn't achieved enlightenment when she awoke the next day. Or when she finally decided it was time to get out of bed. She had lain in bed for a long time after going to bed, too tired and restless to actually sleep. She couldn't find a comfortable position, couldn't lie still, and couldn't calm the chattering of her brain. And all of the other voices in her head. It was like trying to sleep in the middle of a noisy board meeting.

She thought that the only way to make any more progress on the investigation would be to talk to the other warlocks in the coven. They should have a better idea of whether there were anything going on in Davyn's life that had led up to his disappearance. He met with them regularly. They went to him for help and guidance. Surely if he were in the middle of some sticky situation, they would have some idea about it. Even if it wasn't something that he had been open about. Reg didn't see how the warlocks could be that close and not get an inkling of what the other coven members were up to. Especially when they had been attending coven together for years. Maybe even decades or centuries. It was hard to believe that Corvin and some of the others were centuries old, like they claimed. They certainly didn't look like it. But something about their use of magic—

or some dang good cosmetic potions—kept them looking as if they were still in the prime of their lives.

For Reg's plan to succeed, she needed some help. She had spent a lot of time during the night trying to work things out to find another way, how to proceed with the investigation by herself, but she kept circling back to the original plan. The one that involved her calling Damon Knight.

Reg poured coffee into her largest mug and sighed.

"You see the lengths that I'm willing to go to in order to find you?" she asked Davyn aloud. It was the third day after his disappearance, and Reg knew they had passed a critical milestone. Seventy-two hours since Davyn had left the coven to return home.

It wasn't like Damon was that bad. But there had been... misunderstandings. Miscommunications. Just plain lies. While Reg was willing to bend the truth when it suited her, Damon's distortions had put her in danger. He had sabotaged the project right from the start. And not only that, but he had repeatedly tried to influence her with visions. She couldn't trust anything that was in her head when she was with him. Anything she saw, heard, or thought might have been placed there by him.

She didn't think he was evil, like Kareem or the Witch Doctor, but he wasn't good for her.

But Reg went ahead and dialed his number anyway. She hadn't deleted it from her phone, so maybe she had known all along that she wasn't going to eliminate him from her life completely. Maybe subconsciously, she had known that sooner or later she was going to end up calling him again.

The phone rang a few times, and Reg tried to think of what she would say to his voicemail. If he weren't available, would she even leave a message? What was the point? The thing with Davyn was time sensitive. She couldn't wait around for Damon to free himself up.

"Knight Security."

"Oh. Damon? It's Reg."

"Reg!" Damon sounded surprised, but not displeased to hear from her. Maybe it had been long enough that his wounded pride had healed. It seemed like a lot had happened since the search in the

Everglades and the Spring Games. Maybe he felt the same way. "How can I help you today?"

"Well… this is sort of last-minute, so I understand if you can't help me out. I don't know if you heard that Davyn Smithy is missing?"

"Yeah, I sure did. Don't tell me that you had something to do with that," Damon teased.

"No, not me!" Reg didn't laugh about it. She'd forgotten how Damon's sense of humor and hers were frequently out of sync. "But I've been trying to help the police with their investigation. Psychic consultation."

"Uh-huh. I'm not sure why anyone bothered reporting it to the police. There's not much they could do, bumbling around as they do. How are you supposed to convince them of anything around the case that is… not conventional?"

"Jessup has been doing fairly well." Reg found herself defending Jessup, despite the fact that she'd thought pretty much the same thing. "They've narrowed down the time he was kidnapped to about a seven-hour window."

"And how does that help? I'm sure he wasn't kidnapped by terrorists or for a million-dollar ransom. When the leader of a coven goes missing, I think it's pretty obvious that there is magic involved."

"Well, you're right. But what I called you for was… I would like to talk to the members of the coven. Find out what they might know about Davyn and what might have been going on in his life that led to this. I think that someone must know something. The members of a coven are pretty close, aren't they?"

"Sure. Of course. They might be able to point you in the right direction."

"My psychic gifts will help me a little. Maybe I can read their auras and catch a stray thought here and there. But if any of them were involved or are protecting the person involved, they're going to be pretty careful to block me, and I can't force my way into their minds, since…"

"That's against the rules and would get you into big trouble, even though you were trying to save a life."

"Yeah. But your gift as a diviner—you would be able to tell when they were lying to me and when they were telling the truth, right?"

"Mm-hmm…" Damon's answer was a bit tentative, more like a *yes, but…* "It isn't as black and white as you may think."

"You can tell when they're lying. Even if they're sociopaths. Can't you?"

Mechanical lie detectors couldn't tell that someone was lying if they didn't feel guilty or show any emotional response to a lie. Reg was hoping that the same did not apply to a diviner like Damon.

"Yes. But like I told you before… everybody lies. Big or little. Everybody is going to shade the truth a little bit when answering questions. And my gift does not tell me *why*. Is someone lying because he is guilty? Because he wants to portray himself in a better light? Because he is a pathological liar? He wants attention? He's protecting someone else?"

Reg hadn't thought about all of that. But for a good number of those things, she would be able to use her psychic abilities to tell why someone was lying. Emotions were fairly easy to read, even without her gift. Guilt, embarrassment, attention-seeking—she could discern those.

"Do you think you could help me out? You probably had other plans today, but he's been missing for three days, and I'm worried we might not have much time."

"You want me along while you interview members of his coven. In hopes that one of them knows something, and between the two of us, we can figure out who and why." His question was flat and, Reg thought, implied that he didn't think it had a chance of working.

"Well… yes."

"Why not?" Damon surprised Reg with his quick reply. "Davyn is a good guy. The coven needs him. I think Black Sands as a whole needs him."

"So… you don't mind? You can get out of whatever you had planned today?"

"I'll make a couple of calls to get jobs covered, but yes. I'm my own boss, so I can play hooky if I want to."

Reg let out her breath. "I didn't think it would be that easy to talk you into it."

She could tell that Damon was smiling when he responded. A slight uplift in his voice. She could picture his face and the humor she'd seen in his eyes before. "Well then, where do you want to start? Do you have a list of the coven members?"

"Um... no. I was hoping that you would have some idea of who is in the coven. But I guess since you're not a member..."

"Well, we know that Corvin is. We can always start with him. I know a couple of names, and he can give us the names of others. Or maybe Marta Jessup, since you're working with her. She'll have the full list."

"I'm not sure how she would feel about me talking to the warlocks in the coven. She didn't exactly ask me to, and I didn't tell her that I was."

"Ah, I see. Don't worry about it. I'm sure it won't be too hard to get them. We'll start with what we have and work our way out. If nobody wants to share, I can get someone to do some research to find the rest of the members out. It isn't usually too hard. Luckily, witches and warlocks no longer have to operate in secret. A lot of the covens have websites or online groups that are accessible. They frequently put events in the community newsletter."

"Good."

"You want me to pick you up?"

"Yeah, I guess that would be the best." If Reg tired herself out with reading people or trying to reach Davyn again, it was probably best if she had a ride and didn't have to port or drive herself. No point in driving tired and ending up in an accident.

"I'll be there in fifteen. Have you had coffee?"

Reg looked down at her large mug. "Only one."

Damon chuckled. "I'd better pick up some more on the way, then. I'll be twenty minutes."

"Text me when you're here and I'll come out."

CHAPTER TWENTY-SIX

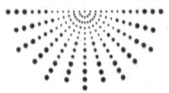

*R*eg remembered not to wear a skirt to go with Damon. He had a big truck that was difficult to get into when hampered by a skirt, and Reg preferred not to have to lift it to her waist in order to climb up into the cab. She didn't often wear pants, so it felt strange to be going out dressed like that. It felt like she was missing something.

"Corvin's house?" Damon asked. He gestured to the takeout cup in the holder next to Reg. "That's yours."

Reg picked up the cup and sipped the coffee appreciatively. No matter how many times she made coffee at home, it never quite tasted like coffeehouse brew. "Perfect. Yeah, I guess we try Corvin first."

She tried to decide how to engage Damon in small talk on the way there, but decided that just wouldn't work. She had no desire to talk about the weather or other inconsequential things on the way.

"You should know going in there that Corvin has an alibi for the time that Davyn disappeared," she informed Damon. "He was with the coven. Davyn left alone. So they all have alibis, unless we find out they were involved and are just covering for each other. Or covering for Corvin. But I can't think of why they would do that."

"If he charmed them into it."

"I suppose… but once he's not with them anymore, I don't think they would stick to the party line. Corvin has to be there to influence them."

Damon nodded. "I wasn't sure if that would work or not. But are you sure of his limitations? Since you first met him, he's grown a lot in his powers."

"I guess. But I don't think that has changed. He can't charm someone if they aren't in the same room with him."

"You know that for a fact?"

"He's tried enough times to influence me."

Damon cocked his head slightly, which Reg presumed meant she'd made her point. "Do you know what powers he *has* acquired? The fact that he drained the Witch Doctor of most of his powers has always irked me. That immortal was very powerful. For Corvin to get him on the run..."

Reg remembered the moment when the Witch Doctor had fled Corvin, sending his essence into each of nine draugar. Francesca, a white Haitian witch, had bound each of the draugar into their kattakyn form, so that to all the world, they appeared to be nothing more than pure black cats. Then she and Reg had sent each of the kattakyns to new homes around the world. Binding the kattakyns was supposed to keep the Witch Doctor's essence imprisoned for a thousand years. But one of the kattakyns, Horace, had already been separated from the piece of the Witch Doctor he had held, so now they weren't so sure.

Damon didn't know about Horace's portion of the Witch Doctor's spirit being lost. At least, Reg hadn't told him about it.

Damon wanted to know what powers Corvin had taken from the Witch Doctor, and Reg still wasn't sure of the answer.

"It's hard to say. I think he is getting in better control of them, but I'm not sure what he is capable of. He wouldn't exactly tell me. But I know... he's getting stronger."

"But he isn't in full control of them. He hasn't been pulling any of the same tricks as the Witch Doctor?"

The Witch Doctor had been able to raise and control nine draugar, something that was unheard of. Draugar were something like zombies. Reanimated corpses, but nothing like the ones she had seen on TV. They could look just like regular men or grow into giants. Or shrink down into kattakyns, making it harder to detect them. They could kill in either form and had terrorized Black Sands until Corvin, Francesca, and the others had banded together to defeat the Witch Doctor.

"No zombies that I'm aware of," Reg said lightly. "And I think I would know."

"Would you?" Damon glanced away from the road to look at Reg.

"Yes. I did last time."

"You don't think that he would be able to cloak them from you?"

"No."

But Corvin *had* been hiding something from Reg. She had felt the walls he had built. But just like she wasn't able to keep him out of her mind completely, he couldn't keep her completely away from reading him either. Raising an army of draugar would have been too big of a thing for him to hide from her. She would not only feel the same dread she had felt when the Witch Doctor was raising them. She would have known that Corvin had something to do with it.

She was pretty sure, anyway.

Damon looked back at the road. Of course he could sense the difference between the absolute truth and Reg trying to shade the truth a little. And she honestly didn't know what Corvin was capable of. But she was as sure as anyone could have been. More than anyone else could have been.

"But you don't know what other powers he has. What else he might be hiding."

"Well... no. I know he tries not to let everything leak out. I can tell he is stressed out. That's what I think it is, anyway. He's been kind of crabby lately, not quite like himself. It's been since the announcement that he could rejoin the coven."

She worried over the dark aura surrounding Corvin. Did it signify depression? Some other dark mood? It wasn't anger. She had seen the red glow around him when he grew angry. Sadness? Anxiety?

"He's always seemed pretty crabby to me." Damon grinned.

Reg couldn't help but give a short laugh at that. "That's just because you guys rub each other the wrong way."

"I don't like predators. There are predators in any community, and there are protectors. I am one of the protectors."

Reg shrugged. She didn't know how to argue with that. She herself had referred to Corvin that way many times. It felt like a betrayal to let Damon call Corvin a predator without defending him, but how could she? By definition, he was. It wasn't *all* he was. But his hunger for magical gifts compelled him to prey on those who were weaker.

CHAPTER TWENTY-SEVEN

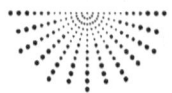

hey arrived on Corvin's street and Damon took a minute to find a space he could park his truck in. The lot wasn't as wide as Sarah's property and there were more vehicles parked on the street. But it wasn't the slums; Corvin still lived in a very nice house. Reg had been there once or twice before.

She was glad that she hadn't decided to go there alone. All of the talk of Corvin's increased powers had put her on edge. She had been able to protect herself from Corvin on most occasions recently, but if he became as strong as the Witch Doctor, she didn't think she would be able to resist him. Not for long.

There was no need to ring the doorbell. Corvin was standing at his open door by the time they made it up the sidewalk. His eyes were dark. As Reg had noticed, he and Damon did not get along.

"What is this?" he demanded. "Selling cellular plans door to door? Missionary outreach?"

"I think you know why we're here," Reg countered.

Corvin stood there looking at them, glowering. Reg didn't know if he was waiting for a full explanation or just trying to intimidate her. She gestured behind him.

"Shall we?"

Corvin grunted and stepped back, allowing them to enter. Reg and Damon crossed the threshold.

Reg took a deep breath and looked around. What had she been expecting? Booby traps? For Corvin to slam the door and magic her away to where Davyn was trapped? She had sort of expected things to be a mess, for it to look like there had been a fight or some other kind of violence. Corvin's demeanor had been so different recently that she was expecting there to be some sign of it in his house. A mess. A corkboard with newspaper articles or ancient texts pinned to it and red yarn running from one to another, showing wildly unlikely connections between them—some sign of a disordered mind.

But everything was as it had been the last time she had been to Corvin's house. Dark, heavy furniture. Not as neat and orderly as Davyn's house. More lived-in and bachelor-esque. But certainly not the disaster area she had imagined it might have devolved into. Corvin sat down on a large wingback chair that made Reg think of a throne. He didn't ask them to sit or if they wanted drinks. He just crossed one leg over the other and continued to glare at them.

Reg and Damon each took seats anyway.

"We're trying to figure out what happened to Davyn," Reg told him. Of course he already knew that, but she felt like they needed at least a short introduction before diving straight into the questions. Corvin might not be up for small talk, but just diving straight into an interrogation seemed rude.

"Why don't you just leave that to the police? They've already been around asking questions. You're not exactly law enforcement, Regina."

"I've been retained as a consultant on the case," Reg informed him, her voice even.

"As an investigator?"

"As... a consultant."

"As a psychic."

Reg nodded. "Well, yes."

"Psychics don't conduct interviews."

"Well... psychics do readings. I can talk to people and see if I get any impressions... the more people I can talk to about Davyn, the better the chances are that I might get some impression or some answer that the police can follow up on."

"You're not going to get any impressions from me."

She didn't point out that he was the person she was most likely to get impressions from, since his mind was open to her.

Or mostly open. Partially open.

"I guess you were at the coven on Monday night before Davyn disappeared?"

"I might have been. Did the police tell you that?"

"I am working with the police," Reg repeated. "I know they've already talked to you about it, but can you run through it once more with me? Maybe I can get something…"

"The workings of the coven are private."

"Why?"

He looked taken aback at her question, showing a reaction other than crankiness for the first time. "We are a private group. Conducting our spiritual practices. The state doesn't have any right to be involved in our religious beliefs."

Reg shrugged. "I didn't ask you about your religious beliefs. And who cares if I did? They're not exactly a secret, are they? Or have you started some new cult that worships you as their messiah?"

"You're mocking us now?"

"Come on. The coven was gathered. I don't care what kind of ceremony or practice it was for. Unless you were offering human sacrifices. Or cats. I just want to know about Davyn. If he was there, what kind of a mood he was in, if he said anything that seemed strange or out of character. What happened before he left. What happened after he left. You don't have to tell me your beliefs or what kind of ritual you were there for. I'm not challenging any of your 'spiritual practices.'"

"Practitioners of magic have been persecuted for centuries. Just because there is a superficial acceptance of our beliefs and our right to gather, that doesn't mean that the prejudice and persecution have stopped. And just because you are a witch, that doesn't mean that you accept our beliefs or practices either."

"I said I don't care about that."

He sat there staring at her.

"Davyn was there, right?" Reg persisted.

"Yes, of course he was."

"He was the leader of your coven, so he must have always been there."

"Sometimes, if he was busy with something else important or was sick, he would appoint someone else to lead the practices that night. But yes, he was almost always there when coven was held."

Reg nodded. One answer down. It would be a lot easier if she could just get him to let down his barriers and have a regular conversation with her. His defenses were so high that she felt like she was trying to reach him through a brick wall. Or a tornado.

"And what was he like?"

Corvin raised his brows. "What was he like?"

"I don't want to put any words in your mouth. Did he act like he normally did? Was there anything *off*? Was he emotional or distracted? Did he say anything strange?"

Corvin's shoulders were rigid, despite his studied casual posture. "He seemed fine. I didn't notice anything out of the ordinary."

"Do you guys… socialize while you are there? I mean, is it all business, just the practice you are there for, or do you hang out and talk about yourselves and see how everyone is doing?"

Corvin looked at Damon. "And why is he here? I thought the two of you weren't seeing each other anymore."

"We're not *seeing* each other." Reg shifted uncomfortably, looking at Damon. "I just asked Damon if he would come along with me. Be a second set of ears, in case there was anything I missed."

"You don't need to be protected."

She shrugged. "That's not what I said. So… do you socialize?"

"Some."

"Did Davyn say what was going on in his life? Anything he was working on or planning to do later?"

"Not that I recall. He wasn't that open about his private life. He might mention work now and then, or some significant anniversary or date. But he didn't talk about himself much."

"And he didn't say anything that night about himself or about something that was coming up?"

"Not that I recall."

"Did he lead the ceremony that night?"

Corvin studied her. "He was our leader."

"And he led whatever was going on that night? Or did you guys rotate and take turns? Was it someone else's thing, or was it all Davyn?"

"Bernie led the ritual. Bernie Sayer. And after that, Davyn had... some other things to announce. Rules, procedures, that kind of thing."

Reg could sense what he wasn't saying. And even if she hadn't been able to feel it, she would have been able to guess what he was talking about. "The election campaign?"

He cleared his throat, which sounded like an angry growl of protest. "Yes."

"Were the two of you the only ones running?"

Corvin pressed one fist into the palm of the other hand. Like he wanted to sock someone and was either preparing himself or trying to hold himself back. She wasn't sure which. "Yes, thus far."

Reg waited for more information before pressing. "Did you... expect someone else to join in the race?"

"No."

"So it was just the two of you."

"That's what I said."

And with Davyn out of the way, it was now only Corvin. But there must be some kind of procedure in place before Corvin could just take over the coven. A vote of confidence from the members. His appointment written down in a book. Maybe some kind of offering made or ceremonial clothing given.

Reg looked at Damon. She didn't expect him to say anything or to jump into the interview. It was her show. But she wanted to make sure she wasn't missing anything. That Corvin wasn't telling a huge lie about anything she had questioned him about so far.

Damon's lips tightened slightly and he gave a tiny shake of his head. Reg looked back at Corvin.

"Was there any... discussion of the rules? Any objections?"

"That's private."

So... maybe there was. Maybe someone had challenged the new rule that would allow Corvin to run for the group's leadership. Or maybe there was an objection not to a cursed warlock running for leadership, but to a warlock who had just been reinstated into the coven being allowed to run for leadership so quickly.

"Was this your first coven since your reinstatement? The first time you had met with them since... the judgment?"

"Yes. It was."

"Was the ceremony to bring you back in? Did you get a big 'welcome back'? Or did they just treat it like you had never been gone?"

"I don't see what that has to do with Davyn's disappearance."

"Well... maybe not. I just wondered. I'm trying to get a full picture of what happened that night."

"As I said, it was a private practice of our faith. Not something that I would share with an outsider, especially someone working for the non-magical authorities."

"Okay. Fine. So Davyn participated in the rituals, then talked to everyone about the leadership race, answered any questions or objections to the new rules or how it was being run, is about right?"

Corvin shrugged with one shoulder.

"And then...?"

"I'm sure you already know. What do you need me to tell you for?"

"I want to hear the story. You were there. I might get a feeling about something if I hear about it firsthand. Hearing about something second or third hand is like reading it in the newspaper. There are no emotions attached to it."

CHAPTER TWENTY-EIGHT

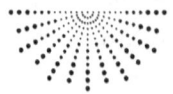

*C*orvin sighed loudly and rolled his eyes. "As I'm sure you heard, he got a phone call."

Reg waited.

"He said it was the police and that something had happened to his house. He'd been broken into. So, he lit out of there and went home."

"He said it had been broken into?"

"Yes."

"Because it wasn't. Everything was fine at the house. No sign of any broken windows or door."

"And Marta said that the police never called him. Yeah. But that's what Davyn said. I assume that was the message he was given."

"You think someone was trying to draw him away from the coven."

Corvin flashed a look at her. "I never said what I thought."

"But is it?"

He twitched his chin slightly in an upward nod. "That's what it sounds like. If I have to have an opinion about it, then yes, someone called him to pull him away from the coven."

"Who do you think did that?"

"I have no idea. How would I?"

"You knew each other. You were in the same coven. I assume you knew things about each other's lives. If someone had threatened him or there was something seriously wrong in his life, then I assume you would have heard about it."

"Like I said, Davyn doesn't share much. If there's something messy going on in his life, I have no idea what it is."

"You were running against him for the leadership of the coven."

"So?" He shrugged. "What does that have to do with anything?"

"You were competitors. You wanted to take over from him."

"I don't see what that has to do with anything."

"With Davyn out of the way, it makes it that much easier for you to take over leadership of the coven."

"It makes no difference." At Reg's skeptical raised eyebrow, he shook his head. "Okay, *marginally* easier. But I wasn't seriously worried about it."

"Why not?"

"Davyn had been in there long enough. He was ready to pass it off to someone else. He didn't want to have to do all the work. Thought it would be nice to have some more time with his… family. And his persuasive powers…?" Corvin looked up at the ceiling and shook his head again. "He could give a logical argument. Nothing wrong with his brain. But it takes more than logic to win an election." He looked smug. "You need other gifts to really be able to influence people."

The thought of Corvin using his charms to influence the other warlocks in the coven made her feel a little sick. How could it be a fair election if one of the candidates had the ability to magically charm the voters, and the other did not? Remembering how she had allowed herself to be influenced by him in the past made her feel more nauseated. Knowing that he had that magical influence over her, why did she keep doing things with him?

Not that she could help it if he showed up at The Crystal Bowl when Reg was eating. But she didn't have to agree to eat with him. She could still refuse. It was hard to stay convinced that he was a danger to her when she had been able to fend off his advances and use his own magic against him in the past. But she couldn't let herself become complacent. Corvin was constantly growing in power, learning how to use more of the gifts he had acquired and stealing more to supplement them. She couldn't assume that he had the same powers from one day to the next.

Reg played with the end of one of her braids, running it between her fingers and feeling the bumpy, woven pattern. "How many people are in the coven? Is it a big group or a little one?"

Corvin leaned forward slightly. "The core membership of the coven is thirteen. That is a common number of members to form a coven. We do have other members as well. Neophytes who have not yet been initiated into the order. They form a part of the coven, but not the core."

"And can everyone vote?"

"No. Only the core members. And of course, you cannot vote if you are running. With Davyn and I both in the race, that leaves eleven voting members."

"Is it majority rules? Or does it have to be unanimous?"

"Simple majority." Corvin smiled, showing his teeth. "Six people."

He only had to charm or persuade six people to get himself elected leader of the coven. And without Davyn there to present what he thought was best for the coven, it wouldn't be hard to make people forget what he might have already said. Corvin was very good at making her forget everything else, all of the logic and warnings she had been given, so that all she wanted was to be in his arms. Davyn had said that Corvin wouldn't have as strong an influence over other warlocks, but Reg didn't see that it would make much difference. When he put all of his efforts into changing someone's mind, it was pretty overwhelming. She had gotten in trouble a lot more times than she would like to admit. Times when others had to step in to assist her, or when Reg only managed at the last moment to escape his wiles.

"But the leadership race doesn't have anything to do with Davyn's opinion," Corvin said with a shrug. "You've already been told I was there the whole time. I did not make that phone call to Davyn. I did not follow him home." He leaned his head against the back of the chair, looking like a king surveying his kingdom. Smug and superior.

Reg looked over at Damon. He shrugged and nodded. Corvin was, apparently, telling the truth.

But truth or not, Reg could still see the darkness that oozed out of him and became part of his aura, shifting between red and black. There was still something very disturbing going on with Corvin. He had changed over the past weeks.

"What about the rest of the warlocks? Did any of them leave before or right after Davyn?"

Corvin closed his eyes and thought about it. He shook his head. "No, not that I recall. If anyone had left... it was probably just a neophyte. No one in the inner circle."

"Can I get the names of the others that are part of this core group?"

"Why would I give you that?"

"So that there is someone else who can verify your alibi."

"I don't need to prove my alibi to you. I've already talked to the police."

"I want to talk to some of the other members, see if any of them might have been closer and know anything about what Davyn might have been having problems with. Maybe he didn't share anything with you, but you had been shunned until recently. Maybe he was friends with someone else. Someone that he did share things with."

"He wasn't the type to share personal information. Do you know how long it took for him even to mention Julian Sabat? He eventually had to because people had seen the two of them together and wanted to know more about Sabat and their relationship. He was very private."

Reg could remember Davyn blushing when she had asked him about Julian. In all of the time that she had spent practicing her fire-casting with him, she had not known anything before then about any of his past relationships. And it was Julian who had told Reg that Davyn had grown up in a non-magical home. Reg would have expected Davyn to have at least mentioned that during their fire-casting lessons. It would have been nice to hear from him how he had grown up as a firecaster among people who had no idea of his gift, just as Reg had. They had something else in common. Yet Davyn had never mentioned it himself. Lessons had always been professional, with Davyn asking after Reg's health and progress, but not telling her anything about his own.

"He still might have said something to someone. If you don't have phone numbers for these guys, that's fine. I just want names. I can find the rest. Track them down and talk to them to find out whether they know anything about problems Davyn had been having in his life. Or whether anyone had motive to hurt him."

"You mentioned Bernie Sayer," Damon contributed.

Corvin glared at him and nodded.

Corvin, Davyn, Bernie. That left ten more.

"Don't you want me to find Davyn?" Reg asked. "He's the leader of your coven. Don't you have some loyalty to him? Don't you care what happens to him?"

"I can't be responsible for what happens to everyone else."

"I'm not talking about everyone else. I'm talking about Davyn and the fact that he's missing. He would look for you if you were missing, you know."

Corvin opened his mouth to argue, then closed it. He considered for a few seconds before nodding. "Yes, he probably would."

"Exactly." Reg nodded. "If you want to prove to your coven that you're a good spiritual leader, that you care about the members of the coven and will help to take care of their needs, then don't you think you should cooperate and help us find Davyn? Otherwise... they're going to think that you're just a big jerk and don't care for anyone but yourself. And why would they elect you if you don't care about anyone else? Isn't the whole point of being a leader to help them?"

Corvin's eyes were dark as he stared straight ahead, not looking at Reg or Damon. Reg could feel the anger bubbling beneath the surface. Just under the surface, ready to erupt at any time. And with the powers that Corvin held, she didn't want to have to deal with him angry.

"I supposed you're right," he finally grumbled.

"I am. You should be demonstrating how much you care about the people in your coven right now, not how little."

Damon nodded his agreement.

"There's a meeting this afternoon. I'm sure they'll all be there." Corvin cleared his throat. "A blessing for Davyn."

"Oh. Like a group prayer?"

Corvin nodded. "Yes. Drawing on the powers of the coven. Positive thoughts directed toward Davyn. However we can use our powers to help to keep him well and safe."

"What a great idea. Where is it? I'll go talk to them. Catch them all in one place."

"We don't typically tell outsiders where or when we are meeting."

"Sure. That's understandable. You don't want that kind of information getting into the hands of the wrong people."

Reg waited. They might not tell "outsiders" most of the time, but he would tell her. If he wanted to look like he cared about helping Davyn, whether he really did or not, he needed to share the information so that Reg could talk to the coven, pick up any clues or impressions that she could, and figure out how to reach Davyn and bring him back. If she knew what was holding him there... or who was holding him there... or how... any of those things would lead her one step closer to figuring out how to get him back.

"Two o'clock," Corvin finally told her. "In the temple orange grove."

CHAPTER TWENTY-NINE

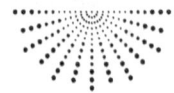

*I*t was Florida. There were a lot of orange groves.

In the car, Damon explained to Reg that the temple orange grove was a nature preserve where there had once been a pagan temple. It had been long enough ago that no one could remember much about it, other than that it had been a temple. Its particular purpose or deity was long forgotten, as were most traces of the temple itself.

There were some rocks that had been part of the foundation of the temple. Someone looking very carefully could find where the outer walls had stood so many years before. Other than that... it was an orange grove carefully maintained by a foundation that had received a grant from an anonymous donor for just that purpose.

"Do you think we'll be able to find anything out?" Reg asked.

"Well, you have as much a chance as anyone. Maybe more so. And if Corvin is going to show that caring attitude that you talked to him about, then he can encourage the other members of the coven to support you and tell you everything they can. I don't know if that will result in the clue that lets you find Davyn and bring him home safely, but it's at least worth trying."

"Yeah."

Damon looked at the time on his radio panel. "Do you want to get some lunch before we go over? Kill some time until they start showing up?"

"I guess so, yes. That would make sense." Reg's stomach gave a rumble. She hadn't realized that she was hungry. But all that she'd had so far was coffee, and she had obviously burned that off during the session with Corvin.

They found a cafe nearby and ordered. Reg still found it difficult to talk to Damon. First of all, because of the social distance between them, when they had previously been feeling out the possibility of a romantic relationship. Reg didn't want to say anything too intimate or familiar, but she didn't want to give him the cold shoulder either. He had agreed to ditch his regular work and help her out, when she had offered nothing in return but an interesting day. Reg paid for his lunch, and figured that was something, anyway. At least there was a free lunch.

But she also had never really clicked with Damon. He had been interested in her and had sent out clear signals, offering her an escort and giving her his business card when they had first met, the day of Corvin's tribunal. But their first attempts at dating did not turn out well. They didn't seem to speak the same language. Reg could get along with Corvin, whose life experience had been nothing like Reg's, and she still found him interesting and attractive. But Damon tended to do things that triggered negative emotions and memories for Reg. And he put visions into her head, which, as far as she was concerned, was very creepy. Especially when she couldn't tell at the time whether they were real or imagined. It was pretty disconcerting to play along inside a vision for a while, thinking it was reality, and then to find out that it had all just been something some guy had stuck into her head.

"I hope you'll be able to find Davyn. He's a good guy. Seems like he would be a good, solid, stabilizing leader for a coven. Hunter, on the other hand…"

"You don't think he's stable?" Reg asked, heavy with irony.

Damon snorted. "No. Stable is not the word I would use for Hunter ever—and even more so now. I don't know what is going on, but he seems like he could blow at any time."

"Yeah, I've been worried lately. I think maybe it's just the stress of being reintegrated into the coven and trying to run for leadership right away. Maybe he should have waited a year, or however long would have been customary to get settled back in first."

"Maybe he thinks this is his only chance."

Reg frowned. "Why would he think that?"

"The rules are shifting. Right now, they're in his favor, but all it is going to take is a single report that one of these, umm…"

"Power drinkers?" Reg suggested. Damon was clearly uneasy even naming Corvin's condition. That was what came of making it taboo even to discuss. People had to tiptoe around the issue. Reg didn't like to tiptoe.

"Right. Power drinkers… all it is going to take to swing the pendulum back the other direction is for one of these power drinkers who has been allowed to lead a coven to make a mistake, and they'll shut all the rest down. Corvin has this one small window before someone steps out of line. And then, if he isn't the leader of the coven already, it will be too late. He'd be closed out again for decades, maybe longer."

Reg was sure that one of those cursed leaders would step out of line sooner or later. It was only a matter of time until one of them let go of his self-control and wrested the powers from one of the other warlocks in their coven. She knew Corvin's hunger, and she knew how difficult it had been for him to follow the magical community's laws in the past. He had failed before. He would fail again. Or one of the other leaders would. And the ramifications would be heard all around the practicing world.

* * *

Damon drove to the temple orange grove, pointing out a couple of other landmarks on the way there. Reg had been in Black Sands for close to a year, but there was a lot she still didn't know. The town had a lot of history for such a small, sheltered place. It had been around for a long time and some of the residents were very long-lived.

"Here we are."

At first, there was nothing to set the site apart from any other grove Reg had seen. They had a short distance to walk from the parking lot. When Reg entered the grove she drew her breath in quickly in surprise. She found herself holding her breath, afraid to let it out again in case anything should change.

Damon looked at her curiously. "What is it?" he asked in amusement.

"This is amazing." Reg looked at the edifice in shock. "I've never seen anything like it."

Damon looked around at the trees and shook his head. "It's a grove of trees. You'll find them all over. Granted, not every state has oranges, but you've been here long enough that you must have seen a few."

"Oh, it's not the trees. It's the temple."

Damon raised an eyebrow. "The temple."

Reg breathed slowly out and then in again, afraid that she would do something that would make it all disappear. It was clear that Damon did not see the same sight she did.

"It's a beautiful building," she explained. "It looks like… it's made out of silver and gold light."

"Really." He gazed at the air in front of him. "What does it look like?"

Reg did her best to describe the structure. They walked into the grove and Reg walked around the temple structure without looking down at the ground at the stones still visible from the foundation. She stopped at the doorway and pointed it out to him.

"This is really something."

She had been so wrapped up in the temple that she hadn't noticed the warlocks arriving while she toured Damon around it. They stood quietly at a distance around her, listening with interest to her descriptions. Reg suddenly became aware of their presence and her cheeks grew hot.

"Oh… I'm sorry. I was just…"

"Can you really see all of that?" a young-looking warlock asked skeptically.

Reg rolled her eyes and didn't bother engaging with him.

"I've seen pictures of what they think the old temple looked like," another contributed, "and she's pretty much bang on."

"She's probably seen the same pictures," the young skeptic pointed out.

They all looked at each other. Reg knew that there was no point in trying to convince nonbelievers. It just made them more likely to attack and to try to recruit others on their side. Things could get very messy very fast.

"Sorry about this, but we have a meet-up planned here," a warlock with a white handlebar mustache and red face told Reg. "So when you're done…"

Reg felt like pointing out that there was no way to book the site and she had as much of a right to be there on a pilgrimage as they did to meet there as a coven. But the guy had at least been polite about it.

"Are you Davyn's coven, then?"

He raised his brows, surprised at this. "Yes, we are. And you are…?"

"I'm helping with the investigation. I was hoping you could answer a few questions about the night he disappeared."

CHAPTER THIRTY

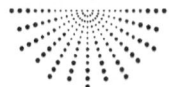

*T*he man looked around at some of the other warlocks, standing in a rough circle around the temple site. "The police have already been making their rounds asking questions. You don't look like a cop."

"I'm not, obviously, but I was hired on as a consultant. So I'd like to follow up with those who were here Monday night to get their impressions of how Davyn was and what happened after he left here. I know that no one knows, but I'm used to dealing with more... speculative ideas."

"A psychic?" a man standing close to Reg, wearing what looked like a long black raincoat, suggested. The raincoat looked like it would be incredibly uncomfortable in the Florida heat. Like a portable sauna.

"Yes. Reg Rawlins, Psychic Investigator." Reg patted her pockets, looking for her business cards.

The warlock waved away her attempts to find them. "I don't need any proof."

"I have business cards. I should hand them out so that if any of you need to contact me later if one of you remembers something that might be relevant—"

"I don't need your number. I'll just reach out to you telepathically." The warlock made a show of putting his fingers to his temples and concentrating hard, mocking her.

There was laughter from the group. Reg shook her head. "You do that," she said. "And for those of you who *don't* want to make a fool of yourselves..." She found a stack of business cards in one of the pockets of her purse and started handing them around. "You might want to try a more conventional method. Of course, if you're not up on current technology, like *telephones*, you could always send me a message by raven..."

The laughter of the warlocks was now directed at the unfortunate warlock who had decided to tease her, rather than at Reg. Most of them took a card from her, encouraged by the fact that others in the group were doing so. Peer pressure working in Reg's favor.

"We *do* have a ceremony scheduled," the warlock who seemed to have taken it upon himself to lead the group reminded everyone. "So maybe after you've finished handing those out, you could go back home and people can contact you if they have anything to report..."

Reg shook her head. "I wanted to ask a few questions while you're all together here. That saves me running around trying to track everybody down individually. I can ask now or wait until after your prayer thing."

Damon was still there, hanging at the edges of the group, keeping a sharp eye out for anything suspicious. Reg was happy to have him there and grateful that he knew when to keep quiet and just hang back. His job providing security for private and public functions had trained him to stay in the background until she needed him.

The warlocks looked at each other, not liking the idea of Reg staying there to watch their rituals. But they couldn't kick her off of property that wasn't theirs. It was open to the public and could not be booked for one particular group. They could ask her to leave nicely, as they had, but she didn't have to leave.

"Why don't we just do it?" one of the younger men asked. "Let her ask her questions, and then we'll be alone for the ritual."

There were several nods and voiced agreements. Reg looked around at them to make sure that there was a consensus. Corvin was not there, and she didn't know whether he would be coming to put on a show of concern over Davyn's disappearance or not. She figured he would. And she preferred to ask her questions before he got there, when he might influence their answers.

"Fine. If that's what everyone wants to do," the leading warlock conceded, not sounding too happy about it. "But let's make it quick. Some of us have other places we need to be and only have a short time for this meeting."

"Can I get your names?" Reg asked.

He looked at her. "Are you going to write them down?"

He might have been against her writing them down, or might just have wondered how she could be conducting such an investigation without the aid of a notebook to record her findings. Reg really didn't like reading or writing. Both were difficult for her, and writing down all of the names would take up all of the time she had before Corvin's arrival. She had developed a pretty good memory for names and the relevant points she would pick up in the investigation to compensate for her disabilities.

At least, she had a good memory for things that had happened since Wilson's death. The things that had happened before that were still scattered in her brain.

"No, I'm not writing it down."

There were relieved reactions from a number of the warlocks. So, despite the fact that there was greater acceptance of those who practiced in magic, especially in Black Sands, there were apparently a few of them who would prefer not to have their names made public. Or who did not want to be associated with a police investigation.

"I'm Wilf Martin," the de facto leader introduced himself curtly.

John Saunders was the young skeptic, Hershel Benson the man in the black raincoat, and so on around the circle. Reg did her best to commit them all to memory.

"So, is everyone who was there Monday night here today?" Reg asked. She wasn't sure whether she could tell the core eleven members of the coven from those who were in junior positions. She could go by age and confidence, but that wouldn't necessarily be accurate, since some of those who practiced magic managed to stay very young-looking.

"There are a few missing," Benson advised. "People tend to work during the day. Some of us can get the time off for something like this, and others can't."

"Who is missing?"

They exchanged looks. "Corvin Hunter," Saunders pointed out. "Uh… Jeremy Frederick. Marshall Brown."

Reg would try to follow up with them later. Although if everyone in the grove could vouch for them, Reg could at least be confident that they had been there Monday night and had not been the person who had called Davyn.

It might be a good idea to catch a couple of them separate from the group. They could be more open about what they saw and thought than the warlocks who were present and would have to watch what they said in front of their peers and to toe the party line.

Reg didn't whip out a notebook to write these names down, and again, there seemed to be a collective sigh as they saw that she wasn't going to record any of what she heard there. They were gradually getting more relaxed about talking to her.

"Those of you who were at the coven on Monday… can you confirm that those three were present the whole time? Including when Davyn got the phone call and headed home?"

They looked around at each other, nodding, gradually forming a consensus. "Yes," Benson agreed. "We were all there. They were there. They never left the group."

"And no one who was there had to go… to get something he forgot out of his car, or to find a restroom, or get refreshments? Nothing like that?"

She had no idea how the coven operated, but those all seemed like reasonable excuses to leave the group for a few minutes. And maybe to be a little longer than expected. It wouldn't be hard to drive a mile or two to a phone or a remote area and then place the call to Davyn while he was still there with everyone else.

The warlocks shook their heads, apparently sure of themselves.

"Okay, great. That's really helpful."

It pretty much eliminated the chances that anyone in the coven had been involved in Davyn's disappearance.

"And Corvin Hunter was with the group the whole time?"

More definite nods. Of course people had paid attention to Corvin. It had been his first time back with the coven since he had been shunned.

"How did he seem?"

Wilf Martin shrugged. "He seemed just the same as ever. It was nice to have him back in the coven. We have missed him. You know about, err…" he cleared his throat, looking awkward.

"About his sentence, yeah."

"She was the one," Saunders said. "She was the one that pressed charges against him for trying to take her powers by force."

There were dark looks from a number of the warlocks, and Reg cursed her bad luck. Of course someone had recognized her from the tribunal. It wasn't that big of a community. Several of the others had probably been there too.

"I never pressed charges," Reg reminded him. "That was the fairies. The tribunal called me to testify about what had happened, but I wasn't the one who started it."

Nods and grunts of acknowledgment from around the circle as others remembered this detail.

"It had nothing else to do with me," Reg insisted. "I just answered their questions about what happened. That's all. I've seen Corvin plenty of times since then. He'd tell you that himself. He doesn't hold a grudge against me."

There was silence for a few minutes. Then others began to answer her last question. "Yeah, he seemed just the same as ever. As glad to be back in the coven as we were to have him back."

"He didn't seem stressed at all? Angry?"

She was surprised by the negative answers around the group. Corvin *hadn't* been stressed on Monday? That didn't make any sense. She had seen him both before and after that. His negative mood had been going on for several weeks. Had they been so happy to see him that they had just overlooked his crankiness? Or had he been able to put it aside and remain good-humored for the night's rituals? Maybe he was just so happy to be back there that he'd been able to stay in a good mood while he was with them. She imagined that it would have been quite encouraging to have all of his peers talking to him again after the long months of silently ignoring him even if they saw him at the grocery store or in some other setting.

"And he was definitely there when Davyn got his phone call?"

"Sure." Lots of heads bobbed up and down. People's eyes had been on Corvin that night, his first night rejoining the coven and, Reg assumed, announcing his candidacy in running for leadership of the coven. He would not have been able to wander off without their noticing, even for a few minutes.

"Corvin said that there was some discussion about picking a new leader for the coven that night," she said, introducing it as something Corvin had brought up with her, so they wouldn't think they had to protect a secret for him. "How did that discussion go?"

"Everything was fine," Benson growled. "If you're trying to imply that there was division in the coven over the candidates, you're wrong."

Reg feigned surprise. "No, not at all. Why would there be division?"

Benson was caught wrong-footed. His eyes flashed to Martin and then back to Reg. "Some people might not think that Corvin was a good candidate for leadership, that's all. But the coven was united on letting him run. There were no dissenting voices."

Reg could feel the unrest around the group at his assertion. He might be telling the truth. It might be that no one had spoken up in opposition to allowing a power drinker to run for the leadership position. But there were those who did not think it was a good idea. Reg scanned the faces of the warlocks, trying to identify which ones had the strongest feelings about it. It surprised her that the strongest dissenters seemed to be the young warlocks, not the core group. She had thought that the core group would be more likely to be rigid and set in their ways, still carrying on prejudices about those with Corvin's condition. But they all seemed relaxed about it. Maybe, since they were the ones who could vote, they were confident that Corvin would not be elected, despite allowing him to run. They would just vote for Davyn instead. The youngsters had no control over the situation and might be more anxious about what the outcome would be.

"Has any of that changed now that Davyn is missing? How will the election be handled if Davyn isn't found and Corvin is the only one running? I guess he just automatically gets it?"

Benson looked around at the others, hoping that someone would jump in.

Martin stroked his white mustache. "If Davyn is not found… I'm sure someone else will throw his hat into the ring to run against Corvin."

CHAPTER THIRTY-ONE

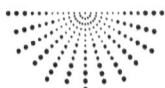

ill he?" Corvin said from behind Reg. "Do you speak for yourself, Wilf? Or someone else?" His voice was gravelly and testy. Certainly not the unstressed warlock they had described to Reg, happy just to be back in the coven.

Wilf's face got redder. "Corvin," he greeted, his voice suddenly hoarse. "I'm glad that you made it. I wasn't sure you were going to be able to."

Reg turned and backed up so that she could see Corvin as well as the rest of the circle. He moved forward to take his place with them, barely glancing at Reg.

"What's this about someone else running for the coven leadership? I thought that Davyn was the only one. And he's clearly on his way out."

Wilf sputtered. "I was just... I'm just speculating. I'm sure Davyn will return and things will go forward just as expected. I just meant that... in the interests of the democratic process and making sure that everyone in the coven can express their preferences, someone else would probably join the race if Davyn wasn't able to. Probably." He ran his hand over his shiny head, sweating under Corvin's gaze.

"I haven't heard anyone express any interest in it. If anyone else is interested in leading the coven, they should have stood up when we discussed it on Monday."

"There's still plenty of time for someone else to change their mind and run," Benson told Corvin. "There's nothing that says they have to declare themselves at the same time as you and Davyn."

"But that's what I would expect."

Benson and Martin looked at each other, shrugging. Neither jumped in to say they would be interested in running against Corvin. Reg didn't imagine that anyone would be too eager to run against him. But it might be necessary if they wanted to keep the leadership of the coven from falling to Corvin.

"Are you done here, Regina?" Corvin growled.

"Well... no, not quite." Reg decided that she'd better move forward in her questions before Corvin could tell her it was time to leave. They might not have the site reserved, but Corvin could be pretty convincing.

"What else, then? I don't think this nonsense concerning the leadership election has anything to do with Davyn's disappearance. Does anyone else?" He glared around at the rest of the warlocks. No one dared to register an objection.

"I wondered whether anyone had any insight into what was going on in Davyn's life lately," she said, finding it more difficult to speak now that Corvin was there, glowering his disapproval over the matter. "Any reason he might have had to be stressed, if there was someone who was bothering him. If he mentioned anything... unusual that had happened recently?"

"Like what?" questioned young Saunders. "What would he tell us about? You think he was being stalked? That someone was following him around, just waiting for the opportunity to kidnap him?"

Reg stared at him, not responding for several long, uncomfortable seconds. She waited until she was sure that Saunders was really squirming about his sarcastic question before saying anything.

"Yes. Because somebody *did* lure him away from the coven in order to kidnap him."

"You don't *know* he was kidnapped. You don't know what

happened to him. He might have just tripped and hurt himself. He might have taken off on vacation. You don't *know*."

"Yes, I do."

They all stared at her, startled by this statement and her confidence in it.

"I *know* it wasn't an accident and that he didn't go on vacation. And that means that someone targeted him. It wasn't just some random kidnapping, because whoever it was called Davyn and got him away from here. He intentionally lured Davyn away from the group, where he was safe."

"It could be a coincidence," Saunders tried, not nearly as loud or certain of himself this time. "He might have just gotten that call from the police like they said, and someone else took the opportunity when they saw him alone."

"The police didn't call him that night. It was a set-up."

"Somebody broke into his house. Maybe it wasn't the cops who called him, it was a neighbor, and he just got it mixed up when he told us."

"Explain to me how he went on vacation after leaving his phone, wallet, and car at home. Or how his house was broken into without any windows or doors being damaged. He didn't misunderstand the caller."

"He might have left his door unlocked and they just let themselves in."

"Then why would the neighbor think that anything was wrong? Why would they think there was anything wrong unless they saw some sign that someone had *broken* into the house? Maybe he just had company and left them a key or left the door unlocked. Why would anyone immediately think it was a break-in, unless they knew that Davyn had been threatened or stalked? *You* wouldn't think that."

"It still could be an accident. He could be in the woods with a broken ankle, waiting for someone to find him."

"He's not in the woods near his house. The police have searched. With dogs."

"They could have missed him," Saunders said, his voice quiet and with a little bit of a whine in it. He knew that he'd been beaten. No one else would believe that it was just an accident or something innocent.

Reg scanned the faces of the rest of the warlocks. "So? Did Davyn tell anyone that he was having trouble with someone? Or that he was worried about something? I don't care whether it was anything to do with the coven. It could be work. It could be personal. It could be something totally bizarre and nonsensical. I just want to know if he mentioned that he was having any issues."

She waited. The men shook their heads and looked at each other, searching for some explanation from the others in the coven. But no one seemed to have anything. Either Davyn didn't share, or he hadn't had any particular worries. Reg looked at Damon, but he shrugged and didn't point her toward anyone he could identify as lying.

"What about... Julian Sabat?" Reg asked, silently apologizing to Davyn for bringing up his private matters. "Did people know about him? Anything about him?"

"His relationship with Sabat was not a secret from the coven," Martin advised. "I think everyone was happy for him. He hadn't had anyone in his life for a long time."

"Was there anyone who... disapproved? Some people can be pretty vocal about same-sex relationships."

Shrugs and head shakes. Reg closed her eyes and stretched out all of her senses, trying to catch any hint of anger or disapproval from the warlocks. But it hadn't been one of them who had kidnapped him. They all gave each other alibis because they had been together when Davyn had disappeared.

"I think you'll find that the members of a coven are far more open-minded than the general public," Benson said. "We subscribe to a culture that... is much more ancient and tolerant of individual differences and sexuality. We don't see sex or same-sex relationships as something shameful. We don't subscribe to the western cultural viewpoint. Shaming people for their innate nature... is not something that we do."

Unless that innate nature was something like siren blood, in which case they egged Reg's door and left spells restricting her movements in the hopes that she wouldn't go out into the world. Corvin had probably put up with that kind of prejudice for years, decades, or even centuries. Being gay might not be a problem for the coven, but they weren't open to allowing *everyone* to express their innate natures.

"No one objected? Did he ever talk about anyone at work who might? A family member? Someone in the community?"

"Not that Davyn spoke of."

"What about jealousies? Was there someone else who was interested in Davyn that he had turned away? Or someone interested in Julian?"

"Everyone was happy for him," Martin repeated. "And Sabat wasn't from around here, so I don't think anyone in Black Sands was attached to him. I think it's a wild goose chase. I don't think that part of Davyn's life had anything to do with… what might have happened to him."

"Are you about finished beating this dead horse, Regina?" Corvin demanded. "Do you think we can go on with our ceremony honoring Davyn before everyone has to go back to work?"

Reg sighed. She *was* about finished beating that particular dead horse, but she wished she could find out more from the coven. "Yes, I'll let you get back to your planned activities. Just remember…" She looked around at the gathered warlocks. "It would do more good to Davyn if you can help me and the police department to find out who did this and how to get Davyn back than it will to dance around and pray for him."

Corvin's face flushed a deep red. The other warlocks avoided Reg's eyes.

"You have my card. Call me if you know anything that could help. I don't know how much longer Davyn has."

CHAPTER THIRTY-TWO

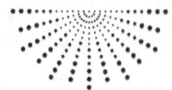

*R*eg and Damon retreated to Damon's truck, leaving the warlocks to their ceremony.

Damon chuckled. "Nothing like mocking someone's spiritual practices to get them to cooperate with you."

"I didn't—" Reg cut herself off and grimaced. "Is that what I did? Sheesh, that wasn't very polite, was it?"

"You may be right. I'm not sure how much nature, God, or the universe is going to do to help Davyn if everybody just sits around on their hands and hopes that things work out for the best. I think things work out for the best when we do everything we can and leave the rest to nature. Without our husbandry, the garden just grows wild."

Reg looked at him, frowning, not sure she understood what he was trying to say. But he seemed to be supporting her plea to the warlocks to help her out, so she couldn't argue with him.

Damon swung himself up into the driver's seat of the truck. Reg clambered up into her seat as gracefully as possible.

"Do you think any of them will take me up on it? Call me with what they know?"

"I don't know. I don't know if any of them even know anything relevant."

"Were any of them lying?"

"No big lies that I could detect. Of course, everyone shades what they say to put themselves in the best light, but I don't think anyone knows of any huge secret Davyn was holding."

"What about a smaller secret?"

"Maybe. Nothing that anyone thought significant, I don't think."

"But they could be wrong. A little thing could be important. Who do you think might know something?"

"The young one with the attitude. A little surprising, since I would expect the more established warlocks to know Davyn better."

"John Saunders?"

"Right, that sounds like the right name. I'm not sure how you could keep all of them straight."

"I have a good head for names. Most of the time."

"And you got the ones who weren't there as well?"

"Yeah. I can follow up with them later. Maybe they'll have more to say if there isn't anyone to overhear. Especially Corvin. Did you see everybody jump when he got there?"

"Yes. They all looked like they'd been caught with their hands in the cookie jar."

"But none of them had been badmouthing Corvin or saying he hadn't been there. So why feel guilty?"

"Who knows? Maybe just because they are private people and what happens at coven is supposed to be held confidential."

"But I wasn't asking about any of the coven's rituals or practices. Just whether anyone knew who might be out to harm Davyn."

Damon shrugged. "I don't know. Maybe they felt like saying anything, even talking about who was there and who was not, was too much."

"It's not like they are doctors or lawyers."

Damon just shrugged again. "I don't run with a coven, so I don't know."

A lone wolf. Was he on his own because he didn't fit in with any of the established groups? Or just because he wanted to be? Or had he done something that had estranged him from the local covens and they wouldn't have him?

* * *

Reg remembered to call Jessup before her evening appointments started to arrive. She had called back each of the clients she had missed the previous night, when she had been caught in her trance, and rescheduled them. She didn't want to have to reschedule anyone else, and didn't want to be interrupted by a phone call from Jessup asking whether she had made any progress on the case.

"Hi, Reg," Jessup answered, still sounding pleasant and welcoming, but not nearly as cheerful as she had been the day before. The case was undoubtedly starting to wear on her. Maybe she was getting pressure from above to either find something or move on to another more pressing case. But Black Sands was not the big city with a ton of crime so, hopefully, there hadn't been any other abductions or murders that would compete with Davyn's case. At least not for another day or two. If they got to a week without any sign of where Davyn had gone, Reg was worried that Davyn would be presumed dead and the case would be set aside until more evidence came in.

"Hi. Did you find anything out today?" Reg got in her question before Jessup could ask the same, hoping that there would be something they could use. She hated to have to report that despite going to visit Corvin and his coven, Reg hadn't made any progress herself.

"Well..." Jessup drew the word out. She didn't seem to be teasing Reg, just thinking about it, but anxiety and irritation shot through Reg at not getting an immediate answer one way or the other. "We have been following up on any of the members of the coven who might have had issues with Davyn, even though they all alibi each other. I'm still not convinced that everyone is being one hundred percent truthful about them all being there at the time of the phone call. Or maybe they think that everyone was, but forgot that someone had gone to take a smoke break or a solitary walk. People don't necessarily mean to lie; sometimes they are just unreliable."

"I thought that all eyewitnesses were unreliable."

"Yes... truer than I would like to think."

"Nothing else?"

"We followed up on the call to Davyn. Got a warrant for his phone records and checked to see where that call had come from."

"Great! Who was it?"

"Not much help, unfortunately. A landline at the gas station a couple of miles down the road."

"Who made the call?"

"The clerk who was on duty at that time of night didn't remember anyone using it. But he says it's not uncommon, and it was probably just so routine that he forgot. Cell coverage is not great out there, so people stop in and ask if they can use the phone. Not like there are any payphones around anymore. They just let whoever needs it use it."

"And the clerk doesn't remember who it was."

"No."

"Could it have been him?"

"I imagine so. But we don't have any evidence that it was, so we can't exactly arrest him for making a phone call to Davyn. Not that there is anything illegal about making a call to Davyn even if he admitted it. We can't prove that the phone call and the disappearance are related. Or that the person on the phone said what Davyn said he did. That could have been a cover for something else. Meeting someone that he didn't want people to know about. A lover. A bookie. Just because he told the coven it was the police, that doesn't mean he really thought that it was."

"But wouldn't he know that people would ask him about it later? I mean... you don't want to attract attention to yourself if you're going to meet someone quietly. You don't want everyone in the community talking about how your house was broken into and then having to maintain that fiction. It's too hard."

"Maybe he's not a very accomplished liar and didn't realize how difficult that would be. How would he know if he'd never done anything like that before? Anyway, I'm not saying he did just make it up as a cover for whatever the call was really about. I'm just saying... there's no proof. We don't know that's really what happened."

"Okay. Well, thanks for the information. I'll keep trying to get any impressions about what happened. It's hard, though. I can't force myself to have an insight or vision."

"You didn't find anything out today?" Jessup asked, sounding disappointed. "I was really hoping that you would be able to get somewhere."

"No. I talked to Corvin and his coven, but you've already talked to them, so you know I didn't get very far with them. Although, they met at that temple orange grove, and the temple is really stunning."

"The temple? I thought that all that was left of it was a few stones in the ground?"

"Physically," Reg agreed. "But I can still see the… psychic impression. It's amazing."

"Oh, well, that's nice. And… you didn't get anything when you talked to anyone in the coven? Any impressions or idea of what might have been going on in Davyn's life?"

"No. According to them, he was well-liked and didn't have any secrets." Reg snorted. "He would be the first one. He must have had something in his past that he didn't want turned up. But… no insight into what happened and who bound him in this… void."

"Or how to get him back?"

Reg shrugged, wishing she had a better answer. "I don't know. Who do you talk to about getting someone back from a place like that? Is there a magical missing persons department? A lost and found for misplaced warlocks?"

"That's not really funny, Reg."

"I know." Reg sighed. "I'm just trying to figure out what to do. It's frustrating to know that he's there, but not how he got there, who imprisoned him, or how to get him back. Really frustrating."

She really was hoping that Jessup would come back with some brilliant suggestion. That there was a special department for dealing with such things or an ancient witch or warlock who could help call Davyn back. It wasn't right that she was the only one who had been able to see him when she had so little knowledge of the workings of the magical world around her. Why couldn't it have been Sarah or someone who would know what to do about it?

"Is there *anyone* who would know what to do?" Reg pressed. "Isn't there... some expert who could see him and get him out?"

"No. I'm not sure anyone has the knowledge or skills of how to retrieve someone who is stuck on another plane. Maybe... he's just in a root cellar or pit somewhere, and it was just too dark or obscure for you to see it. That would be a lot easier to get him out of."

Reg thought of the root cellar in Davyn's house. She knew he wasn't there. She had checked, and there was nowhere to hide him there. Despite what Jessup wished, she was pretty sure that Davyn was not being held in a physical place that she could lead the police to.

CHAPTER THIRTY-THREE

*I*t was after midnight and in the small hours of the morning before Reg went to bed. She was tired out from the long day and happy to be settling in for a good rest.

She had done everything that she could, but didn't feel like she was any closer to figuring out who had sent Davyn to the void and how to get him back. It was incredibly frustrating knowing that she could reach out to him and feel him close to her, but couldn't figure out how to get him out. How long could he survive in that state? Would he die without any food, water, or sleep? Or would he live in a suspended state in the void, tortured but unable to escape or die until the end of time?

It came as no surprise that going to bed worrying about Davyn, she fell into a dream about him as soon as she fell asleep.

Nothing had changed. It was still dark and cold. She could sense Davyn there in the darkness and tried to reach out to him telepathically. Of course they couldn't shout to each other across the void, but thoughts were faster and shouldn't be lost in the nothingness.

Fear.

Trying to connect with Damon, she tapped into his emotions and, of course, the thing that was foremost in Davyn's mind was fear. He was trapped, maybe for the rest of his existence, in this lonely place without light or sound or food or drink. A place that was cold and airless and that no one else could get to.

It was terrifying.

Reg had long associated fear with the physical responses in her body. Heartbeat and breathing, a knot in her stomach, tightly-tensed muscles. But in the void, Davyn did not seem to connect with his body, or Reg with hers, but the fear was still there. Maybe darker and deeper like the void itself.

I'm here. Reg tried to project reassuring thoughts to him. *I'm here, and I'm trying to figure out how to get you home.*

There was no direct answer, no answering words or voice like there were when she was communicating with Corvin or the gnomes. Just the fear. Now his fear enveloped both of them. No longer worried about just himself, but her as well, caught there in the void with him. How was she going to get herself back out?

Reg gasped for breath and awoke in her bed, her whole body rigid. She looked around her and tried to reassure herself. It was just a dream. She was not there with Davyn. Everything was going to be okay. As long as she could find a way to rescue him from that place. Or non-place.

Starlight was snuggled up against her, purring. Reg reached out her fingers to pet him and burrow into his thick black fur for comfort and reassurance. There was a meow from the windowsill at the same time as Reg's fingers met with the cat beside her and she recognized that it was not Starlight. The fur was coarser, the body larger.

Reg sat bolt upright and looked at him. The shape in the darkness beside her was not Starlight's neat, compact form. It was closer to the size of a small panther.

Reg reached over to the bedside lamp and turned it on. By the time her fingers met with the switch and she managed to fumble it on, she knew what she would see. The huge black cat staring back at her was familiar.

"Horace! What are you doing here?" She gave him a hug and buried her face in his fur. "You scared me!"

The kattakyn purred and licked at her hair. Reg pulled back and scratched his ears. He seemed calm and happy, which was a relief.

When she had tried to rehome him with Marian, another psychic in Black Sands, he had not been happy with the match. He had been sad and had returned to her repeatedly while she'd slept. Only rather than being on the bed beside her, he had lain down on her chest, crushing the breath out of her. The kattakyns were known to be able to kill that way, entering people's homes during their dreams, lying on the victim's chest and getting heavier and heavier until the breath was crushed out of them. Starlight had saved Reg from this fate more than once, chasing Horace off before he could kill her.

It wasn't that he had been angry with her and wanted to kill her or had been directed by the Witch Doctor to do so, as other kattakyns had been before Reg and the others had defeated him. Horace had been confused. Disrupted, taken from his home, the piece of the Witch Doctor that he had been carrying torn from him, he couldn't understand why he couldn't stay with Reg and what the consequences of returning to her and lying on top of her would be. Her efforts to find Horace a new home had been unsuccessful until she had come across Merneith on an unrelated quest.

Reg rubbed her fingers around Horace's ears and scratched down his back. "Is Merneith here?" she asked softly, reaching out with her senses and feeling for the long-dead Egyptian queen.

I am here, she heard the reply in her head, similar to when she was speaking to a gnome. *I have no wish to be disembodied again.*

She had apparently had her fill of being a wandering spirit in the several thousand years she had been alone in the tomb.

Are you both happy? Reg directed her question at Merneith's consciousness. *Was this a good arrangement?*

We are at peace, Merneith confirmed. *Both of us together… are much happier.*

Good.

Starlight jumped down from the windowsill to the bed and walked over to Horace to touch noses with him.

"What do you think?" Reg asked him aloud. "He's doing better?"

Starlight began to groom the much larger cat. Starlight, too, was Egyptian in origin and had been there when Merneith and Horace combined, so it was no surprise to him that the big cat was actually two consciousnesses, not just one.

"You didn't lay on top of me this time," Reg observed. "That's a good boy."

Humans are fragile, Merneith observed. *Crushing them is not a good idea.*

"No," Reg chuckled. "I much prefer him just lying beside me."

Reg brushed her fingers against her shirt to make sure they were clean of fur before rubbing her eyes, yawning.

"What time is it? It's too early for me to get up."

Cats are nocturnal.

Right. Reg scratched Horace's ears. "I'm glad you're happier now."

There was a feeling like a sigh from Merneith. *It is good to be at rest. The sah needs a home.*

Sah seemed to be Merneith's word for her spirit or ghost.

Could you leave Horace again if you wanted to? Reg asked curiously. She knew very little about how the world of spirits worked, and if it worked the same for all humans or was different for each human culture. Was there one afterlife or many? Not all spirits remained behind, where Reg could talk to them. The ones who stayed behind seemed to have frequently met with sudden or violent ends. But some just seemed uncertain about where to go or what to do next.

Of course. I have will. But I have no desire to leave.

And if you did, you could just decide to? There doesn't need to be a... call or special ritual done.

It is easiest to move to another body. Being disembodied is... uncomfortable. Merneith seemed amused by her own words. *If one can have discomfort without a body.*

Reg hadn't thought about that before. But she had been uncomfortable in the void where Davyn was, even though she hadn't felt like she had a body there. Did she? Or had it just been the lack of sensory input?

Well, I'm glad that you both found a way to be happy together, Reg acknowledged. She yawned again and lay back down, stroking both Starlight and Horace. She closed her eyes, thinking about Horace and Merneith, and then her mind wandered to Davyn.

If you were without a body, could you go somewhere... I don't know where it is. Somewhere very dark and full of nothing. A friend of mine is there, and I don't know how to get him out.

Her brain was already starting to drift, dozing as she petted the cats.

Where is this? Merneith inquired.

Reg was so close to sleep, it was easy to share what was in her head. If she had been awake, maybe she would have been more careful about opening her mind to such a powerful entity. She tried to recall the times she had been in the void with Davyn with as much clarity as possible. How could she describe it? It was nothing. There was nothing to describe. Nothing to remember except that Davyn had been there, and he had been scared.

Who is using this underworld place? Merneith inquired.

Reg was too close to dreamland to answer. Horace nudged her arm with his nose. She tried to rouse herself for long enough to finish the conversation. *I don't know. But I want to get him out. Can you tell me how to get him out?*

To wrestle the sah binding him there? You do not have the strength.

Who does? Can you help?

Sleep now.

CHAPTER THIRTY-FOUR

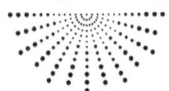

When Reg finally did wake up again, she knew that something had happened in the night but couldn't remember what it was. Everything was vague and shadowy. Maybe she would remember more when she'd had a coffee or three. Or maybe it would be one of those things that just faded the more she tried to remember it.

She put the coffee grounds in the hopper of her machine and pressed the button to brew. Her phone rang. Reg put it to her ear.

"Hello?"

"Good morning, Regina." Corvin's purr filled not just Reg's ear, but went straight to her heart. It had been a while since she had heard that tone from him. She had almost forgotten how it gave her the shivers. Goosebumps spread down her arms.

"Whoa. Good morning!"

He chuckled, apparently sensing her surprise and immediate physical response. "It won't be morning very much longer. You had a good sleep, did you?"

"I don't remember. I think there's something I should be able to remember, but I can't quite put my finger on it."

"Still having memory issues?"

"No. Just when trying to remember something I dreamed."

"Ah. So how about grabbing a coffee together this morning? Or early this afternoon."

"I'm just making coffee now. And you're not coming over here to drink it."

"Then let's go out somewhere else. You can dump that down the drain. It would be so much nicer to go out for coffee."

Just the way he said it made Reg think of a fragrant, high-end coffee house. Coffee from her own machine was one thing. It was enough to do the job and wake her up. But a much higher standard of coffee, a chic little cafe, and Corvin's company...

"No, I shouldn't," Reg objected.

"You should. Let me treat you. I've been a bear to you lately, so let me make it up."

It was true; he'd been incredibly grumpy and annoying, but she didn't think that he'd been aware of it himself.

"I shouldn't waste this."

"Dump it. I won't tell anyone. You need to indulge yourself now and then. And I'm offering to do it today. Take me up on it."

"Where are we going to go?"

Reg had meant to say, "Where are *you* going to go?" but the *we* slipped off her tongue before she was prepared for it. She could at least have led him on for a question or two. Teased him, because he was definitely going to be teasing her.

"We could go to my club. Nice private rooms there," Corvin suggested.

As if she hadn't turned down the private rooms at Corvin's exclusive club a hundred times before. There was no way she could take the chance of being alone with Corvin. Especially since she got the feeling that the ever-accommodating hostesses at the club would happily look the other way. Anything to make Corvin happy. Reg suspected that some very unsavory things went on behind the scenes at that place, hidden under the umbrella of wealth and exclusivity.

Wealth and exclusivity might hide a multitude of sins, but didn't make them right.

"How about The Witches' Brew?" Reg suggested instead.

Corvin sighed, but she knew that he wasn't really upset at going to the coffeehouse instead of his club. He had known that she would turn it down. The fact that she was suggesting somewhere else confirmed to him that she would go, no matter how ill-conceived an idea it was, and that's what he really cared about. The chance to be close to her. So that he might be able to charm her, to get his hands on her gifts once more.

"Will you head over there now?" Corvin asked.

Reg looked down at herself. "I'll be a few minutes. Have to make myself decent."

"Don't do that on my behalf," he snickered. "And you know, I'm perfectly happy to bring coffee to your place. Then you don't have to get dressed or leave your house. Everything in the comfort of your own cottage."

"You can't come in. Don't even think about it."

"One day, Regina…" his words were a low, throbbing purr. "One day…"

"Today is not that day."

"Well then… text or call me when you're on your way and I will meet you there. Don't take too long. I might think you're standing me up."

"I'll be there," Reg promised.

She hung up the phone.

Why was she going? Because she was still tired and wanted some good coffee instead of the stuff she had brewed? To prove to herself that this was not the case, she poured herself a mug of the fresh coffee and took it with her while she got ready. She needed the caffeine boost to actually get her out of the house. Then she could reward herself with one of those really good coffees. It wasn't really about the coffee. She assured herself that it wasn't because of Corvin, either. Just because he was back to himself again and interested in the game once more, that didn't mean she had to play along. Or that she wanted to get caught.

It would give her the opportunity to ask Corvin more about Davyn in a more relaxed environment. He had not been happy when she and Damon had interviewed him in his home. If he were happy, he might give her completely different answers from the ones he had already supplied. She was sure that he knew Davyn better than he was making out. Maybe they weren't best friends, but Davyn was Corvin's spiritual advisor and had gotten him out of some scrapes. They had been in the coven together for years, maybe even decades or centuries. Could Corvin really know someone for that long without knowing something of his personal life and troubles?

That was the only reason she was going.

CHAPTER THIRTY-FIVE

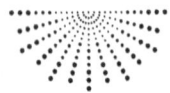

She gave Corvin a heads-up that she was leaving the house and he was at The Witches' Brew ahead of her. He already had a large coffee in front of him. When Reg entered, he stood up from his chair and smiled and beckoned to her. He acted like a gentleman, pulling her chair out for her, seating her, and pushing the chair back in again.

"Now, what can I get you?" he asked, bending down low to whisper in her ear, his warm breath on her throat. Reg's heart raced.

"Uh... let me just look at the board for a minute."

There were way too many densely-printed words on the order board for her to be able to read through them. Corvin didn't want to wait for her all day while she read through the encyclopedia of coffees, other beverages, and sweet treats. Instead, Reg fell back on the trick of just focusing on the few posters with seasonal specials on them.

"That one," she pointed it out to Corvin, "with the caramel in it. That looks amazing."

"It looks like a week's worth of calories," Corvin laughed. But he didn't object to her choice or suggest something else.

Reg sat watching him as he walked over to the barista and started to chat with her. She smiled and fluttered her eyelashes at him, completely ignoring the fact that he was there *with* someone. It took a few minutes for her to ring up his order and then put together all of the ingredients, shots, and added flavors required to create the special. Corvin waited patiently, then smiled and thanked her and returned to Reg.

"That's some drink. I hope you enjoy it."

"I will." Reg inhaled the scent of caramel, chocolate, and coffee. It was heavenly. She took a quick sip, even though she knew it was probably too hot. But it wasn't, maybe because it had taken so long for the barista to put everything together, performing for Corvin. Reg took a longer sip and closed her eyes. "That's good stuff."

"So, how have you been lately?" Corvin asked, taking a sip of his own coffee.

"It isn't like I didn't just see you. You already know how I am. From yesterday."

He looked bemused by this, as if she might be remembering the wrong day. He shrugged. "We didn't really talk about anything personal, though, did we? I don't remember you saying how you are. What's going on in your life."

"Well… no. I'm trying to find my mentor and bring him home safely. How do you think I feel about that?"

"Frustrated that you might have to get a new mentor?" Corvin suggested lightly.

"No! Corvin, I can't believe you would say something like that! I'm not worried about replacing Davyn! I'm worried about him being okay. And it isn't like firecasters are a dime a dozen. I don't know where I would find another one to help train me."

"So you *have* thought about it," he pointed out.

"No, I'm just saying that now. No one could replace Davyn. Not as my mentor and not as my friend. I want to make sure that he gets back safely."

"But first, you have to find him. Figure out what happened to him. Whether someone is responsible for his disappearance."

Reg looked at Corvin over the rim of her coffee cup. He was clearly fishing for what she knew so far. But she wasn't ready to give away to anyone what she knew about Davyn and where he was. Especially not Corvin. He might have an alibi, but Reg still couldn't trust him to be concerned about anyone else but himself. He didn't care about where Davyn was or what had happened to him. He just wanted to make sure that he could get elected. If Reg were going to get Davyn back, he would probably appreciate a heads-up so that he could call for the vote before Davyn's return. Reg didn't know if he had to wait any particular amount of time before the vote, or if the date had already been set. Maybe Corvin could just do it whenever he wanted to and wanted to know how much time he had before Davyn's return, if he were going to return.

"You want him to come back, right?" Reg said. "Because he's your friend."

"Of course I want him to come back."

But that certainly wasn't the vibe she was getting from him.

"This is why you wanted to get together for coffee? Just so you could find out whether I know anything or not?"

"Yesterday, you came to me wanting to know what I thought and what you should do next. Today... I'd like to get your thoughts. Not because I want to harm Davyn, or whatever you have in your pretty little head. I'm concerned about him, just like anyone else. As every day passes, it's hard to remain optimistic that he will ever come back. If you know anything, it would be very reassuring."

"You're so full of hot air, it's a wonder you don't blow away. Do you think I can't tell when you're lying?"

"Yesterday, you brought a diviner, so I have to think that you don't trust your ability to read me as much as you would like."

"Damon was just there to keep me company... to ensure I wasn't alone with you. I can read you just as well as ever."

He smiled, looking at her. It was a delicate dance. If Reg entered his mind, then she put herself at risk. He had access to her thoughts just as much as she did his. She could read his face, his body language, his aura, and any thoughts that he projected outward. But if she went too far, it was just as dangerous as being alone with him. There was no telling how much he would read from her or how much control he might be able to get over her.

His whole aspect was different today. As if something that had been pressing down on him was gone. The darkness she had associated with him lately was gone.

"What happened yesterday after I left?" Reg shook her head.

"What do you mean?"

"You're so different than yesterday. Did they... already elect you or something?"

"No, of course not. I need time to convince everyone that I am the better choice."

Using his charms and influence, paying bribes, offering favors, Reg could imagine all of the ways he had of changing their minds and persuading them to vote for him. Six members. He only had to convince six people that he was the best candidate.

"Then what is different? You weren't like this yesterday."

"Things change."

Was he bipolar? On a new medication? Had he heard some good news? Found out the results of a medical test? It was hard to believe he was the same person.

"What changed?"

Corvin smiled. "Let's just say it's a good day today."

Reg supposed she didn't tell him her secrets either. In fact, she was holding things back from him, not telling him what she knew about Davyn and his abduction.

Reg's mind jumped tracks, and she was suddenly thinking about the first missing person case she had worked on with Jessup. Jessup had brought her the case of Calliopia, an adolescent fairy who had disappeared. Of course, the first thing everyone thought was that she had run away. Kids did that. They rebelled and went out looking for excitement or a different life, or to join a new boyfriend their parents didn't approve of. That's what kids did. But Calliopia had, in fact, been abducted and was being held by the pixies, mortal enemies to the fairies. Reg had been able to see Calliopia in a vision and, with Jessup's help, had been able to figure out where Calliopia was being held.

If only the same thing would work for Davyn.

Reg had learned on that case how the pixies lived on two different planes. They lived in the world of humans, where they were visible, or they could disappear into the world of shades. Most people could not see them in the world of shades, but Reg was sometimes able to make out their shadowy figures. Just like when Davyn was cloaked with his power of invisibility, she could still see a dark, shadowy form where he was.

"What do you know" —a dangerous question to ask Corvin, who loved to lecture— "about other worlds?"

"What other worlds? I'm afraid I don't know much about worlds other than our own. There is speculation but, considering I can't see or touch them, I would have to get information from whoever lives in these other worlds. They would either have to come here or I would have to go there."

"Like... the pixies' world of shades. What do you know about it?"

"I know the pixies exist on two planes. They can disappear into the world of shades, and then we cannot see them. Not much else, I'm afraid."

"Is it just like our world? Does it look the same? Do they eat and drink and sleep there? Or is it... like a place where they are suspended, and nothing changes or progresses?"

"These are very deep questions to be addressing in a coffee shop."

"Do you know?" Reg persisted.

"No. I assume they can move around and do whatever they like. It seemed natural for them to move in and out between the worlds. Despite the name, I don't think it is actually a different world. I think that all pixies simply exist on two planes."

"And what about... the underworld? Or the afterlife? Are they the same thing? Does everyone go there?" She remembered Ruan speculating there might be different worlds of shades for different species.

"Again... nobody is reporting back from the afterlife. We can only speculate."

"But there are people who have come back and described it. Or myths like Persephone or the guy that played the lute."

"Yes. And they have been described very differently by different people. A shining city. A light. Darkness. Fire and brimstone. Are they all the same place? Do different believers go to different places? I don't know. There is not enough evidence."

Reg pondered this. Davyn had seemed to be alone in the place where he was trapped, but was he? Or had she only been looking for him and there had been others that she hadn't been aware of? What if it was the underworld? Would it be possible to get Davyn back like those myths, or was he gone forever? Her eyes prickled, and Reg turned away from Corvin, taking another drink of her coffee, trying to hide her emotion. The idea that Davyn might be dead and never return cut her to the quick.

"Regina," Corvin said softly. He put his hand over her arm, not touching her, just pushing waves of heat in her direction, healing and comforting warmth. She wanted to let go and let the tears flow, but she couldn't do that in front of Corvin. "Reg, there is no reason to believe that Davyn is dead. I know he has been missing for what seems like a long time, but that doesn't mean he is gone. There is still hope."

"Really? What do you think happened to him?"

"I don't know. But you must not give up hope."

CHAPTER THIRTY-SIX

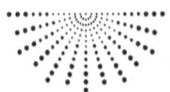

*T*here wasn't anything for Reg to do but go about her day and hope that she would be able to figure something out that would help Davyn.

As much as she would have liked to confide in Corvin what she knew about Davyn being held prisoner in the void, she didn't trust him. Even though he had not had anything to do with Davyn's disappearance, she couldn't rely on his help in getting Davyn back. It would be against Corvin's interest in taking over leadership of the coven. He could make some feeble attempt and tell her that he had done everything he could, and happily go on to assume Davyn's role. He didn't have any reason to bring Davyn back. Even if they were friends, and Reg went back and forth on whether Corvin and Davyn actually were friends, she still couldn't assume that Corvin would put Davyn's interests before his own. She didn't believe he would. She couldn't tell him anything about what she knew, and even thinking about it around him was dangerous.

Back in her car, Reg rested her forehead on the top of the steering wheel and closed her eyes, finally letting the tears of frustration and grief flow.

Her phone rang.

Unbelievable.

Reg lifted her head and wiped tears from her face and eyes. She pulled out her phone and looked at the call display.

Francesca.

Francesca, a white Haitian, the charmer who had bound the pieces of the Witch Doctor's soul to each of the nine kattakyns and then sent them around the world to live with new owners, as far away from each other as possible. The owner of Nicole (NEE-cole, in Francesca's lilting accent), a kitty friend of Starlight's, who they some-times set up playdates with. Reg really wasn't in the mood for a kitty playdate. Until she found a way to get Davyn out of the place where he was being held, she didn't want to deal with such trivial things.

She took a couple of deep breaths and then answered the phone. "Francesca—"

"I need you to come here right away, Reg. Can you please come?"

"I'm kind of busy."

"I need to talk to you."

"So, talk."

"I need you to come here. There is… someone here you need to see."

"What?"

"Just come, please."

Reg couldn't find a reason not to. If Francesca needed her that badly, then she should go.

She worried about who it was Francesca wanted her to see. Kareem, the warlock who had initially owned Horace, before taking the Witch Doctor's spark from him? Someone who knew something about one of the other kattakyns? Maybe another of the owners had unbound their kattakyn. Reg needed to know what was going on with them. The one thousand years that Francesca's binding spell was supposed to last for was shrinking far more rapidly than Reg was comfortable with. If more of the practitioners they had sent the kattakyns to interfered with Francesca's spell, they would be in trouble.

She drove over to Francesca's house. There were no cars parked on the street in front of it. But that didn't necessarily mean anything. Not everybody traveled by car.

Francesca must have been watching for her because she opened the door when Reg was only partway up the sidewalk. She waited on the threshold impatiently.

"Hi. What's up?"

"You need to come in here. *Talk* to him."

Reg shook her head and entered the house.

She should have guessed. Harrison sat on the couch, his long legs looking even longer in vertically striped pants. He wore a puffy pink shirt and held a black cat in his arms, stroking it. Reg took a closer look to ensure that it was Nicole and not one of the kattakyns.

"What's going on? What are you doing here?"

Harrison had been to Francesca's house before, when they had discovered that Weston, Reg's immortal father, was secreted in the basement under the stairs. When she had released him. Which had probably been a huge mistake. So far, Weston hadn't caused a lot of trouble, as far as Reg knew, but he and Harrison were like a couple of little boys encouraging each other to get into mischief. It was only a matter of time.

"Reg," Harrison's expression was serious. Usually, petting a cat and talking with Reg was when he was the happiest. But their relationship had experienced some strain since Kareem had unbound Horace.

"Hi. What's up?"

His eyes lifted toward the ceiling, then he shook his head. "It is not what is up that is important."

"Well, no... I guess not."

Reg sighed and sat down on the couch, studying Harrison. Francesca stood with her arms folded across her chest, looking stubborn and angry.

"Is he bothering you?" Reg asked. "You need to fill me in on what's going on here."

"It did not start with him. He apparently just decided to join the party and make everything twice as interesting. It started with Marian."

Marian. A competitor to Reg's psychic services business. But they had mostly put their differences aside and tolerated each other, helping each other from time to time or making referrals when a client needed something specific. They wouldn't likely ever be fast friends, but they had come a long way from the animosity that had existed between them when they first met.

"With Marian. What happened?"

"She came here… looking for a cat."

"Oh. Yes, her cat recently died, so she is looking for a new one."

Reg had tried to rehome Horace with Marian, but that hadn't worked. Horace just kept transporting himself back to Reg. Until she had found a better home with him in Egypt with Merneith. Marian still needed a replacement for the familiar she had recently lost.

"Why would she come here?" Francesca asked pointedly.

"I don't know. I guess maybe she heard that you had kittens you were looking for homes for."

Francesca shook her head. "How would she know that?"

"I guess someone talked to her." Reg shrugged. "What's wrong? I don't understand what you're upset about."

"You told her about the kattakyns?"

Reg's stomach knotted. "What? No!"

"She knew about the kattakyns. There are only a few of us who know about them, and you are the only one who has anything to do with her."

"I didn't tell her. Why would I? I tried to give Horace to her, but you know how that worked out."

"And you told her what he was."

"No. I didn't. I never said he was anything other than just a regular cat. I couldn't explain why he suddenly got so much bigger, but I can't understand why *that* happened even with him being a kattakyn. Dwarf magic, maybe? Or just the draugrs being able to appear in different sizes?"

"She *knew*, Reg."

Reg rubbed her forehead. "What did she say, exactly?"

"She said that Horace hadn't worked out, but she wanted to buy one of the other kattakyns. She was very insistent. She said she would pay any price. It did not matter who the cat had gone to; she wanted to get it back and adopt it herself."

"That doesn't make sense."

"No. Where did she find out about the kattakyns? If not from you, then who? Out of the few of us who know, who would have told her?"

It didn't make any sense. They all knew that it had to stay a secret. To save the world from the Witch Doctor, they had to keep him bound. To keep him bound, they had to keep anyone who would wish to free him from finding out where each part of him was, keeping the circle of people who knew about it very small.

Francesca was the only person who knew where each of the kattakyns had gone. Reg had been involved in the process, but had only looked at pictures and discussed the practitioners that the cats were going to. She hadn't known their addresses. In some cases, she knew what country each kattakyn was going to. But a lot of that had become lost or scrambled in her memory, as she had dealt with certain challenges of her own. Corvin had tried to get that information from her, but she couldn't give it to him, even if she had wanted to. He had gone to Francesca and she had refused him. Harrison, too, had tried to get information from Francesca. He said it was because he wanted to make sure that all of the other kattakyns were okay and had not been interfered with like Horace. But Reg couldn't help but be suspicious that he wanted to free all of them so that the Witch Doctor could be re-formed once more. He objected to another immortal being bound.

"Samyr Destine," Harrison said abruptly.

Reg and Francesca looked at him.

"His name is Samyr Destine. Not *the Witch Doctor.*"

"I know," Reg agreed, shrugging. "But I knew him as the Witch Doctor first."

Harrison snorted. "Witch Doctor. A Witch Doctor is human. Destine is not."

"Did *you* tell Marian about the kattakyns?" Reg demanded. "When did you come into this story?"

He petted the cat and shook his head innocently. "I would not tell a human. They... make mistakes."

"And your kind doesn't?"

"Humans make *many* mistakes."

"And immortals only make a few big ones?"

Harrison tilted his head slightly to the side, considering, then nodded. "Yes."

"Who else knows about the kattakyns?" Francesca asked. "All of the immortals? Only you?"

"He is my kind. What happens to one of us affects all."

"But you can't automatically tell," Reg argued. "You don't know everything. You didn't know where Weston hid himself. You didn't know what happened to Destine until you saw the kattakyns. You're not all-knowing."

Corvin had tried to drill that into her. Not to give the immortals the attributes that Christians gave to their god. Immortal was not the same as all-seeing and all-knowing.

Now she was coming to understand that. Harrison didn't automatically know what the other immortals were doing. Maybe they had to hide their activities if they didn't want to be seen. Or perhaps they were just like humans, only more powerful and living longer lives.

"You didn't tell Marian? Are you sure? You're telling me the truth?"

"I told no human."

"Okay." Reg shrugged and looked back at Francesca. "I don't know who it was, then, but I swear it wasn't me. Maybe it was Damon. Or maybe Corvin bragged to her about the whole thing. Maybe he bribed her to find out where the kattakyns were. Told her she could have one of them if she helped him out. She wants a new cat. Maybe he used that."

"Nobody had to tell Destine," Harrison contributed offhandedly, scratching Nicole's ears.

CHAPTER THIRTY-SEVEN

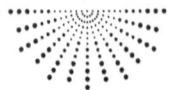

For a minute, it seemed like the world stood still.

Everything was silent. Even the voices in Reg's head went quiet, as if understanding what an important moment this was. Francesca turned her head slowly to look at Reg, her eyes going wide. At first, neither of them understood. On one level, it was clear what Harrison was saying. No one had to tell Destine what had happened because it had happened to him. On the other, Reg couldn't quite fit this piece into the puzzle she had been building.

Destine knew what had happened.

Destine knew about the kattakyns. He was the one who had created the draugar. He was the one who had animated them and given them the ability to shift into their cat form. He was the one who had sent the last remnants of his essence out in nine different directions, split among the nine kattakyns so that they couldn't completely kill him.

And he knew Francesca had been the one to bind the kattakyns. Because he had been there. She had bound him.

But it wasn't Destine who had gone back to Francesca to find out where each of the kattakyns had been sent carrying their little sparks of Destine's soul. It was Marian. And Reg knew that Marian was not Destine. Destine couldn't have gone anywhere, couldn't have told anyone anything, because he was bound. That was the whole point of the exercise, wasn't it?

"Was it not really Marian?" Reg asked, trying to sort out the logic of the situation. "Maybe it wasn't Marian; it was the Witch Doctor? But how could it be? We bound him. *You* bound him, I mean."

"This could not be," Francesca agreed, her Haitian accent thick, betraying her concern despite her calm tone. "It was not Destine."

"Why did I come here?" Harrison asked, staring off into space, not looking directly at Francesca or Reg.

"Why *did* you come here?" Reg repeated. "Explain it to me."

"Destine was here."

"No. He couldn't have been. Destine was split into nine pieces."

"Yes."

"He couldn't come here."

Harrison made a pinching gesture to indicate a small portion. "A bit of Destine."

Reg swallowed. "Another one of the kattakyns has been unbound? Which one?"

Harrison shook his head. As he continued to pet the cat, Reg took a closer look to make sure that it was really Nicole and she hadn't been fooling herself. But she could feel the cat's aura and personality. It was Nicole, not one of the kattakyns.

"But the piece of Destine that was bound to Horace was lost. When Kareem attacked me and we had to fight back. That piece was… dispersed."

They hadn't been able to determine what had happened to that part of the Witch Doctor. They had speculated, but no one had been able to find it, and Reg had believed that it had simply been dispersed into the universe, as Corvin had suggested.

Marian hadn't been with them. She could not be the one who had received his essence. There were only a few of them there who could have received that insubstantial piece. Harrison. Corvin. Reg herself. The elves would not have been able to receive it. *Would they?*

"Was it you?" Reg asked Harrison. "Were you the one who held that piece?"

In her heart of hearts, she couldn't believe it. The Witch Doctor and Weston had proven that the immortals could be immoral and devious, but Harrison had always been childlike in his communications and behavior toward Reg. Guileless. Transparent. Could he have lied to her about holding the piece of the Witch Doctor? She didn't believe that he could have. Maybe he could have lied with his words but, as with a child, his actions would have given him away. He wouldn't blame Corvin or someone else for something that he himself had done. He wouldn't see the need for it.

"I am whole," Harrison told her, gesturing to himself. "No more and no less than one."

"Where is the piece of Destine now?"

"It is no longer hidden."

"Hidden…" Reg knew that it would take powerful magic to hide a part of an immortal from Harrison. Harrison might not be all-seeing, but if the piece were obvious, as it was when Marian held it, Harrison would know where it was.

And there was only one person she knew who was powerful enough to do that. Someone who already held most of Destine's powers.

Corvin.

She hadn't thought that he would be able to hide such a big secret from her. The conduit between the two of them would not allow it. She had been able to keep certain pieces of information from him, it was true. The locations of the kattakyns. The fact that she knew where Davyn was. Or at least, that she could sense where Davyn was. But she didn't know how he could hide a piece of the Witch Doctor from her. To hold it, with all of the power it represented, and not to give himself away to her.

It took a lot of magic to hide it from her and Harrison. The type of magic that only Corvin had.

When Merneith had told Reg that she needed a body to rest her spirit in, she had mentioned Corvin. Her words came back to Reg, as strong and clear as if Merneith were standing in front of her today.

"This no home for my *sah*. I need a receptacle. A *khet*. to be able to hold my being. Like this one." She motioned to Corvin.

Reg had thought that, like Norma Jean, Merneith had admired

Corvin's physical form and wanted to transfer her being into him. But she hadn't meant that. She had meant that Corvin was already holding another being, another sah, within him, and Merneith had recognized this, even though none of the others had.

"How did Marian get the sah?" Reg asked, looking from Harrison to Francesca.

Her lips pressed into a long, thin line, and Francesca shook her head. "Disembodied, it could not just 'land' on her. Such a spark must be transferred deliberately from one form to another... physical touch is necessary. It was no accident."

"It has to be Corvin, then, doesn't it?"

Francesca was nodding.

"He had to touch Kareem to pull it out of him. And he had to... touch Marian to give it to her."

"That is how it is done," Harrison agreed.

"And... does that fragment, that little piece of what was left of the Witch Doctor... does it have a *will*? When it is held by a human, can it still... act independently?"

"This is very bad magic," Francesca warned, making a claw shape with her fingers to ward off evil spirits. "This kind of magic should not be practiced."

"But can it...? I don't know what happens when the sah enters a new person. Does it affect their actions?"

"They still have some influence," Francesca said. "They magnify the host's personality. How much *will* they have... I don't know."

"So when Marian came to ask about the location of the kattakyns, it wasn't really *her* asking."

Francesca met Reg's eyes. They both stared at each other for a few seconds, working it out. The Witch Doctor was the one who had formed the kattakyns and transferred his consciousness to them. And he was the one who had come by Francesca's house to find out where the other pieces were. It wasn't *Marian's* inquiry; the sah had been in control of the khet.

CHAPTER THIRTY-EIGHT

*R*eg thought about Corvin. For weeks, he had not been himself. He had been angry and demanding, impatient with everyone around him. He had struggled to remain civil to her, when he had always pursued her and been so charming before. She had seen the darkness bleeding off of him and had never wondered what was inside of him that was releasing that inky blackness.

She had thought it was Corvin being Corvin. But of course it wasn't. She had known Corvin since arriving in Black Sands and, while he had a certain devil-may-care attitude and that dark, predatory hunger, he had not been so full of darkness then. And it had not been a gradual increase. He added powers, he charmed and pursued Reg, but his frustration and anger and the blackness inside him, had not been there until recently.

Until he had saved Orri and taken the powers from Kareem. And the sah.

"I need to go."

Francesca shook her head. "Where? Do not do anything reckless."

"I need to talk to someone. I need to figure this out."

She was missing something. She knew she was. She needed to figure out what it was before it was too late.

"Talk to Harrison," Francesca encouraged, motioning to him. "He should know all of the answers."

Reg looked at Harrison, who raised his brows politely, waiting for her questions. But she already knew that when it got down to it, Harrison would give her misleading and ambiguous answers, and she would be no further ahead than if she had not asked in the first place.

"I'll talk to you later. Come by my house tonight. Right now, I have to go."

"Humans must not interfere," Harrison warned.

"Humans have already interfered."

"Yes," he agreed.

Reg bolted for the door. "Thank you, Francesca. Sorry to ditch you like this."

* * *

She drove her car as quickly as she dared, and did not get pulled over by the cops and given a speeding ticket. Despite their name, speeding tickets were never quick. The cops always seemed to take a remarkably long time to write them. Maybe it was on purpose. Knowing that people were late or rushing, the police officer decided that to teach them a lesson, they needed to be slowed down. Maybe even to miss whatever it was they were hurrying to.

Reg didn't know for sure where the sah would take Marian. Reg was operating from instinct, her unconscious mind a jump or two ahead of her conscious mind. She used hands-free commands to place a call to Corvin.

"Reg," he greeted pleasantly. "I hope your day has been going well since we last saw each other."

"Yes. But I need something."

"I hope I can help."

"Can you go out to Davyn's house? Meet me there?"

"Davyn's house. Why there? Do you think you're going to find something? The police have already searched it."

"I know. But I think... this time will be different."

"Why? What could be different?"

"Did you see Marian this morning? Before we had our coffee?"

"Yes. But I don't see…"

"What happened? What did you talk about?"

"I…" Corvin's voice started strong, but then faded out. "I don't remember it all. Small talk. Just a short consult."

"You went to her for a reading?"

"Yes."

"Why?"

"I wanted to ask her some things about my future."

"What things did you ask her?"

"No, I… I don't know."

"What did she tell you? Did you get the answers you were looking for?"

"She was busy," Corvin said eventually. "She had other things on the go, so we decided to wait until later."

"Then why did she set up an appointment with you?"

"I don't think she did. I just dropped in. But she had to go out somewhere. On an errand."

"To see Francesca?"

"I honestly have no idea, Reg. Could have been. Why does it matter?"

"Just meet me at Davyn's, okay? Follow the path out back. To the altar."

Reg disconnected the call. Either he would come, or he would not. She couldn't control it.

But she thought he would. Corvin had always shown up when she had needed him. He would be too curious about why she needed him to go to the altar behind Davyn's house to ignore her request.

* * *

She was right, and Corvin was close behind her when she got to Davyn's house. Reg eyed him, realizing that maybe it wasn't such a good idea for her to be there alone with him.

If she were in luck, Marian would be there. But Marian would not be on her side.

"This way," Reg called out to Corvin and dashed into the woods, following the path she had taken a few days before. Corvin followed her, quickly catching up and overtaking her. He grabbed her by the arm. They both experienced a sharp jolt of electricity. It took Reg's breath away and she stared at Corvin, slightly stunned.

"Reg! What is this about? What's going on?"

"If you don't already know... you'll find out in a minute. Come on. Not here."

"Where is this altar?"

"Follow me."

Corvin looked at her for a moment. Then made a "go ahead" motion with his hands. Reg turned and hurried on toward the clearing. They reached it in a couple of minutes, both of them puffing a little, out of breath. Reg wasn't sure whether it was from the adrenaline or moving so quickly.

There was a figure kneeling in front of the altar. Reg drew in a quick breath and held it for a moment. Marian. Right where Reg expected her to be.

Marian looked up from the altar and scowled when she saw Reg.

It wasn't the scowl that was so startling. It was the darkness in Marian's countenance and, like with Corvin, the blackness bleeding out into her aura.

Corvin swore sharply under his breath. "What happened?"

"It was partially you."

"What?"

"You saw her this morning, right? Did she look like that when you met?"

"No."

"No," Reg agreed. "Not until you gave her the sah."

"The what?"

"You're the one who is supposed to know Egyptian." Though, of course, she had already found out he didn't speak the same ancient Egyptian that Merneith did. Nor modern Egyptian. Somewhere in between, in something that Reg thought he had called Middle Kingdom. But maybe the word was close enough to the form of Egyptian that he knew that they could skip over that part.

"The sah that you passed on to Marian. The Witch Doctor's spark."

Corvin's forehead creased, and he shook his head. "We've talked about this. You know that I didn't keep the Witch Doctor's sah. You were there. It didn't go into me. It was dispersed."

"It wasn't. And right now, it's in Marian. Just look at her if you don't think so."

Corvin looked back at Marian, whose face was contorted with rage.

"You think she's just upset because she needs a new cat to replace the one that died?" Reg demanded.

"Well, no…"

"I need your help. We need to work together to get Davyn back."

He shook his head. "What does this have to do with Davyn?"

"You kidnapped Davyn and bound him here, on another plane."

"I did *what*?"

"Or maybe you didn't do it, but the sah did it while it was in control of you. How much of what you have done in the last few weeks do you remember clearly?"

"I remember everything. Why wouldn't I?"

"Everything? What happened after the coven met on Monday?"

He shrugged. "Nothing particular. Everyone went their separate ways, back home to bed."

"Is that what you did?"

"Yes, of course."

"You didn't come back here?"

Corvin looked around the clearing. "Why would I?"

"Because you wanted Davyn out of the way. You wanted the leadership of the coven."

"We've talked about this. I only need to get six votes. I don't need to kidnap or kill Davyn to do that. I am quite capable of persuading people on my own."

"The Witch Doctor wanted to be sure. He didn't want to leave it up to an election. He wants the power."

"You talk about the Witch Doctor as if he was still alive. You know he is bound to all of the kattakyns."

"Yes. And I know you wanted to find all of them so that you can free him."

"No. To make sure that they were safe."

"I told you that we had already checked up on them all."

Corvin growled. "You didn't know about Kareem taking the spark from his cat."

"We found out pretty quickly. And *then* where do you think that spark went?"

"It had nothing to do with me."

"Look at Marian! That's where it is. You gave it to her this morning so that she could go ask Francesca where the kattakyns were. You—or the sah—thought that Francesca would be more likely to tell Marian than you."

"Maybe she had this spirit from the start. You have no reason to think that I had it or used it."

"I know how you've been lately. You haven't been yourself. And Marian wasn't there when the sah was lost. *You* were."

"You could have taken it. Or Harrison." He shook his head. "Where *is* Harrison in all of this?"

"I just talked to him. He and Francesca said that the sah had to be passed through physical contact. Like you had with Kareem. And like you had when you passed the sah on to Marian this morning."

Corvin shook his head, frowning.

"And like you passed the sah on to the gas station attendant on Monday on your way to the coven, so that he would make that phone call to Davyn to make it look like someone else was out to get him. Everybody would see you at the meeting and know that you had not been the one to make that call."

Corvin made a noise of disbelief.

Reg took a couple of steps closer to Marian. "Are you the great wizard who bound Davyn?"

Marian glowered at her. Reg had never seen the woman exude such hate. Marian used to be jealous and resentful of Reg, but this was way beyond that.

"You! What are you doing here?"

"I came to see if it was really you who bound Davyn."

"What I do is none of your business. Stay out of it, or you will regret it!"

"You must be very powerful to have bound such a powerful warlock. And to control *that* one." Reg jerked her head toward Corvin.

Marian snorted. "As if anyone would be difficult for me to control. That one holds my powers and doesn't even know how to use them. He's like a child. Like you."

Reg didn't look at Corvin's face to see how he felt about that. But she could feel the heat radiating off of him. Not the attraction that he emanated when he was trying to seduce Reg, but fury.

"How could any mortal challenge you?" Reg asked, putting as much admiration and subservience in her tone as possible. A fangirl. Make the sah think that she was cowed by his power, impressed by what he had done. Put him off guard.

"No mortal could," Marian replied, her eyes alight. "You are right."

"Look at what we did. We tried to bind you, and yet, here you are. A thousand years? Francesca could not even bind you for a thousand days!"

"I will gain back all that I lost and more. Stupid humans, thinking that you can take down one such as I!"

Reg wanted to challenge this statement, reminding him of all of the ancient gods who were no more. Somehow, humanity had wiped them out over the centuries. She didn't know how many immortals were left, but it seemed to be a pretty limited population. Maybe even more limited than the sirens.

"And Davyn... what is this place you have him trapped in? Is it the underworld?"

Reg was moving closer to Marian, and she could feel Corvin following close behind her and off to the side. Drifting closer, as if he only wanted to hear all of what was being said, mildly curious about the conversation.

"The underworld," Marian repeated. Her face looked thoughtful.

"At first, I thought it was," Reg said, "but then I realized... there was no fire."

"No fire?"

Reg nodded eagerly. "Hades, hell, whatever you call it—there are always flames. It's full of fire and brimstone to torment the souls who are sent there. But where Davyn is… I didn't see any flames."

"There are flames," Marian countered.

Reg was pulled into the void. She could feel Davyn close by. His strength was beginning to fail. She didn't know if his body was actually in that place or if it was somewhere else, but whether the damage had been done to his body or his soul, lingering there for days was not doing him any good. Reg reached out, trying to touch his consciousness with hers. They knew each other. He should be able to hear or sense her when she tried to touch his mind.

The edges of the world began to burn.

CHAPTER THIRTY-NINE

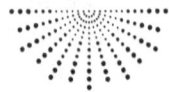

*R*eg's heart thumped faster as the fire began to close in on them. Leaping, roaring flames. They would have been intimidating to anyone in real life. And in the void, in the sharp darkness, they quickly overcame the icy coldness and warmed Reg to a temperature that would have made her sweat in real life. Or would have made other people sweat.

Other people who were not firecasters.

"It's burning!" She wasn't sure whether she shouted the words out loud or just imagined that she did. Her voice wouldn't carry in the void. She could feel Davyn being warmed and strengthened by the flames. It was not well known in the community that he was a firecaster. Reg knew, of course, because he had identified her as a firecaster and trained her. He had other powers and was the leader of the coven, and that was what people knew him for. Marian must not know or had not allowed the Witch Doctor to access that information. Corvin had probably not had any reason to think about it.

Are you okay? Reg sent the thought to Davyn, trying to keep it from everyone else.

The fire… is good.

She was glad to hear his response in her head. He was still there, still fighting against the power that held him there.

Wait until you are strong, she told him.

She didn't want to alert the Witch Doctor that what he was doing was counterproductive to his goal. He wasn't tormenting Davyn by filling the void with fire. He was giving him more strength and focus.

Reg tried to pull herself back out of that world, back to where she was talking with Marian and Corvin in the glade. It was difficult to focus on the cool, pleasant glade when the fire was calling to her. She took a few deep breaths, drawing in as much strength from the fire as she could, and then tried again.

She snapped back into place in the clearing in the woods. "You're hurting him," she protested to Marian. "You can't do that! Don't burn him. He's suffering! Please put out the fire."

She could feel Corvin's amusement over her ploy and hoped he didn't give it away to Marian and the Witch Doctor's sah. But Marian was paying no attention to Corvin. The sah had already discounted him as being unworthy, unable to exercise the Witch Doctor's powers he held. Instead, with a look of enjoyment on Marian's face, the Witch Doctor turned up the heat even further in the void where Davyn was struggling and growing in strength. She could sense Davyn from the mortal plane now instead of having to go into the void to find him. He was getting stronger and would be able to break the bonds that held him there before too long.

Ah. She felt the thought from Corvin. *I can feel him now.*

Reg took a few deep breaths and then, focusing on Davyn and his struggles, issued a clear call. *Davyn Smithy. Come to me.*

* * *

Davyn drew strength from the fire, letting it feed his own inner fire and revive him. He had been growing so weak, but the appearance of fire in the void had been a boon. He could sense more around him than he had been able to since he was brought there. He could sense not only the darkness of the place he was bound, but also the physical world around him. The glade where he meditated and offered sacrifices. The people who were there, shining like beacons. Or in the case of one of them, swirling in inky blackness.

Come to me.

He heard Reg's call and felt the tug on his consciousness. She was there, and if the two of them had been strengthened enough by the fire, he might be able to break free of the bonds that held him and go to her. He took in deep drags of the fire, as if inhaling oxygen deep into his lungs, and let the strength expand throughout him.

* * *

For a few long seconds, Reg could feel the pull of the spell she cast and the resistance of the power holding Davyn bound. She poured more strength into it, drawing on the fire burning in the void. And then Davyn tore loose. She felt the kaleidoscope of color and sensation as he was pulled toward her. And then he was there, in the mortal plane. Davyn made a loud grunt as he landed on the ground, and a heap of clothing and warlock was sprawled on the grass of the clearing in front of her. It was a good thing he hadn't dropped right on top of the stone altar. That could have hurt.

Davyn scrambled as quickly as he could to his feet.

"Reg." He put his hand on her arm and squeezed. "Thank you!"

Reg nodded and indicated Marian. "He's in there, now. We need to do something. What can we do?"

Davyn looked at Marian's furious face, his eyes popping in comical surprise. "What is it?" he demanded.

"The Witch Doctor. One piece of him. He's the one who bound you. But I don't know what to do and how to prevent him from doing more damage. What can we do?"

"I can do this," Corvin said boldly. He reached out and grabbed Marian by the arm.

"Don't!" Reg warned, but it was too late. He already had his hand on her.

Marian's face froze in an expression of shock and surprise. And Corvin again changed from the warlock she was familiar with to the angry, irritable version that she had put up with for the past few weeks.

"You think you can fool me?" he roared. "Overcome me?" He

swept his arm across, knocking Davyn to the ground with his unexpected blow. "You think you can undo what I have done?"

Reg watched him, staying out of reach. But she knew that his power would extend much farther than his physical reach. And now that the sah was back in Corvin, it had access to the Witch Doctor's powers. With knowledge of how to use them.

"What do we do?" she asked Davyn. "There must be something we can do to stop him."

Davyn got to his feet again, clearly shaken. After being in the void for days, his reactions seemed slow, his brain lagging as he tried to get back up to speed on what was going on in the mortal world.

"We work together," he said, but didn't come up with a game plan. Marian was looking around at everything, clearly out of her depth. Maybe with the sah now gone, she didn't even remember how she had ended up there.

Corvin surveyed Reg coldly. "You cannot take him from me. That one may not have had the power to let me hold him," he jerked his head in Marian's direction. Then he smoothed his hand down his front. "But this one *does*."

"There is no point in you holding Davyn anywhere. Why would you even bother? What does the leadership of a little coven matter to you?" Reg tried to appeal to his ego.

"This little coven," Corvin said, his face twisted into a snarl, "was one of the first ever established in the new world. One of the longest-surviving covens in the history of this planet. It has far greater importance and influence than you could ever imagine."

Reg rolled her eyes. "A bunch of old guys getting together to pray and dance around? That's the most important thing in the world for you to tackle?"

Corvin glared. "I have to start somewhere. In order to gain in power, I must move one step at a time, gaining a foothold with every new project I tackle." His nostrils flared, and he looked down at Reg. "Something that you would know nothing about."

"Oooh," Reg taunted back. She was stung, but she knew it wasn't really Corvin who was speaking to her and that she had, in fact, been gaining in power since she had arrived in Black Sands. Far more than she had ever expected to. She had gone from a drifting con artist with barely a penny to her name to having a home, a familiar, and wealth she had never imagined and had no idea what to do with. And the gifts which she had previously thought were attributable to coincidence, cold reading, and mental illness had flourished in the magical community. She had been acknowledged as powerful by several different practitioners and magical species, something that she could never have imagined. "Is that your brag? That you're more powerful than me?" She snickered. "More powerful than a psychic?"

"You will not stand in my way." He stepped toward Reg, his body drawn up to its full height to be as intimidating as possible. "I will not allow you to unwind what I have achieved. I will become as powerful again as I once was. Even greater."

Reg shrugged with one shoulder. "Big man." She yawned. "Why don't you get elected by the warlocks in a fair and square race against Davyn? Removing him from the picture makes it obvious that... you're afraid of him. You don't think you have what it takes to get elected on your own merit. The only way for you to get elected is to eliminate the competition first."

"That is a lie! This warlock is nothing compared to me."

Davyn faced Corvin straight on, not letting himself show any fear. "Reg is right. It's obvious you can't win the election on your own merits."

CHAPTER FORTY

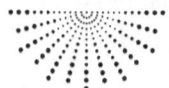

*C*orvin's hand flashed toward Davyn as if he were going to hit him. Davyn moved at the same time, seemingly much slower, but he managed to raise a wall of fire between them, which so startled Corvin that he stepped back to avoid contact with it. Reg could feel the heat pouring off of the flames. It wasn't any hallucination or optical illusion. It was a real fire, capable of burning Corvin to a crisp. And it called to Reg.

Corvin raised both hands and was able to dampen the flames a little. But he couldn't put it out like Davyn or Reg could. Davyn grinned at Reg, enjoying himself despite the danger. After being bound by Corvin and the sah, he relished the opportunity to retaliate.

Corvin dismissed the danger from Davyn with a flick of his wrist, an unseen force hitting Davyn and knocking him to the ground. He faced Reg, his pupils dilating wide.

"Do you think you are able to fight me? Both of you together could do nothing. The whole coven together couldn't do anything to harm me."

He stepped closer to Reg and grabbed her with both hands, demonstrating his physical prowess.

"You are nothing, witch. Do you hear me?"

Reg tried to pull away from him, but didn't have the strength. But her physical strength was not her only weapon. She pushed back against Corvin with her mind. She had fought him before. She was just as eager as he was to prove that she was not the weaker. He had already expended energy in starting the fire in the netherworld and in trying to keep Davyn there. Now he had to fight against Davyn and his fire. And against Reg and hers. And Marian… well, Marian wasn't going to be any help. Reg had to admit that. They would need to protect her. To make sure that the sah couldn't get back to her again.

"Stay back," she warned Marian. "No matter what he tells you, don't do what he says."

Marian nodded, wide-eyed. She took a few paces back from them. Not far enough, Reg didn't think. But it was a start.

Corvin took no notice of this exchange. He stared into Reg's eyes, his gaze hard and unwavering. Like he could see right into her soul. Reg did her best to shut him out. The shared experiences the two of them had been through together made it impossible to keep the connection completely closed. She tried to throw up a psychic shield and to reflect some of his energy and aggression back to him. She had found it a very effective move when battling an opponent with stronger gifts.

"You are mine," Corvin told her, pushing back. Reg tried to keep her focus. The smell of roses floated up to her nostrils, and she knew he was trying to use his charms to seduce her. If he managed it, she would be unable to stop him from anything. She would quite happily nestle in his arms and do whatever he asked her to.

"Do you really think that's going to work?" Reg demanded.

He smiled, clearly feeling that it was only a matter of time until Reg gave in. But Reg was in the open air, not inside where the pheromones could build up and overcome her. She swept a blast of fire through the air to purify it. Everyone took a step back, eyes wide, even Davyn. Reg laughed.

"You think you can charm me?" Reg asked, "that's not going to work today."

He switched tactics and, instead of trying to entrance her with his charms, he wrenched open the door to her mind, making Reg gasp with the violence and reel back, trying to avoid him reading her or taking control. She could feel the sah, separate from Corvin's mind, strong, gathering to it the Witch Doctor's powers that had been little used since Corvin had absorbed them.

"No!" Reg tried to push back, but he was too strong. Even stronger than the force she had fought in the void when she had tried to call Davyn back the first time. He had an iron will, not willing to budge an inch. He would overcome her. She could feel Davyn trying to help her, feeding her fire with his in an effort to overbalance the Witch Doctor's power.

But Reg's grip was slipping. She wouldn't last long. She tried to call on Corvin's power as well. She had been able to channel his strength in the past. Corvin was still there; maybe he could still help give her his strength, draining his own, until she was strong enough to overcome the Witch Doctor's sah.

But she couldn't seem to reach Corvin. He was there, but he was blocked from helping her. Or he was enjoying the battle, the feeling of overcoming Reg. It was, after all, what he had wanted since he'd first met her.

Reg was losing ground. She tried to think of everything she could do to strengthen herself or take from his power. She was momentarily distracted by the rising cry of the sirens. Norma Jean and the other siren sisters were going wild, shrieking to her, making it almost impossible to think in an already impossible situation.

"Take him. Mark him. He is yours!"

Reg shook her head, irritated. It was like being menaced by a mosquito when playing a well-matched game of tug-of-war.

I can't right now, she told the voices in her head. *I'm sort of busy!*

What kind of mother would encourage her to pursue a romantic relationship—or a fine meal—or a combination of the two when she was fighting for her life?

But as she continued to lose ground to the Witch Doctor, her mind started to clear, and she began to see what the siren voices were trying to tell her. The voices and music created pictures that flowed into her mind. She started to see how it all worked. She stepped closer to Corvin, and he didn't object, thinking that she was doing want he wanted her to. Getting closer and succumbing to him. Reg reached out to him, touching his arms and shoulders, running her hands over his muscles as if she had been ensorcelled and wanted nothing more than to join with him.

Closer. Closer.

Reg could hear Corvin's blood singing in his veins.

Before he could sense what she was thinking or planning to do, Reg kissed him on the throat.

CHAPTER FORTY-ONE

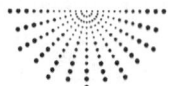

*R*eg's heart was pounding hard. She could feel and smell Corvin's blood pumping just beneath the surface. It was all she could do to restrain herself from any further action. She knew that one contact would be enough. Corvin had already proven himself susceptible to the siren's kiss. That one touch of her lips was all that it would take.

But he didn't know it yet.

He held her against him, expression exultant. "You are mine," he insisted. "And now your powers are mine too."

"That's not what you're supposed to say," Reg told him.

He frowned, looking at her. "What?"

"You're supposed to say, 'yield to me.' The rule is you have to get consent before stealing the powers of a conquest."

He shook his head. "Why would I do that?"

"It's the rule. You have to get me to say that I yield to you, before you can take my powers."

"That's just stupid," Corvin spat. "I am not human. I don't have to get consent for anything. I can enter. I can take. I can create and destroy. I don't follow human rules."

"You're in a human body. I think you have to."

"No. I take what I want."

223

"And you want my stupid little human powers? Didn't you say that they were inconsequential? That they are too small for you to care about?"

"Stuck on this planet with such weak inhabitants, I am forced to build upon what I have. One step and then another. Until I can destroy all of you."

Reg never could understand the desire to destroy everything. Why did those seeking powers often want to destroy rather than build? Someone with the Witch Doctor's power could do a lot of good in the world. Once he had had what he needed, he could help others. Change things for the better.

Corvin's grip around her tightened. "Yield to me."

He had, apparently, decided to follow the rules to get what he wanted. It would be faster. There would be fewer roadblocks. Reg breathed deeply a couple of times. Even though there was plenty of air, she was starting to get a little light-headed from the pheromones. She gripped Corvin tightly and looked into his eyes, looking for signs that he was succumbing to the trace of her saliva on his throat.

"No."

"You must!"

Reg smiled and shook her head. "No. It has to be my free will and choice. And you haven't convinced me yet. Corvin is usually better at this. You are... not very good."

"I will take what I want—"

Corvin's body suddenly shifted, and Reg clutched at him, trying to keep him from falling over. Some men were like that. They could barely stay on their feet once they were overcome by the siren's venom. Lame. It was much easier to direct a man who stayed on his feet than to drag one who was too wobbly even to walk. Reg looked around. Something was missing. She hadn't thought things through properly before deciding to pit her siren powers against Corvin's abilities and the Witch Doctor's powers.

"What is it?" Davyn asked.

"Umm... I need something."

"What did you do? How did you...?" Davyn stared at Corvin's blank expression. "What's wrong with him?"

"It wears off. Don't worry. But we need to figure out how to get the sah to leave him."

"What... sah?"

"The Witch Doctor. Horace's piece. You saw it move from Marian to Corvin?"

Davyn nodded, but it was clear that he didn't yet understand the full impact of what he had seen. It might take him a while to catch up after being trapped in the void for so long.

"It was the sah that wanted you out of the way. He trapped you in the void so you couldn't get in the way of his advancement. So he could lead the coven. Maybe steal the powers of everyone in the coven. And then use it as a steppingstone to... whatever the next thing is."

"Right."

Reg looked around again. "Is there a pond or something close by?"

Davyn considered. He pointed in one direction. "It's a few miles away... there is a little creek and a slough. But... he's not going to be able to walk that far. He can barely stand."

Reg pointed her nose in the direction of the slough and concentrated. She could detect the scent of the water, very faint, on the breeze. With that smell in her nostrils, she could picture the body of water in her mind. She had two choices. She could transport herself and Corvin there, or...

Calling a body of water from two miles away was harder than making Mike's ribs appear in her fridge, but when Reg opened her eyes, there it was in front of her. Davyn's mouth hung open.

"What...?"

Reg dragged Corvin forward. He was compliant, moving with her as she pulled him. She grabbed his shoulder and threw him to the ground, falling to her knees. In a split second, she had an arm around his neck to force his face down into the water.

"What are you doing?" Marian shrieked, finally coming out of her daze. She hurried forward and pulled ineffectually at Reg, trying to stop her from what she had to do.

"Reg," Davyn spoke urgently, also startled by her plan and the swiftness with which she put it into action. "Reg, you can't do this. You'll kill him."

Reg turned her head toward Davyn, looking at him sidelong. "Do you have a better idea?"

"It's murder. You can't."

"He kidnapped you. Tried to kill you."

"But... you can't."

"Besides, it's not murder. I'm a siren. Man is my natural prey. As long as I follow the human laws..." She pressed Corvin's face firmly into the stagnant water and mud. He tried to escape her grasp, but his movements were sluggish. The sedating siren venom was doing its work. "They can't charge me with anything."

"You don't want to do this."

"Watch—and see—" Reg insisted.

"Corvin is your friend."

"Mmm. Acquaintance," Reg corrected. "He was trying to charm me. He wanted to consume *my* powers."

"I know, but..." Davyn sounded miserable. "The two of you have been closer than I've ever known Corvin to be with anyone before. You... understood each other."

Reg recognized the final struggles of the prey beneath her. Maybe her plan wasn't going to work after all.

Corvin. Now!

The exchange happened so fast Reg could have missed it. Even expecting it, the sah transferred to her so quickly that she could barely shut the doors of her mind in time. She released Corvin and pushed herself into the void.

It had been easier when Davyn had been there. She'd at least had a reference point. But she had been into the void a few times, so she eventually found her way, slipping through the cracks of the plane she was in, into that netherworld.

So far, so good.

The emptiness of the void, with Davyn no longer there, was terrifying. He must have been out of his mind when he had first woken up there.

Francesca had said that the sah couldn't come out of the air and enter into a person. Reg hoped that the opposite was not true. Corvin had suggested that the sah he had retrieved from Kareem had simply dispersed into the atmosphere. Harrison had not said that was impossible. She hoped she hadn't misjudged the situation.

She used all her strength to push the foreign entity out of her head. The Witch Doctor's sah had willingly left his powers behind in Corvin when it had appeared that Reg was going to kill him. He did not want that piece of himself to die with Corvin. Reg was no longer fighting against the piece of the Witch Doctor's consciousness and his combined powers, but only against that one small spark.

He left her, escaping into the void. Reg lit the void on fire once more. She surrounded the small spark with walls of fire and then slipped through the cracks back to her own reality. She did what she could to seal those cracks once more, feeding flames in until she could do no more.

CHAPTER FORTY-TWO

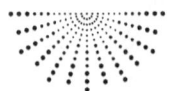

*R*eg!"

Reg lay on her back on spongy ground, water soaking into her clothing. She stared up at the leaves on the trees and the fluffy white clouds floating in the sky. Everything was quiet and peaceful.

Except for the people around her who wouldn't shut up and leave her alone.

"Reg, are you okay? She was under for a long time."

"I think she's okay. Reg? Can you talk? Can you sit up?"

Reg sat up, but only because hands pulled her up by her arms and stabilized her behind her back. She really would prefer to just lie in the grass for a while.

She saw Corvin in front of her. Squatting or kneeling in front of her so that her eyes were at a level with his. His hair was no longer wet, but stood up in untidy spikes. His face was smudged with mud. But at least he was alive. Reg cleared her throat.

"Hey."

"Are you okay? Talk to me."

Reg closed her eyes, wishing she could just go to sleep.

Talking is too hard.

"Okay. What do you need? Is it... gone?"

He's gone.

"How? Where did he go? You just… were in a trance. We didn't know if you were still fighting with him. I couldn't reach you."

"Give her water," Davyn suggested. "She's been working with fire."

"Do I look like I have water on me?"

Reg opened her eyes and looked at Corvin, laughter bubbling out of her. "Yes!"

Corvin chuckled at this. He smoothed his hands over his messy hair. "Some crazy siren tried to drown me."

"Normal siren behavior," Reg told him.

"Well… maybe so, but I can tell you, I'd rather not have to go through that again."

Reg closed her eyes. She wanted to go back to sleep, but the hands behind her still kept her sitting up.

"There's water there," she told Corvin, making a weak gesture toward a six-pack of water bottles beside him.

"I don't think you want to be drinking the slough water. To be honest, it doesn't taste that good." Then Corvin saw the bottled water. His brows came down and he looked back at her. "Where did those come from?"

"Don't know. Prob'ly the grocery store."

He removed a bottle from the pack, cracked it open, and handed it to her. After all of her exertions, it felt very heavy. Corvin helped her to lift and steady it. Reg took several swallows before lowering it. She waited for the water to do its work, and looked around. Davyn was the one holding her up, watching her with great concern.

"You were out for a long time," he explained, when he caught her eyes on him.

"Yeah. Can't sense time in there. Or time is different."

"In where, exactly?"

Reg shrugged with one shoulder. "I don't know… not in this world. In space? Under the earth? Another plane? I don't get how it works."

"It wasn't in a basement or something, then. It was… out there."

Reg gave a slight nod. "And now, he is trapped there. I hope."

"How?" Corvin asked. "Do you know a binding spell? It isn't something I have known you to do before."

It was interesting to note that he was unsure what she could do or had done before. Corvin had always been so sure of himself before, especially where she was concerned. He had held her powers. He should know her abilities just as well as she did. But maybe there were only certain things that he could take. Not her siren nature. Or maybe he could only know of the powers he had been able to wield during that short time. He had not known when he had held her powers that she could do a call or that she was a siren.

"I used fire." Reg gave Davyn a smile. "I trapped him inside a cage of fire. I think it will burn for a long time there... there isn't anything to stop it."

Davyn shook his head, frowning. "But there is no fuel. Is there?"

"There must be, in order for me to kindle fire there."

He nodded slowly. "Well... I guess. Sometimes it's best not to question the possibility of what you have already seen or done..."

Corvin offered Reg the water again, and she took a few more swallows. "You made the Witch Doctor's sah kindle a fire there earlier? Why? For yourself or for Davyn?"

"Both of us. I figured... we needed something to give us more strength. I had already tried to get Davyn out on my own, and I couldn't." She had another sip of the water. "I was worried you were going to give me away."

"I wouldn't say anything."

"But you were *thinking* it."

He nodded, conceding this point. Reg leaned forward, testing her strength. She could sit up on her own as long as she braced her elbows against her knees for support. Davyn stayed in position for a moment, making sure she wasn't going to collapse again, then circled around her to crouch down beside Corvin so that she could see them both. Reg looked around and spotted Marian, sitting on the altar stone, her head in her hands. Violets grew thickly around the stone.

"Is she okay? Marian?"

Marian looked up momentarily. Her face was streaked with tears.

She looked tired and haggard. Being possessed by the sah or the stress of the events that had followed had worn her out.

"I just want to go home," Marian said. She rubbed her eyes. "I don't understand this. What just happened?"

Reg tried to figure out how to tell it all to Marian succinctly. Marian didn't look like she could handle too much detail. "We just… were trying to free Davyn from where he was being held."

"But you drowned him," Marian looked at Corvin. "Why were you trying to drown him?"

"Uh…" Reg's cheeks heated. There was no point in trying not to blush. That never worked. "It was the only way I could think of to get the sah to leave him. If he thought that Corvin was going to die, he would want to get out. I don't really know how it all works, but I figured if the host died, the sah would too. Or at least, he would have to go somewhere else." Reg glanced at Corvin, apologetic. "I didn't think anything else would make him leave you again. Not when you held all of his powers."

"Probably the right call," Corvin admitted. "But I can't say I'm happy with putting the theory into practice."

"Are you happy he's not in your head anymore?"

"Well… yes. Although the feeling that I had when he was there was…" He searched for words. Reg could sense the emotions he was projecting, but also had a hard time saying what it was. He hadn't been happy. In fact, he had been very angry and irritable when the sah had been in him.

"Powerful?" she suggested.

"Yes… I suppose. Confident, maybe? We go through this life always wondering about our choices. Whether we did the right thing. Questioning our successes and blaming ourselves for our failures. But with him in my head, there was none of that. Just… strength and confidence. Not confidence that I was making the right choice, but… that anything I did was right."

Marian looked at Corvin with wide eyes. "Yes," she agreed. "I've never felt that way before."

CHAPTER FORTY-THREE

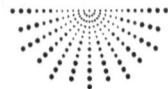

*D*avyn sat on the garden bench with Reg. The sun shone brightly through the trees and it was warm and pleasant. Reg listened to the sound of the tiny waterfall that dribbled into the goldfish pond. It was soothing. She liked to be close to water, even if it was just a little pool.

Davyn didn't have much to say. Reg supposed he was still trying to process what had happened to him. It would have to be pretty traumatic to be kidnapped and bound like that, held in nothingness for days.

"I can't believe it was five days," Davyn said. "It didn't seem like that long. I don't know what I thought... maybe a day, or a night. It was so dark and empty; there was nothing to mark the passage of time."

"I know," Reg agreed. "Every time I went into it, it took much longer than I thought. Maybe they just operate on a different time scale. You know, an hour there is a day here, or something like that."

"Maybe. I appreciate everything you did. I don't think I can express that enough. You did something I don't think anyone else could have done."

Reg shrugged. "There aren't a lot of firecasters around here. I just... did what I could. I didn't think I did that great a job. And it took so long. I didn't think I was going to be able to get you out in time." Reg's throat constricted and hot tears prickled in her eyes. She did her best to push away the unwelcome burst of emotion. Everything was fine. She didn't have to worry about how things might have turned out, because they hadn't. She had helped Davyn to escape his prison. End of story.

"You *did* do a great job. You should be proud of yourself."

Reg shrugged it off. There were footsteps on the path, and Reg looked up to see Julian approaching. "Oh. Hi."

Davyn stood up. He gave Julian a quick bro hug, slapping him on the back. His face was pink.

"Ready to go home?" Julian asked.

"Yes. I think I'm still catching up on my sleep." He gave a little laugh. "You wouldn't think that it would take so much energy, doing nothing for that length of time…"

"You have been through an ordeal," Julian responded, shaking his head. "There's nothing weak about needing to recover from what you have been through."

Davyn shrugged. He gave Reg a little wave. "We'll get back together for some more instruction once I'm feeling back to myself."

Reg was relieved about that. She had been a little worried that he would be embarrassed about her saving him or say that she was ahead of him in her abilities and he couldn't mentor her anymore. She was glad that he was still planning to continue the sessions.

"Okay. Thanks. Feel better soon."

He nodded and left with Julian. Reg remained sitting on the bench, looking at the beautiful blooms and lush greens of the garden, listening to the tinkling of the running water. It was a lovely little oasis there, a place she found herself more and more inclined to go to sit and think or just relax for a while. She had never been much of an outdoors person.

There were footsteps on the path again, and Reg looked up, expecting to see Davyn or Julian. One of them had forgotten to tell her something, or Davyn had dropped something out of his pocket while he was sitting there. Or maybe he had another question about what had happened while he had been kidnapped.

But it wasn't Davyn or Julian. It was Corvin.

At first, Reg thought nothing of it. She was feeling nice and relaxed and, since she had kissed him and tried to drown him, he seemed to have developed a new respect for her. Like maybe he saw her as a person now, instead of just as potential prey or a low-level psychic who could not compete with him in the magic department. Or maybe that was just how Reg had seen herself, and now she was learning that it wasn't true.

Then, in a rush, she realized that he had somehow gotten past all of the wards Sarah had set against him. The backyard was supposed to be protected from enemies and intruders, and specifically from Corvin. In the past, he hadn't been able to get past the gate. Had Davyn and Julian somehow let him into the yard, inviting him in before they left? She didn't think Davyn would be so clueless, but Julian might. Reg jumped to her feet, ready to defend herself.

"There, there," Corvin said, making a downward calming movement with both hands, "no need to get worked up."

"What are you doing here? You are not allowed entrance here!"

Corvin smiled. "Wards are not infallible. I think you will agree that I did, in fact, get in past your wards. So I am allowed entrance here."

"No—how did you get past them?"

He shrugged and sat down on the bench where Davyn had previously been. "No need to get worked up. I'm not here to harm you."

Reg stared at him. She was both horrified that he had gotten past all of the blocks that had been put in place against him and impressed that he had managed to do it. She wasn't as afraid of Corvin as she had once been. Despite his impressive powers, she had been able to defend herself against him under most circumstances.

The encounter with the Witch Doctor's sah had reinforced to her that he had powers that were far beyond what she was able to defend against, yet that didn't worry her. She had still been able to outwit the Witch Doctor and lock his sah behind the fiery wall. And she had still been able to overcome Corvin with nothing more than a kiss, letting the chemical or magical properties of the siren's kiss do its work.

At the moment, Corvin did not appear to be intent upon

charming her. She was not sensing an increase in his body heat or the smell of roses that accompanied his charms. She slowly sat back down beside him.

"There's a pond right there," she pointed out, nodding to the water.

"Trust me, I have no interest in being drowned again," he assured her. "I'm still coughing up bits of grass and algae." He wiped his mouth and beard as if they were still sticking there and made a face.

Reg laughed, a little more relaxed. "So… what are you doing here? I would have thought you would have a lot of other things to do. Running for leadership of the coven or world domination. Whatever."

"There is much to do," he agreed with a smile. "And I will beat Davyn. Trust me on that. It won't be so hard to convince the other members of the coven to elect me." He looked smug and self-satisfied.

"You don't think there's any chance Davyn could win? I would think that everyone would want to see him back in his accustomed place. After him going missing like that, people will want to know that everything is back to normal."

"After an ordeal like that, he really deserves a rest, don't you think? Leading the coven is not exactly a stress-free job."

"Well, sure, but—"

Corvin grinned. "You see, even you agree, after just one reason."

"But—"

"And I can't think of anyone who would be more against me taking over the leadership of the coven than you."

"There are those who believe that someone… from your line cannot be allowed into a leadership position."

"You're right. But if they speak up, they are going to be accused of being prejudiced. Racist. Speciesist. In today's climate, those arguments are enough to discredit a person. No one wants to be accused of prejudice."

Reg shook her head slowly. He was right, she was sure. Those with biases knew enough not to speak up about it now. Sooner or later, the pendulum would start to swing back the other direction and they would be praised for being insightful and forward-looking. But until then, it would be difficult to argue anything against Corvin's kind.

"So, what will you do when you're the leader?" She was afraid of the answer. "Will you make changes?"

"Not immediately. But change is in the air. In time, I will institute some long-overdue adjustments."

Call her prejudiced, but Reg didn't think any of those changes would be for the general good of the coven. The Witch Doctor was not the only one looking to increase his power and influence one step at a time.

Reg looked around the garden, pleasant and buzzing with life.

Change *was* in the air.

Did you enjoy this book? Reviews and recommendations are vital to making a book successful.

Please leave a review at your favorite book store or review site and share it with your friends.

Don't miss the following bonus material:
Sign up for mailing list to get a free ebook
Read a sneak preview chapter
Other books by P.D. Workman
Learn more about the author

Sign up for my mailing list at pdworkman.com and get
Gluten-Free Murder for free!

PREVIEW OF THRICE SPARED

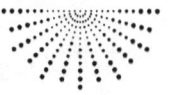

CHAPTER 1

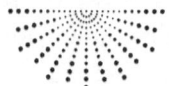

*R*eg watched Corvin walk away from her down the path out of the backyard. Almost as soon as he was gone, the back door of the big house banged and Sarah was striding toward Reg with great purpose. Reg was momentarily thrown back to her childhood when an older woman coming toward her like that almost certainly presaged a slap across the head and punishment for whatever real or perceived infraction the current foster mom thought she had committed.

And the red aura around her landlady was not a comfort.

Sarah stopped in front of Reg, a crease between her eyebrows, her mouth turning down in a stern frown. Her gray hair was in disarray, as if she had been running her fingers through it.

"What was *he* doing here?"

Reg sighed and let out her breath. She gathered her red box-braids in a bunch and released them behind her back. "Just came over for a visit, I guess."

"He came over for a visit. And you let him in!"

Reg shook her head. "I didn't let him in."

"The only way he could get by the wards that protect this yard and the guest cottage is if you let him in, one way or the other. What did you do?"

"I didn't do anything. I was just sitting here. I didn't invite him in; I didn't even call him on the phone. He just showed up here on his own."

"That isn't possible."

Reg raised her brows at Sarah. "I didn't do anything to let him in."

"Did you have something of his here that he could come back to retrieve? Or you gave him a key?"

"I know better than that now," Reg pointed out. She hadn't known all of the rules in the beginning when she had first arrived in Black Sands. But she knew all of the sneaky ways Corvin, a handsome warlock with evil purpose in his heart, could get past the wards that Sarah had set. He had managed to finagle his way around them a few times, and Reg had helped set the new wards, using her newly discovered gifts under Sarah's direction.

But now...

Sarah stared at her, expecting more information about how Corvin had managed to worm his way in again, sure that it had to be something that Reg had done wrong. Reg just shook her head helplessly.

The creases on Sarah's face deepened. Her normally pleasant, grandmotherly demeanor was gone. This new development was definitely of concern to her.

"But if Corvin got past the wards without any action on your part..."

Reg nodded. "You said before that it could happen. That you could not protect the yard from someone whose powers were greater than yours."

CHAPTER 2

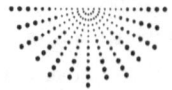

$\mathcal{S}$arah sank onto the bench beside Reg. Her face went slack and Reg grabbed for her, afraid that she would faint and fall right off the bench.

"Sarah!"

Sarah held onto Reg's arm, steadying herself, then let go. "It's all right, dear. I'm fine." Even so, she put her hand over her heart, breathing heavily. "Is it possible?" She closed her eyes. "Of course it is. Corvin has been growing in strength. He has all of the powers that he has been able to absorb from others and from the artifacts he has acquired. And he has apparently grown enough…"

That he was stronger than Sarah.

Reg had relied upon Sarah's wards as she had gotten used to living in Black Sands and all of the possible dangers that lurked there. Black Sands was home to a large population of witches, psychics, and other magical races, and not all of them were good. Sarah said that there was no black magic or white magic, just the intentions of the individuals who wielded the powers. And not all of the individuals who wielded powers in Black Sands had good intentions.

Reg had learned this the way she learned most things. From personal experience. She had always been told that she should listen to the advice of others, to learn from their experiences and trust that they knew better than she did. But she had not been able to trust. She always had to try things for herself.

The breaching of Sarah's wards meant that Reg was exposed to Corvin and his wiles and charms once more. She had to be able to withstand all of the pheromones and stolen magical powers that he could bring to bear against her. She had not always succeeded in the past and had been caught in dangerous circumstances more than once.

But *she* was stronger now too. She had grown into powers and gifts that she had known nothing about before moving into the guest cottage in Sarah's backyard. She had learned that there was more to her success in conning unsuspecting clients out of their money doing psychic readings than just being able to cold read them. She wasn't just observant; she had gifts that she had never understood or suspected.

"Corvin's star is rising and mine is waning," Sarah said in a soft, flat tone. As if she were talking in her sleep, unaware that Reg still sat beside her.

"No," Reg told Sarah sternly. "It doesn't have anything to do with you. It's just because Corvin has been able to drink the powers of the Witch Doctor and Kareem."

"It is only natural that sooner or later, my powers begin to weaken. Even though this body has lasted a long time..." She indicated her apparently middle-aged body. Reg would have put her in her sixties, but she knew that others had said Sarah was centuries old. Only magic had kept her looking so young.

Sarah rubbed her forehead, the third eye position between her brows. She looked suddenly tired and older than she had been since she'd been restored by her powerful emerald.

"You're not old," Reg insisted. "You're not weakening."

Sarah lifted her head and looked around the garden. "We will need to reset and strengthen the wards. You are young and strong and are growing into your powers. Together, we should be able to keep them strong. You have been able to resist Corvin before; that shows that you and he are nearly matched in strength."

Reg nodded. Though she knew it wasn't just her magical gifts that had allowed her to resist Corvin in the past. She had other weaponry in her arsenal. While Sarah knew about Reg's siren heritage, she didn't know that Reg had used the physical traits and instincts that came from that heritage to defeat Corvin the last time. She wasn't sure Corvin would try to seduce her again. Knowing what she could do and how he was just as vulnerable to her wiles as she was to his, would he dare make another attempt?

Who was she kidding? Of course he would. The fact that he had sat on the bench with her and not made any attempt to charm her did not mean that he was finished trying. He was just taking some time to re-evaluate his prey and her weaknesses.

Sarah was quite a powerful witch. Her wards had kept Corvin at bay for quite a while, and if Reg helped, then surely he wouldn't be able to get past them again.

"You'll need to be more vigilant now," Sarah advised. "Strengthen the wards every day. I will do what I can to maintain them, but it will be up to you to see that Corvin can't get past." She shook her head, looking around at the peaceful garden, full of blooms and every imaginable shade of green, and the little burbling waterfall and pond in front of the bench they rested on. "He cannot have the run of this place. Not to access you and not to disturb any of the wildlife or the peace of the garden."

"Okay." Reg nodded. "If you'll show me what to do, I'll do my best."

She didn't point out that she wasn't particularly reliable. Remembering to strengthen the wards every day? Reg found establishing new habits, especially good habits, difficult. She remembered to feed Starlight, her black and white tuxedo cat, every day because he wouldn't let her forget, getting underfoot, yowling, biting her ankles, jumping up on the kitchen island. Whatever he had to do to get her to feed him.

If he had been a goldfish, it would be a different story.

Or a plant.

Sarah was constantly rolling her eyes and telling Reg she needed to take care of the plant that Fir had given her. Sarah watered it, turned it, and kept it close to the window so that it got enough light, but not so much that it would burn. She occasionally took it outside to the garden to be with the other plants and for Forst, the garden gnome, to use his gifts to keep it healthy. Otherwise, Reg was sure that the plant would have shriveled up into a brown, crispy mass of leaves before she realized she had been neglecting it.

"You have to be diligent," Sarah insisted, perhaps understanding Reg's silence too well. "This could be a matter of life and death."

* * *

Thrice Spared, book #17 in the Reg Rawlins, Psychic Investigator series, is available for order now.

ABOUT THE AUTHOR

P.D. Workman is a USA Today Bestselling author, winner of several awards from Library Services for Youth in Custody and the InD'tale Magazine's Crowned Heart award, and has published over 90 mystery/suspense/thriller and young adult books, including stand alones and these series: Auntie Clem's Bakery cozy mysteries, Reg Rawlins Psychic Investigator paranormal mysteries, Zachary Goldman Mysteries (PI), Kenzie Kirsch Medical Thrillers, Parks Pat Mysteries (police procedural), and YA series: Tamara's Teardrops, Between the Cracks, and Breaking the Pattern.

Workman loves writing about the underdog, who the reader may love or hate. She has been praised for her realistic details, deep characterization, and sensitive handling of the serious social issues that appear in all of her stories, from light cozy mysteries through to darker, grittier young adult and mystery/suspense books.

> P. D. Workman, does not shy from probing the deep psychological scars of childhood trauma, mental illness, and addiction. Also characteristic of this author, these extremely sensitive issues are explored with extensive empathy, described with incredible clarity, and portrayed with profound insight.
>
> — —KIM, GOODREADS REVIEWER

Some of Workman's titles have been translated into Spanish, French, Portuguese, German, and Italian.

Workman began writing at an early age and is a prolific reader as well as writer. She is also passionate about teaching and learning, expresses her creativity through art and cooking, and loves exploring the Calgary parks and green spaces where the Parks Pat Mysteries are set. She was a legal assistant for many years and has done extensive charitable work.

Workman was born and raised in Alberta, Canada, and is married with one adult son.

* * *

Please visit P.D. Workman at pdworkman.com to see what else she is working on, to join her mailing list, and to link to her social networks.

* * *

If you enjoyed this book, please take the time to recommend it to other purchasers with a review or star rating and share it with your friends!

facebook.com/pdworkmanauthor

twitter.com/pdworkmanauthor

instagram.com/pdworkmanauthor

amazon.com/author/pdworkman

bookbub.com/authors/p-d-workman

goodreads.com/pdworkman

linkedin.com/in/pdworkman

pinterest.com/pdworkmanauthor

youtube.com/pdworkman

Find P.D. Workman's books at

PDWORKMAN.COM

Scan the QR code below